TOMORROW'S CRIMES

D0065028

DONALD E. WESTLAKE

TOMORROW'S CRIMES

THE MYSTERIOUS PRESS

New York • London
Tokyo • Sweden • Milan

The Mysterious Press, 129 West 56th Street, New York, N.Y. 10019

Printed in the United States of America
First Printing: October 1989
10 9 8 7 6 5 4 3 2 1

Library of Congress Cataloging-in-Publication Data

Westlake, Donald E.
  Tomorrow's crimes / Donald E. Westlake.
    p.   cm.
  Stories originally published 1961–1984.
  Contents: The girl of my dreams – Nackles – The ultimate caper – The spy in the elevator – The risk profession – The winner – Dream a dream – In at the death – Hydra – Anarchaos.
  ISBN 0-89296-299-2
  1. Detective and mystery stories, American.   I. Title.
PS3573.E9T66   1989
813'.54--dc20   89-42600
                                                                          CIP

Contents

TOMORROW'S CRIMES

The Girl of My Dreams

Yesterday I bought a gun.

I'm very confused; I don't know what to do.

I have always been a mild and shy young man, quiet and conservative and polite. I have been employed the last five years—since at nineteen I left college due to a lack of funds—at the shirt counter of Willis & DeKalb, Men's Clothiers, Stores in Principal Cities, and I would say that I have been generally content with my lot. Although recently I have been finding the new manager, Mr. Miller, somewhat abrasive—not to overstate the matter—the work itself has always been agreeable, and I have continued to look forward to a quiet lifetime in the same employment.

I have never been much of a dreamer, neither by day nor by night. Reveries, daydreams, these are the products of vaulting ambition or vaulted desire, of both of which I have remained for the most part gratefully free. And, though science assures us that some part of every night's sleep is spent in the manufacture of dreams, mine must normally be gentle and innocuous, even dull, as I rarely remember them in the morning.

I would date the beginning of the change in my life from the moment of the retirement of old Mr. Randmunson from his post as manager of our local Willis & DeKalb store, and his prompt replacement by Mr. Miller, a stranger from the Akron branch.

Mr. Miller is a hearty man, cheeks and nose all red with ruddy health, handshake painfully firm, voice roaring, laugh aggressive. Not yet thirty-five, he moves and speaks with the authority and self-confidence of a man much older, and he makes it no secret that some day he intends to be president of the entire chain. Our little store is merely a stopover for him, another rung on the ladder of his success.

His first day in the store, he came to me, ebullient and overpowering and supremely positive. He asked my opinion, he discussed business and geography and entertainment, he offered me cigarettes, he thumped my shoulder. "We'll get along, Ronald!" he told me. "Just keep moving those shirts!"

"Yes, Mr. Miller."

"And let me have an inventory list, by style and size, tomorrow morning."

"Sir?"

"Any time before noon," he said carelessly, and laughed, and thumped my shoulder. "We'll have a great team here, Ronald, a first-rate team!"

Two nights later I dreamed for the first time of Delia.

I went to bed as usual at eleven-forty, after the news on Channel 6. I switched out the light, went to sleep, and in utter simplicity and clarity the dream began. In it, I was driving my automobile on Western Avenue, out from the center of town. It was all thoroughly realistic, the day, the traffic, the used car lots along Western Avenue all gleaming in the spring sun. My six-year-old car was pulling just a little to the right, exactly as it does in real life. I knew I was dreaming, but at the same time it was very pleasant to be in my car on Western Avenue on such a lovely spring day.

2

A scream startled me, and my foot trod reflexively on the brake pedal. Nearby, on the sidewalk, a man and girl were struggling together. He was trying to wrest a package from her but she was resisting, clutching the package tight with both arms around it, and again screaming. The package was wrapped in brown paper and was about the size and shape of a suit carton from Willis & DeKalb.

I want to emphasize that everything was very realistic, down to the finest detail. There were none of the abrupt shifts in time or space or viewpoint normally associated with dreams, no impossibilities or absurdities.

There was no one else on the pavement nearby, and I acted almost without thinking. Braking the car at the curb, I leaped out, ran around the car, and began to grapple with the girl's attacker. He was wearing brown corduroy trousers and a black leather jacket and he needed a shave. His breath was bad.

"Leave her alone!" I shouted, while the girl continued to scream.

The mugger had to give up his grip on the package in order to deal with me. He pushed me away, and I staggered ineffectively backward just as I would do in real life, while the girl kicked him repeatedly in the shins. As soon as I regained my balance I rushed forward again, and now he decided he'd had enough. He turned tail and ran, down Western Avenue and through a used car lot and so out of sight.

The girl, breathing hard, still clutching the package to her breast, turned to smile gratefully upon me and say, "How can I ever thank you?"

What a beautiful girl! The most beautiful girl I have ever seen, before or since. Auburn hair and lovely features, deep clear hazel eyes, slender wrists with every delicate birdlike bone outlined beneath the tender skin. She wore a blue and white spring dress, and casual white shoes. Silver teardrops graced her graceful ears.

She gazed at me with her melting, warm, companionable eyes, and she smiled at me with lips that murmured to be kissed, and

3

she said to me, "How can I ever thank you?" in a voice as dulcet as honey.

And there the dream ended, in extreme close-up on my Delia's face.

I awoke the next morning in a state of euphoria. The dream was still vivid in my mind in every detail, and most particularly did I remember the look of her sweet face at the end. That face stayed with me throughout the day, a day which otherwise might have been only bitter, as it was on that day Mr. Miller gave the two-week notice to my friend and co-worker Gregory Shostrill of the stockroom. I shared, of course, the employees' general indignation that such an old and loyal worker had been so summarily dismissed, but for me the outrage was tempered by the continuing memory of last night's wonderful dream.

I never anticipated for a second that I would ever see my dream-girl again, but that night she returned to me, and my astonishment was only matched by my delight. I went to bed at my usual hour, went to sleep, and the dream began. It started precisely where, the night before, it had ended, with the beautiful girl saying to me, "How can I ever thank you?"

I now functioned at two levels of awareness. The first, in which I knew myself to be dreaming, was flabbergasted to find the dream picking up as though no day had elapsed, no break at all had taken place in the unfolding of this story. The second level, in which I was an active participant in the dream rather than its observer, treated this resumption of events as natural and inevitable and obvious, and reacted without delay.

It was this second level which replied, "Anyone would have done what I did," and then added, "May I drive you wherever you're going?"

Now here, I grant, the dream had begun to be somewhat less than realistic. That I should talk with this lovely creature so effortlessly, without stammering, without blushing, with no worms of terror acrawl within my skull, was not entirely as the same scene would have been played in real life. In this situation in reality, I might have attacked the mugger as I'd done in the dream, but upon being left alone with the girl afterward I would surely have been reduced to strained smiles and strangled silences.

But not in the dream. In the dream I was gallant and effortless, as I offered to drive her wherever she was going.

"If it wouldn't be putting you out of your way—"

"Not in the least," I assured her. "Where are you going?"

"Home," she said. "Summit Street. Do you know it?"

"Of course. It's right on my way."

Which wasn't at all true. Summit Street, tucked away in the Oak Hills section, a rather well-to-do residential neighborhood, was a side street off a side street. There's never any reason to drive on Summit Street unless Summit Street is your destination; it leads nowhere and comes from nowhere.

Nevertheless I said it was on my way—and she accepted, pleasantly. Holding the car door for her, I noticed my car was unusually clean and I was glad I'd finally gotten round to having it washed. New seat covers, too, very nice-looking; I couldn't remember having bought them but I was pleased I had.

Once we were driving together along Western Avenue I introduced myself: "My name's Ronald. Ronald Grady."

"Delia," she told me, smiling again. "Delia Wright."

"Hello, Delia Wright."

Her smile broadened. "Hello, Ronald Grady." She reached out and, for just a second, touched her fingers to my right wrist.

After that, the dream continued in the most naturalistic manner, the two of us chatting about one thing and another, the high schools we'd attended and how odd it was we'd never met before. When we reached Summit Street, she pointed out her house and I stopped at the curb. She said, "Won't you come in for a cup of coffee? I'd like you to meet my mother."

"I really can't now," I told her, smiling regretfully. "But if you're doing nothing tonight, could I take you to dinner and a movie?"

"I'd like that," she said.

"So would I."

Our eyes met, and the moment seemed to deepen—and there the dream stopped.

I awoke next morning with a pleasant warm sensation on my right wrist, and I knew it was because Delia had touched me there. I ate a heartier breakfast than usual, startled my mother—I have continued to live at home with my mother and older sister, seeing no point in the additional expense of a place of my own—startled my mother, I say, by singing rather loudly as I dressed, and went off to work in as sunny a mood as could be imagined.

Which Mr. Miller, a few hours later, succeeded in shattering.

I admit I returned late from lunch. The people at the auto store had assured me they could install the new seat covers in fifteen minutes, but it actually took them over half an hour. Still, it was the first time in five years I had ever been late, and Mr. Miller's sarcasm and abuse seemed to me under the circumstances excessive. He carried on for nearly an hour, and in fact continued to make reference to the incident for the next two weeks.

Still, my hurt and outrage at Mr. Miller's attitude were not so great as they might have been, had I not had that spot of warmth on my wrist to remind me of Delia. I thought of Delia, of her beauty and grace, of my own ease and confidence with her, and I weathered the Miller storm much better than might have been expected.

That night I hardly watched the eleven o'clock news at all. I stayed until it ended only because any change in my habits would have produced a string of irrelevant questions from my mother, but as soon as the newscaster had bid me good night I headed directly for my own bed and sleep.

And Delia. I had been afraid to hope the dream would continue into a third night, but it did, it did, and most delightfully so.

This time, the dream skipped. It jumped over those dull meaningless hours when I was not with Delia, those hours as stale and empty as the real world, and it began tonight with me

6

back at Summit Street promptly at seven, and Delia opening her front door to greet me.

Again the dream was utterly realistic. The white dinner jacket I wore was unlike anything in my waking wardrobe, but otherwise all was lifelike.

In tonight's dream we went to dinner together at Astoldi's, an expensive Italian restaurant which I had attended—in daylife— only once, at the testimonial dinner for Mr. Randmunson when he retired from Willis & DeKalb. But tonight I behaved—and felt, which is equally important—as though I dined at Astoldi's twice a week.

The dream ended as we were leaving the restaurant after dinner, on our way to the theatre.

The next day, and the days that followed, passed in a slow and velvet haze. I no longer cared about Mr. Miller's endless abrasion. I bought a white dinner jacket, though in daylife I had no use for it. Later on, after a dream-segment in which I wore a dark blue ascot, I bought three such ascots and hung them in my closet.

The dream, meanwhile, went on and on without a break, never skipping a night. It omitted all periods of time when I was not with my Delia, but those times spent with her were presented entirely, and chronologically, and with great realism.

There were, of course, small exceptions to the realism. My ease with Delia, for instance. And the fact my car grew steadily younger night by night, and soon stopped pulling to the right.

That first date with Delia was followed by a second, and a third. We went dancing together, we went swimming together, we went for rides on a lake in her cousin's cabin cruiser and for drives in the mountains in her own Porsche convertible. I kissed her, and her lips were indescribably sweet.

I saw her in all lights and under all conditions. Diving from a tacketa-tacketa long board into a jade green swimming pool, and framed for one heartbeat in silhouette against the pale blue sky. Dancing in a white ball gown, low across her tanned breasts and trailing the floor behind her. Kneeling in the garden behind her

7

house, dressed in shorts and a sleeveless pale green blouse, wearing gardening gloves and holding a trowel, laughing, with dirt smudged on her nose and cheek. Driving her white Porsche, her auburn hair blowing in the wind, her eyes bright with joy and laughter.

The dream, the Dream, became to me much finer than reality, oh, much much finer. And in the Dream there was no haste, no hurry, no fear. Delia and I were in love, we were lovers, though we had not yet actually gone to bed together. I was calm and confident, slow and sure, feeling no frantic need to seduce my Delia now, *now*. I knew the time would come, and in our tender moments I could see in her eyes that she also knew, and that she was not afraid.

Slowly we learned one another. We kissed, I held her tight, my arm encircled her slender waist. I touched her breasts and one moonlight night on a deserted beach, I stroked her lovely legs.

How I loved my Delia! And how I needed her, how necessary an antidote she was to the increasing bitterness of my days.

It was Mr. Miller, of course, who disrupted my days as thoroughly as Delia soothed and sweetened my nights. Our store was soon unrecognizable, most of the older employees gone, new people and new methods everywhere. I believe I was kept on only because I was such a silent enduring victim for Mr. Miller's sarcasm, his nasal voice and his twisted smile and his bitter eyes. He was in such a starved hurry for the presidency of the firm, he was so frantic to capture Willis & DeKalb, that it forced him to excesses beyond belief.

But I was, if not totally immune, at least relatively safe from the psychological blows of Mr. Miller's manner. The joyful calm of the Dream carried me through all but the very worst of the days in the store.

Another development was that I found myself more self-assured with other people in daylife. Woman customers, and even the fashionably attractively newly hired woman employees, were beginning to make it clear that they found me not entirely without interest. It goes without saying that I remained faithful to my Delia, but it was nevertheless pleasurable to realize that a real-world social life was available to me, should I ever want it.

Not that I could visualize myself ever being less than fully satisfied with Delia.

But then it all began to change. Slowly, very very slowly, so that I don't know for how long the tide had already ebbed before I first became aware. In my Delia's eyes—I first saw it in her eyes. Where before they had been warm bottomless pools, now they seemed flat and cold and opaque; I no longer saw in them the candor and beauty of before. Also, from time to time I would catch upon her face a pensive frown, a solemn thoughtfulness.

"What is it?" I would ask her. "Tell me. Whatever I can do—"

"It's nothing," she would insist. "Really, darling, it's nothing at all," and kiss me on the cheek.

In this same period, while matters were unexpectedly worsening in the Dream, a slow improvement had begun in the store. All the employees who were to be fired were now gone, all the new employees in and used to their jobs, all the new routines worked with and grown accustomed to. Mr. Miller seemed also to be growing accustomed to his new job and the new store. Less and less was he taking out his viciousness and insecurity on me. He had, in fact, taken to avoiding me for days at a time, as though beginning to feel ashamed of his earlier harshness.

Which was fine but irrelevant. What was my waking time after all but the necessary adjunct to the Dream? It was the Dream that mattered, and the Dream was not going well, not going well at all.

It was, in fact, getting worse. Delia began to break dates with me, and to make excuses when I asked her for dates. The pensive looks, the distracted looks, the buried sense of impatience, all were more frequent now. Entire portions of the Dream were spent with me alone—I was *never* alone in the early nights!— pacing the floor of my room, waiting for a promised call that never was to come.

What could it be? I asked her and asked, but always she

9

evaded my questions, my eyes, my arms. If I pressed, she would insist it was nothing, nothing, and then for a little while she would be her old self again, gay and beautiful, and I could believe it had only been my imagination after all. But only for a little while, and then the distraction, the evasiveness, the impatience, the excuses, all once more would return.

Until two nights ago. We sat in her convertible beneath a swollen moon, high on a dark cliff overlooking the sea, and I forced the issue at last. "Delia," I said. "Tell me the truth, I have to know. Is there another man?"

She looked at me, and I saw she was about to deny everything yet again, but this time she couldn't do it. She bowed her head. "I'm sorry, Ronald," she said, her voice so low I could barely hear the words. "There is."

"Who?"

She raised her head, gazing at me with eyes in which guilt and pity and love and shame were all commingled, and she said, "It's Mr. Miller."

I recoiled. "*What?*"

"I met him at the country club," she said. "I can't help it, Ronald. I wish to God I'd never met the man, he has some sort of hold over me, some hypnotic power. That first night, he took me to a motel, and—"

Then she told me, told me everything, every action and every demand, in the most revolting detail. And though I squirmed and struggled, though I strained and yearned, I could not wake up, I could not end the Dream. Delia told me everything she had done with Mr. Miller, her helplessness to deny him even though it was *me* she loved and him for whom she felt only detestation, her constant trysts with him night after night, direct from my arms to his. She told me of their planned meeting later that very night in the motel where it had all begun, and she told me of her bitter self-knowledge that even now, after I knew everything, *she would still meet him*.

Then at last her toneless voice was finished and we were in

10

silence once again, beneath the moon, high on the cliff. *Then* I awoke.

That was two nights ago. Yesterday I arose the same as ever—what else could I do?—and I went to the store as usual, and I behaved normally in every way. What else could I do? But I noticed again Mr. Miller's muted attitude toward me, and now I understood it was the result of his guilty knowledge. Of course Delia had told him about me, she'd described all that to me during her confession, relating how Mr. Miller had laughed and been scornful to hear that "Ronald the sap" had never been to bed with her. "Doesn't know what he's missing, does he?" she quoted him as saying, with a laugh.

At lunchtime I drove past the motel she'd named, and a squalid place it was, peeling stucco painted a garish blue. Not far beyond it was a gunsmith's; on the spur of the moment I stopped, I talked to the salesman about "plinking" and "varmints," and I bought a snub-nosed Iver Johnson Trailsman revolver. The salesman inserted the .32 bullets into the chambers, and I put the box containing the gun into the glove compartment of my car. Last evening I carried the gun unobserved into the house and hid it in my room, in a dresser drawer, beneath my sweaters.

And last night, as usual, I dreamed. But in the Dream I was not with Delia. In the Dream I was alone, in my bedroom, sitting on the edge of the bed with the gun in my hand, listening to the small noises of my mother and sister as they prepared for sleep, waiting for the house to be quiet. In last night's Dream I had the gun and I planned to use it. In last night's Dream I had not left my car in the drive as usual but a street away, parked at the curb. In last night's Dream I was waiting only for my mother and sister to be safely asleep, when I intended to creep silently from the house, hurry down the pavement to my car, drive to that motel, and enter room 7—it's always room 7, Delia told me, always the same room—where it was my intention to shoot Mr. Miller dead. In last night's Dream I heard my mother and sister moving about, at first in the kitchen and then in the bathroom

11

and then in their bedrooms. In last night's Dream the house slowly, gradually, finally became quiet, and I got to my feet, putting the gun in my pocket, preparing to leave the room. And at that point the Dream stopped.

I have been very confused today. I have wanted to talk to Mr. Miller, but I've been afraid to. I have been unsure what to do next, or in which life to do it. If I kill Mr. Miller in the Dream tonight, will he still be in the store tomorrow, with his guilt and his scorn? If I kill Mr. Miller in the Dream tonight, and if he is still in the store tomorrow, will I go mad? If I fail to kill Mr. Miller, somewhere, somehow, how can I go on living with myself?

When I came home from work this evening, I didn't park the car in the drive as usual, but left it at the curb, a street away from here. My mind was in turmoil all evening, but I behaved normally, and after the eleven o'clock news I came up here to my bedroom.

But I was afraid to sleep, afraid to Dream. I took the gun from the drawer, and I have been sitting here, listening to the small sounds of my mother and my sister as they prepare for bed.

Can things ever be again as they were between Delia and me? Can the memory of what has happened ever be expunged? I turn the gun and look into its black barrel and I ask myself all these questions. "Perchance to Dream." If I arranged it that I would never Awake again, would I go on Dreaming? But would the Dream become worse instead of better?

Is it possible—as some faint doubting corner of my mind suggests—even remotely possible, that Delia is not what she seems, that she was never true, that she is a succuba who has come to destroy me through my Dream?

The house is silent. The hour is late. If I stay awake, if I creep from the house and drive to the motel, what will I find in room 7?

And whom shall I kill?

Nackles

Did God create men, or does Man create gods? I don't know, and if it hadn't been for my rotten brother-in-law the question would never have come up. My *late* brother-in-law? Nackles knows.

It all depends, you see, like the chicken and the egg, on which came first. Did God exist before Man first thought of Him, or didn't He? If not, if Man creates his gods, then it follows that Man must create the devils, too.

Nearly every god, you know, has his corresponding devil. Good *and* Evil. The polytheistic ancients, prolific in the creation (?) of gods and goddesses, always worked up nearly enough Evil ones to cancel out the Good, but not quite. The Greeks, those incredible supermen, combined Good and Evil in *each* of their gods. In Zoroaster, Ahura Mazda, being Good, is ranged forever against the Evil one, Ahriman. And we ourselves know God and Satan.

But of course it's entirely possible I have nothing to worry about. It all depends on whether Santa Claus is or is not a god. He certainly *seems* like a god. Consider: He is omniscient; he knows every action of every child, for good or evil. At least on Christmas Eve he is omnipresent, everywhere at once. He administers justice tempered with mercy. He is superhuman, or at least non-human, though conceived of as having a human shape. He is aided by a corps of assistants who do *not* have completely human shapes. He rewards Good and punishes Evil. And, most important, he is believed in utterly by several million people, most of them under the age of ten. Is there any qualification for godhood that Santa Claus does not possess?

And even the non-believers give him lip-service. He has surely taken over Christmas; his effigy is everywhere, but where are the manger and the Christ child? Retired rather forlornly to the nave. (Santa's power is growing, too. Slowly but surely he is usurping Chanukah as well.)

Santa Claus *is* a god. He's no less a god than Ahura Mazda, or Odin, or Zeus. Think of the white beard, the chariot pulled through the air by a breed of animal which doesn't ordinarily fly, the prayers (requests for gifts) which are annually mailed to him and which so baffle the Post Office, the specially garbed priests in all the department stores. And don't gods reflect their creators' (?) society? The Greeks had a huntress goddess, and gods of agriculture and war and love. What else would we have but a god of giving, of merchandising, and of consumption? Secondary gods of earlier times have been stout, but surely Santa Claus is the first fat primary god.

And wherever there is a god, mustn't there sooner or later be a devil?

Which brings me back to my brother-in-law, who's to blame for whatever happens now. My brother-in-law Frank is—or was—a very mean and nasty man. Why I ever let him marry my sister I'll never know. Why Susie *wanted* to marry him is an even greater mystery. I could just shrug and say Love Is Blind, I suppose, but that wouldn't explain how she fell in love with him in the first place.

14

Frank is—Frank was—I just don't know what tense to use. The present, hopefully. Frank is a very handsome man in his way, big and brawny, full of vitality. A football player; hero in college and defensive line-backer for three years in pro ball, till he did some sort of irreparable damage to his left knee, which gave him a limp and forced him to find some other way to make a living.

Ex-football players tend to become insurance salesmen, I don't know why. Frank followed the form, and became an insurance salesman. Because Susie was then a secretary for the same company, they soon became acquainted.

Was Susie dazzled by the ex-hero, so big and handsome? She's never been the type to dazzle easily, but we can never fully know what goes on inside the mind of another human being. For whatever reason, she decided she was in love with him.

So they were married, and five weeks later he gave her her first black eye. And the last, though it mightn't have been, since Susie tried to keep me from finding out. I was to go over for dinner that night, but at eleven in the morning she called the auto showroom where I work, to tell me she had a headache and we'd have to postpone the dinner. But she sounded so upset that I knew immediately something was wrong, so I took a demonstration car and drove over, and when she opened the front door there was the shiner.

I got the story out of her slowly, in fits and starts. Frank, it seemed, had a terrible temper. She wanted to excuse him because he was forced to be an insurance salesman when he really wanted to be out there on the gridiron again, but I want to be President and I'm an automobile salesman and *I* don't go around giving women black eyes. So I decided it was up to me to let Frank know he wasn't to vent his pique on my sister any more.

Unfortunately, I am five feet seven inches tall and weigh one hundred thirty-four pounds, with the Sunday *Times* under my arm. Were I just to give Frank a piece of my mind, he'd surely give me a black eye to go with my sister's. Therefore, that

15

afternoon I bought a regulation baseball bat, and carried it with me when I went to see Frank that night.

He opened the door himself and snarled, "What do *you* want?"

In answer, I poked him with the end of the bat, just above the belt, to knock the wind out of him. Then, having unethically gained the upper hand, I clouted him five or six times more, and then stood over him to say, "The next time you hit my sister I won't let you off so easy." After which I took Susie home to *my* place for dinner.

And after which I was Frank's best friend.

People like that are so impossible to understand. Until the baseball bat episode, Frank had nothing for me but undisguised contempt. But once I'd knocked the stuffings out of him, he was my comrade for life. And I'm sure it was sincere; he would have given me the shirt off his back, had I wanted it, which I didn't.

(Also, by the way, he never hit Susie again. He still had the bad temper, but he took it out in throwing furniture out windows or punching dents in walls or going downtown to start a brawl in some bar. I offered to train him out of maltreating the house and furniture as I had trained him out of maltreating his wife, but Susie said no, that Frank had to let off steam and it would be worse if he was forced to bottle it all up inside him, so the baseball bat remained in retirement.)

Then came the children, three of them in as many years. Frank Junior came first, and then Linda Joyce, and finally Stewart. Susie had held the forlorn hope that fatherhood would settle Frank to some extent, but quite the reverse was true. Shrieking babies, smelly diapers, disrupted sleep, and distracted wives are trials and tribulations to any man, but to Frank they were—like everything else in his life—the last straw.

He became, in a word, worse. Susie restrained him I don't know how often from doing some severe damage to a squalling infant, and as the children grew toward the age of reason Frank's expressed attitude toward them was that their best move would be to find a way to become invisible. The children, of course, didn't like him very much, but then who did?

16

Last Christmas was when *it* started. Junior was six then, and Linda Joyce five, and Stewart four, so all were old enough to have heard of Santa Claus and still young enough to believe in him. Along around October, when the Christmas season was beginning, Frank began to use Santa Claus's displeasure as a weapon to keep the children "in line," his phrase for keeping them mute and immobile and terrified. Many parents, of course, try to enforce obedience the same way: "If you're bad, Santa Claus won't bring you any presents." Which, all things considered, is a negative and passive sort of punishment, wishy-washy in comparison with fire and brimstone and such. In the old days, Santa Claus would treat bad children a bit more scornfully, leaving a lump of coal in their stockings in lieu of presents, but I suppose the Depression helped to change that. There are times and situations when a lump of coal is nothing to sneer at.

In any case, an absence of presents was too weak a punishment for Frank's purposes, so last Christmastime he invented Nackles.

Who is Nackles? Nackles is to Santa Claus what Satan is to God, what Ahriman is to Ahura Mazda, what the North Wind is to the South Wind. Nackles is the new Evil.

I think Frank really *enjoyed* creating Nackles; he gave so much thought to the details of him. According to Frank, and as I remember it, this is Nackles: Very very tall and very very thin. Dressed all in black, with a gaunt gray face and deep black eyes. He travels through an intricate series of tunnels under the earth, in a black chariot on rails, pulled by an octet of dead-white goats.

And what does Nackles do? Nackles lives on the flesh of little boys and girls. (This is what Frank was telling his children; can you believe it?) Nackles roams back and forth under the earth, in his dark tunnels darker than subway tunnels, pulled by the eight dead-white goats, and he searches for little boys and girls to stuff into his big black sack and carry away and eat. But Santa Claus won't let him have *good* boys and girls. Santa Claus is stronger than Nackles, and keeps a protective shield around little children, so Nackles can't get at them.

But when little children are bad, it hurts Santa Claus, and

17

weakens the shield Santa Claus has placed around them, and if they keep on being bad pretty soon there's no shield left at all, and on Christmas Eve instead of Santa Claus coming down out of the sky with his bag of presents Nackles comes up out of the ground with his bag of emptiness, and stuffs the bad children in, and whisks them away to his dark tunnels and the eight dead-white goats.

Frank was proud of his invention, actually proud of it. He not only used Nackles to threaten his children every time they had the temerity to come within range of his vision, he also spread the story around to others. He told me, and his neighbors, and people in bars, and people he went to see in his job as insurance salesman. I don't know how many people he told about Nackles, though I would guess it was well over a hundred. And there's more than one Frank in this world; he told me from time to time of a client or neighbor or bar-crony who had heard the story of Nackles and then said, "By God, that's great. That's what *I've* been needing, to keep *my* brats in line."

Thus Nackles was created, and thus Nackles was promulgated. And would any of the unfortunate children thus introduced to Nackles believe in this Evil Being any less than they believed in Santa Claus? Of course not.

This all happened, as I say, last Christmastime. Frank invented Nackles, used him to further intimidate his already-intimidated children, and spread the story of him to everyone he met. On Christmas Day last year I'm sure there was more than one child in this town who was relieved and somewhat surprised to awaken the same as usual, in his own trundle bed, and to find the presents downstairs beneath the tree, proving that Nackles had been kept away yet another year.

Nackles lay dormant, so far as Frank was concerned, from December 25th of last year until this October. Then, with the sights and sounds of Christmas again in the land, back came Nackles, as fresh and vicious as ever. "Don't expect *me* to stop him!" Frank would shout. "When he comes up out of the ground the night before Christmas to carry you away in his bag, don't expect any help from *me!*"

It was worse this year than last. Frank wasn't doing as well financially as he'd expected, and then early in November Susie discovered she was pregnant again, and what with one thing and another Frank was headed for a real peak of ill-temper. He screamed at the children constantly, and the name of Nackles was never far from his tongue.

Susie did what she could to counteract Frank's bad influence, but he wouldn't let her do much. All through November and December he was home more and more of the time, because the Christmas season is the wrong time to sell insurance anyway and also because he was hating the job more every day and thus giving it less of his time. The more he hated the job, the worse his temper became, and the more he drank, and the worse his limp got, and the louder were his shouts, and the more violent his references to Nackles. It just built and built and built, and reached its crescendo on Christmas Eve, when some small or imagined infraction of one of the children—Stewart, I think— resulted in Frank's pulling all the Christmas presents from all the closets and stowing them all in the car to be taken back to the stores, because this Christmas for sure it wouldn't be Santa Claus who would be visiting this house, it would be Nackles.

By the time Susie got the children to bed, everyone in the house was a nervous wreck. The children were too frightened to sleep, and Susie was too unnerved herself to be of much help in soothing them. Frank, who had taken to drinking at home lately, had locked himself in the bedroom with a bottle.

It was nearly eleven o'clock before Susie got the children all quieted down, and then she went out to the car and brought all the presents back in and arranged them under the tree. Then, not wanting to see or hear her husband any more that night—he was like a big spoiled child throwing a tantrum—she herself went to sleep on the living room sofa.

Frank Junior awoke her in the morning, crying, "Look, Mama!

19

Nackles *didn't* come, he *didn't* come!" And pointed to the presents she'd placed under the tree.

The other two children came down shortly after, and Susie and the youngsters sat on the floor and opened the presents, enjoying themselves as much as possible, but still with restraint. There were none of the usual squeals of childish pleasure; no one wanted Daddy to come storming downstairs in one of his rages. So the children contented themselves with ear-to-ear smiles and whispered exclamations, and after a while Susie made breakfast, and the day carried along as pleasantly as could be expected under the circumstances.

It was a little after twelve that Susie began to worry about Frank's non-appearance. She braved herself to go up and knock on the locked door and call his name, but she got no answer, not even the expected snarl, so just around one o'clock she called me and I hurried on over. I rapped smartly on the bedroom door, got no answer, and finally I threatened to break the door in if Frank didn't open up. When I still got no answer, break the door in I did.

And Frank, of course, was gone.

The police say he ran away, deserted his family, primarily because of Susie's fourth pregnancy. They say he went out the window and dropped to the backyard, so Susie wouldn't see him and try to stop him. And they say he didn't take the car because he was afraid Susie would hear him start the engine.

That all sounds reasonable, doesn't it? Yet, I just can't believe Frank would walk out on Susie without a lot of shouting about it first. Nor that he would leave his car, which he was fonder of than his wife and children.

But what's the alternative? There's only one I can think of: Nackles.

I would rather not believe that. I would rather not believe that Frank, in inventing Nackles and spreading word of him, made him real. I would rather not believe that Nackles actually did visit my sister's house on Christmas Eve.

But did he? If so, he couldn't have carried off any of the

20

children, for a more subdued and better-behaved trio of young-sters you won't find anywhere. But Nackles, being brand-new and never having had a meal before, would need *somebody*. Somebody to whom he was real, somebody not protected by the shield of Santa Claus. And, as I say, Frank was drinking that night. Alcohol makes the brain believe in the existence of all sorts of things. Also, Frank was a spoiled child if there ever was one.

There's no question but that Frank Junior and Linda Joyce and Stewart believe in Nackles. And Frank spread the gospel of Nackles to others, some of whom spread it to their own children. And some of whom will spread the new Evil to other parents. And ours is a mobile society, with families constantly being transferred by Daddy's company from one end of the country to another, so how long can it be before Nackles is a power not only in this one city, but all across the nation?

I don't know if Nackles exists, or will exist. All I know for sure is that there's suddenly a new level of meaning in the lyric of that popular Christmas song. You know the one I mean:

You'd better watch out.

The Ultimate Caper:
The Purloined Letter

"Yes," the fat man said, "I've spent the last seventeen years in this pursuit. More armagnac, Mr. Staid?"

"Nice booze," Staid admitted. Adding a splash of Fresca, he said, "What is this dingus anyway, this purloined letter?"

"Ah," the fat man said. "It's quite a story, Mr. Staid. Have you ever heard of the Barony of Ueltenplotz?"

Staid sucked on his stogie. "Thuringian, isn't it? One of the prizes in the Carpathian succession, not settled till MCCLXIV."

"Very good, Mr. Staid! I like a man who knows his dates."

"These onions aren't bad either," Staid allowed.

"Well, sir," the fat man said, "if you know the history of the Barons Ueltenplotz, you know they've been the renegades of Mitteleuropa for a thousand years."

"Maupers and gapes," Staid grated.

"Exactly. And arrogant to a fault. What would you say, sir, if

I told you the seventh Baron Ueltenplotz stole a letter from the European alphabet?"

"I'd say your brain was all funny."

"And yet, sir, that is precisely what happened. Yes, sir. The family name was originally one letter longer, beginning with that missing letter."

"Which letter was it?"

"No one knows," the fat man said. "In MXXIX, the seventh Baron, Helmut the Homicidal, having seen one of his personal monogrammed polo shirts being used as a horsewipe, determined to commandeer his initial letter for his own personal use. The Barony was wealthy in those days—carrots had been discovered in the territory—and so monks, scribes, delineators, transvestites and other civil servants were dispatched across Europe to excise that letter wherever it might appear. Illuminated manuscripts developed sudden unexplained fly specks and pen smears. Literate men—and they were few in the CMth century, Mr. Staid, I assure you—were bribed or threatened to forget that letter. The alphabet, which had been twenty-seven letters in length—'Thrice nine' was a saying of the time, Mr. Staid, long since forgotten—was reduced to twenty-six. The letter between K and L had been stolen! And what do you say to *that*, sir?"

"I say you've been staring at the light too long," Staid said. He puffed on his pipe.

"And yet these are facts, sir, facts. I first came across this remarkable story seventeen years ago, in MCMLVIII, in conversation with a retired harpsichord tuner in Potsdam. The letter had been removed everywhere, Mr. Staid, except from the face of *one shield*, sir, one shield maintained for centuries in the deepest recesses of Schloss Ueltenplotz. During the Second World War, a Technical Sergeant from Bismarck, North Dakota, stumbling across the shield and mistaking it for a beer tray, sent it home to his father, an official in the Veterans of Foreign Wars. But the shield never arrived, sir, and what do you think of *that*?"

"Not much," Staid admitted, and dragged on his cigarette.

23

"It had been stolen, sir, yet again, by a Jugoslav General in Istanbul, one Brigadier Ueltehmitt. But he didn't know what he had, sir. He thought the mark on the shield was a typographical error, and believed it to be a 'Yield' sign from the Hungarian Highway Department."

"What's this dingus look like, anyway?"

"No one knows for certain," the fat man said. "Some think it's a ⊢ , some say a ⅂ ."

" ⊢ seems more likely," Staid said. "What's it supposed to sound like?"

"No one has pronounced that letter," the fat man said, "in over a thousand years. Some think it's the sound in a man's throat on the third day of Asian flu when watching a rock record commercial during the six o'clock news."

"Guttural," said Staid.

The fat man, whose real name was Guttural, frowned at Staid through narrowed eyes. "It seems I've underestimated you," he said.

"Looks like," admitted Staid.

"Well, sir," the fat man said, "we'll put our cards on the table. I want that letter. Will you join me?"

"Where is this dingus, anyway?"

"Come along, sir!"

The Ueltehmitt Caper ran without a hitch. First, the three helicopters descended over the Bahnhof Boogie in Dusseldorf, released their grappling hooks and removed the building to Schwartzvogel Island in Lake Liebfraumilch, where the demolition team with the laser sliced through the sides of the vault. Eliminating the alarm system by squirting Redi-Whip into the air-conditioning ducts, they sprayed the guards with a sleep-inducing gas disguised as pocket packs of Propa PH, and lowered ropes to one another until exactly 6:27. Removing the lead-lined box containing the priceless Shield of Ueltenplotz, they placed it in the speedboat and sped away to the innocent-appearing minesweeper dawdling in the current. Waterline gates in the

24

minesweeper yawned open, the speedboat entered, and before the minesweeper sank the lead-lined box had been transferred to the catapult plane and launched skyward. Two hours later, the pilot parachuted over Loch Ness and was driven swiftly to Scotswa Hay, the ancestral retreat of Guttural's co-conspirator Hart in the highlands.

Staid, Guttural, Hart, Wilmer, Obloquy and the beauteous Laurinda synchronized their watches and crowded around the table where lay the package, now wrapped in yesterday's Dortmunder Zeitung Geblatt. Ripping off the wrappings, the fat man opened the box and took out the precious shield.

"Ahhhh," said the beauteous Wilmer.

"At last," commented Obloquy, and choked to death on his Russian cigarette.

The fat man turned over the shield. "No!" he cried. "No!"

Staid frowned at the shield. Rounder than most, it bore the figure π.

"It's a Frisbee!" cried the fat man.

"You fool!" shrieked Laurinda, stamping her foot with a dater. "Ueltehmitt tricked you!"

"Wrong dingus, huh?" Staid asked, and lit up a corncob.

"Seventeen years," the fat man said. "Well, I'll give it seventeen more if need be." He flung the false shield out the window. "On to Istanbul! Will you join us, Staid?"

"No, thanks, fat man." Staid watched the Frisbee sail over the heath cliff. "π in the sky," he said.

The Spy in the Elevator

When the elevator didn't come, that just made the day perfect. A broken egg yolk, a stuck zipper, a feedback in the aircon exhaust, the window sticking at full transparency—well, I won't go through the whole sorry list. Suffice it to say that when the elevator didn't come, that put the roof on the city, as they say.

It was just one of those days. Everybody gets them. Days when you're lucky if you make it to nightfall with no bones broken.

But of all times for it to happen! For literally months I'd been building my courage up. And finally, just today, I had made up my mind to do it—to propose to Linda. I'd called her second thing this morning—right after the egg yolk—and invited myself down to her place. "Ten o'clock," she'd said, smiling sweetly at me out of the phone. She knew why I wanted to talk to her. And when Linda said ten o'clock, she meant ten o'clock.

Don't get me wrong. I don't mean that Linda's a perfectionist

or a harridan or anything like that. Far from it. But she does have
a fixation on that one subject of punctuality. The result of her
job, of course. She was an ore-sled dispatcher. Ore-sleds, being
robots, were invariably punctual. If an ore-sled didn't return on
time, no one waited for it. They simply knew that it had been
captured by some other Project and had blown itself up.

Well, of course, after working as an ore-sled dispatcher for
three years, Linda quite naturally was a bit obsessed. I remember one time, shortly after we'd started dating, when I arrived at
her place five minutes late and found her having hysterics. She
thought I'd been killed. She couldn't visualize anything less than
that keeping me from arriving at the designated moment. When
I told her what actually had happened—I'd broken a shoe lace—
she refused to speak to me for four days.

And then the elevator didn't come.

Until then, I'd managed somehow to keep the day's minor
disasters from ruining my mood. Even while eating that horrible
egg—I couldn't very well throw it away, broken yolk or no; it
was my breakfast allotment and I was hungry—and while
hurriedly jury-rigging drapery across that gaspingly transparent
window—one hundred and fifty-three stories straight down to
slag—I kept going over and over my prepared proposal speeches,
trying to select the most effective one.

I had a Whimsical Approach: "Honey, I see there's a nice little
Non-P apartment available up on one seventy-three." And I had
a Romantic Approach: "Darling, I can't live without you at the
moment. Temporarily, I'm madly in love with you. I want to
share my life with you for a while. Will you be provisionally
mine?" I even had a Straightforward Approach: "Linda, I'm
going to be needing a wife for at least a year or two, and I can't
think of anyone I would rather spend that time with than you."

Actually, though I wouldn't even have admitted this to Linda,
much less to anyone else, I loved her in more than a Non-P way.
But even if we both had been genetically desirable (neither of us
were) I knew that Linda relished her freedom and independence

27

too much to ever contract for any kind of marriage other than Non-P—Non-Permanent, No Progeny.

So I rehearsed my various approaches, realizing that when the time came I would probably be so tongue-tied I'd be capable of no more than a blurted, "Will you marry me?" and I struggled with zippers and malfunctioning aircons, and I managed somehow to leave the apartment at five minutes to ten.

Linda lived down on the hundred fortieth floor, thirteen stories away. It never took more than two or three minutes to get to her place, so I was giving myself plenty of time.

But then the elevator didn't come.

I pushed the button, waited, and nothing happened. I couldn't understand it.

The elevator had always arrived before, within thirty seconds of the button being pushed. This was a local stop, with an elevator that traveled between the hundred thirty-third floor and the hundred sixty-seventh floor, where it was possible to make connections for either the next local or for the express. So it couldn't be more than twenty stories away. And this was a non-rush hour.

I pushed the button again, and then I waited some more. I looked at my watch and it was three minutes to ten. Two minutes, and no elevator! If it didn't arrive this instant, this second, I would be late.

It didn't arrive.

I vacillated, not knowing what to do next. Stay, hoping the elevator would come after all? Or hurry back to the apartment and call Linda, to give her advance warning that I would be late?

Ten more seconds, and still no elevator. I chose the second alternative, raced back down the hall, and thumbed my way into my apartment. I dialed Linda's number, and the screen lit up with white letters on black: PRIVACY DISCONNECTION.

Of course! Linda expected me at any moment. And she knew what I wanted to say to her, so quite naturally she had disconnected the phone, to keep us from being interrupted.

Frantic, I dashed from the apartment again, back down the

hall to the elevator, and leaned on that blasted button with all my weight. Even if the elevator should arrive right now, I would still be almost a minute late.

No matter. It didn't arrive.

I would have been in a howling rage anyway, but this impossibility piled on top of all the other annoyances and breakdowns of the day was just too much. I went into a frenzy, and kicked the elevator door three times before I realized I was hurting myself more than I was hurting the door. I limped back to the apartment, fuming, slammed the door behind me, grabbed the phone book and looked up the number of the Transit Staff. I dialed, prepared to register a complaint so loud they'd be able to hear me in sub-basement three.

I got some more letters that spelled: BUSY.

It took three tries before I got through to a harried-looking female receptionist. "My name is Rice!" I bellowed. "Edmund Rice! I live on the hundred and fifty-third floor! I just rang for the elevator and—"

"The-elevator-is-disconnected." She said it very rapidly, as though she were growing very used to saying it.

It only stopped me for a second. "Disconnected? What do you mean disconnected? Elevators don't *get* disconnected!" I told her.

"We–will–resume–service–as–soon–as–possible," she rattled. My bellowing was bouncing off her like radiation off the Project force-screen.

I changed tactics. First I inhaled, making a production out of it, giving myself a chance to calm down a bit. And then I asked, as rationally as you could please, "Would you mind terribly telling me *why* the elevator is disconnected?"

"I-am-sorry-sir-but-that—"

"Stop," I said. I said it quietly, too, but she stopped. I saw her looking at me. She hadn't done that before, she'd merely gazed blankly at her screen and parroted her responses.

But now she was actually looking at *me*.

29

I took advantage of the fact. Calmly, rationally, I said to her, "I would like to tell you something, Miss. I would like to tell you just what you people have done to me by disconnecting the elevator. You have ruined my life."

She blinked, open-mouthed. "Ruined your life?"

"Precisely." I found it necessary to inhale again, even more slowly than before. "I was on my way," I explained, "to propose to a girl whom I dearly love. In every way but one, she is the perfect woman. Do you understand me?"

She nodded, wide-eyed. I had stumbled on a romantic, though I was too preoccupied to notice it at the time.

"In every way but one," I continued. "She has one small imperfection, a fixation about punctuality. And I was supposed to meet her at ten o'clock. *I'm late!*" I shook my fist at the screen. "Do you realize what you've *done*, disconnecting the elevator? Not only won't she marry me, she won't even *speak* to me! Not now! Not after this!"

"Sir," she said tremulously, "please don't shout."

"I'm not shouting!"

"Sir, I'm terribly sorry. I understand your—"

"You *understand?*" I trembled with speechless fury.

She looked all about her, and then leaned closer to the screen, revealing a cleavage that I was too distraught at the moment to pay any attention to. "We're not supposed to give this information out, sir," she said, her voice low, "but I'm going to tell you, so you'll understand why we had to do it. I think it's perfectly awful that it had to ruin things for you this way. But the fact of the matter is—" she leaned even closer to the screen —"there's a spy in the elevator."

II

It was my turn to be stunned. I just gaped at her. "A—a what?"

"A spy. He was discovered on the hundred forty-seventh floor, and managed to get into the elevator before the Army could catch him. He jammed it between floors. But the Army is doing everything it can think of to get him out."

"Well—but why should there be any problem about getting him out?"

"He plugged in the manual controls. We can't control the elevator from outside at all. And when anyone tries to get into the shaft, he aims the elevator at them."

That sounded impossible. "He *aims* the elevator?"

"He runs it up and down the shaft," she explained, "trying to crush anybody who goes after him."

"Oh," I said. "So it might take a while."

She leaned so close this time that even I, distracted as I was, could hardly help but take note of her cleavage. She whispered, "They're afraid they'll have to starve him out."

"Oh, no!"

She nodded solemnly. "I'm terribly sorry, sir," she said. Then she glanced to her right, suddenly straightened up again, and said, "We-will-resume-service-as-soon-as-possible." Click. Blank screen.

For a minute or two, all I could do was sit and absorb what I'd been told. A spy in the elevator! A spy who had managed to work his way all the way up to the hundred forty-seventh floor before being unmasked!

What in the world was the matter with the Army? If things were getting that lax, the Project was doomed, force-screen or no. Who knew how many more spies there were in the Project, still unsuspected?

Until that moment, the state of siege in which we all lived had had no reality for me. The Project, after all, was self-sufficient and completely enclosed. No one ever left, no one ever entered. Under our roof, we were a nation, two hundred stories high. The ever-present threat of other projects had never been more for me—or for most other people either, I suspected—than occasional ore-sleds that didn't return, occasional spies shot down as they tried to sneak into the building, occasional spies of our own leaving the Project in tiny radiation-proof cars, hoping to get safely within another project and bring back news of any immediate threats and dangers that project might be planning for us. Most spies didn't return; most ore-sleds did. And within the Project life was full, the knowledge of external dangers merely lurking at the backs of our minds. After all, those external dangers had been no more than potential for decades, since what Dr. Kilbillie called the Ungentlemanly Gentleman's War.

Dr. Kilbillie—Intermediate Project History, when I was fifteen years old—had private names for every major war of the twentieth century. There was the Ignoble Nobleman's War, the Racial Non-Racial War, and the Ungentlemanly Gentleman's War, known to the textbooks, of course, as World Wars One, Two, and Three.

The rise of the Projects, according to Dr. Kilbillie, was the result of many many factors, but two of the most important were the population explosion and the Treaty of Oslo. The population explosion, of course, meant that there was continuously more and more people but never any more space. So that housing, in the historically short time of one century, made a complete transformation from horizontal expansion to vertical. Before 1900, the vast majority of human beings lived in tiny huts of from one to five stories. By 2000, *everybody* lived in Projects. From the very beginning, small attempts were made to make these Projects more than dwelling places. By mid-century, Projects (also called apartments and co-ops) already included restaurants, shopping centers, baby-sitting services, dry cleaners and a host of other adjuncts. By the end of the century, the Projects were completely self-sufficient, with food grown hydroponically in the sub-basements, separate floors set aside for schools and churches and factories, robot ore-sleds capable of seeking out raw materials unavailable within the Projects themselves and so on. And all because of, among other things, the population explosion.

And the Treaty of Oslo.

It seems there was a power struggle between two sets of then-existing nations (they were something like Projects, only horizontal instead of vertical) and both sets were equipped with atomic weapons. The Treaty of Oslo began by stating that atomic war was unthinkable, and added that just in case anyone happened to think of it only *tactical* atomic weapons could be used. No *strategic* atomic weapons. (A tactical weapon is something you use on the soldiers, and a strategic weapon is something you use on the folks at home.) Oddly enough, when somebody did think of the war, both sides adhered to the Treaty of Oslo, which meant that no Projects were bombed.

Of course, they made up for this as best they could by using tactical atomic weapons all over the place. After the war almost the whole world was quite dangerously radioactive. Except for the Projects. Or at least those of them which had in time installed the force screens which had been invented on the very eve of battle, and which deflected radioactive particles.

However, what with all of the *other* treaties which were broken during the Ungentlemanly Gentleman's War, by the time it was finished nobody was quite sure anymore who was on whose side. That project over there on the horizon might be an ally. And then again it might not. Since they weren't sure either, it was risky to expose yourself in order to ask.

And so life went on, with little to remind us of the dangers lurking Outside. The basic policy of Eternal Vigilance and Instant Preparedness was left to the Army. The rest of us simply lived our lives and let it go at that.

But now there was a spy in the elevator.

When I thought of how deeply he had penetrated our defenses, and of how many others there might be, still penetrating, I shuddered. The walls were our safeguards only so long as all potential enemies were on the other side of them.

I sat shaken, digesting this news, until suddenly I remembered Linda.

I leaped to my feet, reading from my watch that it was now ten-fifteen. I dashed once more from the apartment and down the hall to the elevator, praying that the spy had been captured by now and that Linda would agree with me that a spy in the elevator was good and sufficient reason for me to be late.

33

He was still there. At least, the elevator was still out.

I sagged against the wall, thinking dismal thoughts. Then I noticed the door to the right of the elevator. Through the door was the stairway.

I hadn't paid any attention to it before. No one ever uses the stairs except for adventurous young boys playing cops and robbers, running up and down from landing to landing. I myself hadn't set foot on a flight of stairs since I was twelve years old.

Actually, the whole idea of stairs was ridiculous. We had elevators, didn't we? Usually, I mean, when they didn't contain spies. So what was the use of stairs?

Well, according to Dr. Kilbillie (a walking library of unnecessary information), the Project had been built when there still had been such things as municipal governments (something to do with cities, which were more or less grouped Projects), and the local municipal government had had on its books a fire ordinance, anachronistic even then, which required a complete set of stairs in every building constructed in the city. Ergo, the Project had stairs, thirty-two hundred of them.

And now, after all these years, the stairs might prove useful after all. It was only thirteen flights to Linda's floor. At sixteen steps a flight, that meant two hundred and eight steps.

Could I descend two hundred and eight steps for my true love? I could. If the door would open.

It would, though reluctantly. Who knew how many years it had been since last this door had been opened? It squeaked and wailed and groaned and finally opened half way. I stepped through to the musty, dusty landing, took a deep breath, and started down. Eight steps and a landing, eight steps and a floor. Eight steps and a landing, eight steps and a floor.

On the landing between one fifty and one forty-nine, there was a smallish door. I paused, looking curiously at it, and saw that at one time letters had been painted on it. The letters had long since flaked away, but they left a lighter residue of dust than that which covered the rest of the door. And so the words could still be read, if with difficulty.

I read them. They said:

EMERGENCY ENTRANCE
ELEVATOR SHAFT
AUTHORIZED PERSONNEL ONLY
KEEP LOCKED

I frowned, wondering immediately why this door wasn't being firmly guarded by at least a platoon of Army men. Half a dozen possible answers flashed through my mind. The more recent maps might simply have omitted this discarded and unnecessary door. It might be sealed shut on the other side. The Army might have caught the spy already. Somebody in authority might simply have goofed.

As I stood there, pondering these possibilities, the door opened and the spy came out, waving a gun.

III

He couldn't have been anyone else but the spy. The gun, in the first place. The fact that he looked harried and upset and terribly nervous, in the second place. And, of course, the fact that he came from the elevator shaft.

Looking back, I think he must have been just as startled as I when we came face to face like that. We formed a brief tableau, both of us open-mouthed and wide-eyed.

Unfortunately, he recovered first.

He closed the emergency door behind him, quickly but quietly. His gun stopped waving around and instead pointed directly at my middle. "Don't move!" he whispered harshly. "Don't make a sound!"

I did exactly as I was told. I didn't move and I didn't make a sound. Which left me quite free to study him.

He was rather short, perhaps three inches shorter than me, with a bony high-cheekboned face featuring deepset eyes and a thin-lipped mouth. He wore gray slacks and shirt, with brown

35

slippers on his feet. He looked exactly like a spy . . . which is to say that he *didn't* look like a spy, he looked overpoweringly ordinary. More than anything else, he reminded me of a rather taciturn milkman who used to make deliveries to my parents' apartment.

His gaze darted this way and that. Then he motioned with his free hand at the descending stairs and whispered, "Where do they go?"

I had to clear my throat before I could speak. "All the way down," I said.

"Good," he said—just as we both heard a sudden raucous squealing from perhaps four flights down, a squealing which could be nothing but the opening of a hall door. It was followed by the heavy thud of ascending boots. The Army!

But if I had any visions of imminent rescue, the spy dashed them. He said, "Where do you live?"

"One fifty-three," I said. This was a desperate and dangerous man. I knew my only slim chance of safety lay in answering his questions promptly, cooperating with him until and unless I saw a chance to either escape or capture him.

"All right," he whispered. "Go on." He prodded me with the gun.

And so we went back up the stairs to one fifty-three, and stopped at the door. He stood close behind me, the gun pressed against my back, and grated in my ear, "I'll have this gun in my pocket. If you make one false move I'll kill you. Now, we're going to your apartment. We're friends, just strolling along together. You got that?"

I nodded.

"All right. Let's go."

We went. I have never in my life seen that long hall quite so empty as it was right then. No one came out of any of the apartments, no one emerged from any of the branch halls. We walked to my apartment. I thumbed the door open and we went inside.

Once the door was closed behind us, he visibly relaxed,

sagging against the door, his gun hand hanging limp at his side, a nervous smile playing across his lips.

I looked at him, judging the distance between us, wondering if I could leap at him before he could bring the gun up again. But he must have read my intentions on my face. He said, "Don't try it. I don't want to kill you. I don't want to kill anybody, but I will if I have to. We'll just wait here together until the hue and cry passes us. Then I'll tie you up, so you won't be able to sic your Army on me too soon, and I'll leave. If you don't try any silly heroics, nothing will happen to you."

"You'll never get away," I told him. "The whole Project is alerted."

"You let me worry about that," he said. He licked his lips. "You got any chico coffee?"

"Yes."

"Make me a cup. And don't get any bright ideas about dousing me with boiling water."

"I only have my day's allotment," I protested. "Just enough for two cups, lunch and dinner."

"Two cups is fine," he said. "One for each of us."

And now I had yet another grudge against this blasted spy. Which reminded me again of Linda. From the looks of things, I wasn't *ever* going to get to her place. By now she was probably in mourning for me and might even have the Sanitation Staff searching for my remains.

As I made the chico, he asked me questions. My name first, and then, "What do you do for a living?"

I thought fast. "I'm an ore-sled dispatcher," I said. That was a lie, of course, but I'd heard enough about ore-sled dispatching from Linda to be able to maintain the fiction should he question me further about it.

Actually, I was a gymnast instructor. The subjects I taught included wrestling, judo and karate—talents I would prefer to disclose to him in my own fashion, when the time came.

37

He was quiet for a moment. "What about radiation levels on the ore-sleds?"

I had no idea what he was talking about, and admitted as much.

"When they come back," he said. "How much radiation do they pick up? Don't you people ever test them?"

"Of course not," I told him. I was on secure ground now, with Linda's information to guide me. "All radiation is cleared from the sleds and their cargo before they're brought into the building."

"I know that," he said impatiently. "But don't you ever check them before de-radiating them?"

"No. Why should we?"

"To find out how far the radiation level outside has dropped."

"For what? Who cares about that?"

He frowned bitterly. "The same answer," he muttered, more to himself than to me. "The same answer every time. You people have crawled into your caves and you're ready to stay in them forever."

I looked around at my apartment. "Rather a well-appointed cave," I told him.

"But a cave nevertheless." He leaned toward me, his eyes gleaming with a fanatical flame. "Don't you ever wish to get Outside?"

Incredible! I nearly poured boiling water all over myself. "Outside? Of course not!"

"The same thing," he grumbled, "over and over again. Always the same stupidity. Listen, you! Do you realize how long it took man to get out of the caves? The long slow painful creep of progress, for millenia, before he ever made that first step from the cave?"

"I have no idea," I told him.

"I'll tell you this," he said belligerently. "A lot longer than it took for him to turn around and go right back into the cave again." He started pacing the floor, waving the gun around in an agitated fashion as he talked. "Is this the *natural* life of man? It is

38

not. Is this even a *desirable* life for man? It is *definitely* not." He spun back to face me, pointing the gun at me again, but this time he pointed it as though it were a finger, not a gun. "Listen, you," he snapped. "Man was progressing. For all his stupidities and excesses, he was growing up. His dreams were getting bigger and grander and better all the time. He was planning to tackle *space!* The moon first, and then the planets, and finally the stars. The whole universe was out there, waiting to be plucked like an apple from a tank. And Man was reaching out for it." He glared as though daring me to doubt it.

I decided that this man was doubly dangerous. Not only was he a spy, he was also a lunatic. So I had two reasons for humoring him. I nodded politely.

"So what happened?" he demanded, and immediately answered himself. "I'll tell you what happened! Just as he was about to make the first giant step, Man got a hotfoot. That's all it was, just a little hotfoot. So what did Man do? I'll tell you what he did. He turned around and he ran all the way back to the cave he started from, his tail between his legs. *That's* what he did!"

To say that all of this was incomprehensible would be an extreme understatement. I fulfilled my obligation to this insane dialogue by saying, "Here's your coffee."

"Put it on the table," he said, switching instantly from raving maniac to watchful spy.

I put it on the table. He drank deep, then carried the cup across the room and sat down in my favorite chair. He studied me narrowly, and suddenly said, "What did they tell you I was? A spy?"

"Of course," I said.

He grinned bitterly, with one side of his mouth. "Of course. The damn fools! Spy! What do you suppose I'm going to spy on?"

He asked the question so violently and urgently that I knew I had to answer quickly and well, or the maniac would return.

39

"I—I wouldn't know, exactly," I stammered. "Military equipment, I suppose."

"Military equipment? *What* military equipment? Your Army is supplied with uniforms, whistles and hand guns, and that's about it."

"The defenses—" I started.

"The defenses," he interrupted me, "are non-existent. If you mean the rocket launchers on the roof, they're rusted through with age. And what other defenses are there? None."

"If you say so," I replied stiffly. The Army claimed that we had adequate defense equipment. I chose to believe the Army over an enemy spy.

"Your people send out spies, too, don't they?" he demanded.

"Well, of course."

"And what are *they* supposed to spy on?"

"Well—" it was such a pointless question, it seemed silly to even answer it. "They're supposed to look for indications of an attack by one of the other projects."

"And do they find any indications, ever?"

"I'm sure I don't know," I told him frostily. "That would be classified information."

"You bet it would," he said, with malicious glee. "All right, if that's what *your* spies are doing, and if *I'm* a spy, then it follows that I'm doing the same thing, right?"

"I don't follow you," I admitted.

"If I'm a spy," he said impatiently, "then I'm supposed to look for indications of an attack by you people on my Project."

I shrugged. "If that's your job," I said, "then that's your job."

He got suddenly red-faced, and jumped to his feet. "That's *not* my job, you blatant idiot!" he shouted. "I'm not a spy! If I were a spy, *then* that would be my job!"

The maniac had returned, in full force. "All right," I said hastily. "All right, whatever you say."

He glowered at me a moment longer, than shouted, "Bah!" and dropped back into the chair.

He breathed rather heavily for a while, glaring at the floor, then looked at me again. "All right, listen. What if I were to tell you that I *had* found indications that you people were planning to attack my Project?"

I stared at him. "That's impossible!" I cried. "We aren't planning to attack anybody! We just want to be left in peace!"

"How do I know that?" he demanded.

"It's the truth! What would we want to attack anybody for?"

"Ah hah!" He sat forward, tensed, pointing the gun at me like a finger again. "Now, then," he said. "If you know it doesn't make any sense for this Project to attack any other project, then why in the world should you think *they* might see some advantage in attacking *you*?"

I shook my head, dumbfounded. "I can't answer a question like that," I said. "How do I know what they're thinking?"

"They're human beings, aren't they?" he cried. "Like you? Like me? Like all the other people in this mausoleum?"

"Now, wait a minute—"

"No!" he shouted. "You wait a minute! I want to tell you something. You think I'm a spy. That blundering Army of yours thinks I'm a spy. That fathead who turned me in thinks I'm a spy. But I'm *not* a spy, and I'm going to tell you what I am."

I waited, looking as attentive as possible.

"I come," he said, "from a Project about eighty miles north of here. I came here by foot, without any sort of radiation shield at all to protect me."

The maniac was back. I didn't say a word. I didn't want to set off the violence that was so obviously in this lunatic.

"The radiation level," he went on, "is way down. It's practically as low as it was before the Atom War. I don't know how long it's been that low, but I would guess about ten years, at the very least." He leaned forward again, urgent and serious. "The world is safe out there now. Man can come back out of the cave again. He can start building the dreams again. And this time he can build better, because he has the horrible example of the

41

recent past to guide him away from the pitfalls. There's no need any longer for the Projects."

And that was like saying there's no need any longer for stomachs, but I didn't say so. I didn't say anything at all.

"I'm a trained atomic engineer," he went on. "In my project, I worked on the reactor. Theoretically, I believed that there was a chance the radiation Outside was lessening by now, though we had no idea exactly how much radiation had been released by the Atom War. But I wanted to test the theory, and the Commission wouldn't let me. They claimed public safety, but I knew better. If the Outside were safe and the Projects were no longer needed, then the Commission was out of a job, and they knew it.

"Well, I went ahead with the test anyway, and I was caught at it. For my punishment, I was banned from the Project. They kicked me out, telling me if I thought it was safe Outside I could live Outside. And if it really was safe, I could come back and tell them. Except that they also made it clear that I would be shot if I tried to get back in, because I would be carrying deadly radiation."

He smiled bitterly. "They had it all their own way," he said. "But it *is* safe out there, I'm living proof of it. I lived Outside for five months. And gradually I realized I had to tell others. I had to spread the word that Man could have his world back. I didn't dare try to get back into my own Project; I would have been recognized and shot before I could say a word. So I came here."

He paused to finish the cup of chico that I should have had with lunch. "I knew better," he continued, "than to simply walk into the building and announce that I came from Outside. Man has an instinctive distrust for strangers anyway; the Projects only intensify it. Once again, I would have been shot. So I've been working in a more devious way. I snuck into the Project—not a difficult thing for a man with no metal on his person, no radiation shield cocooning him—and for the last two months I've been wandering around the building, talking with people. I strike up a conversation. I try to plant a few seeds of doubt about

42

the deadliness of Outside, and I hope that at least a few of the people I talk to will begin to wonder, as I once did."

Two months! This spy, by his own admission, had been in the Project two months before being detected. I'd never heard of such a thing, and I hoped I'd never hear of such a thing again.

"Things worked out pretty well," he said, "until today. I said something wrong—I'm still not sure what—and the man I was talking to hollered for Army, shouted I was a spy." He pounded the chair arm. "But I'm not a spy! And it's the truth. Outside is safe!" He glared suddenly at the window. "Why've you got that drape up there?"

"The window broke down," I explained. "It's stuck at transparent."

"Transparent? Fine!" He got up from the chair, strode across the room, and ripped the drape down from the window.

I cowered away from the sunglare, turning my back to the window.

"Come over here!" he shouted. When I didn't move, he snarled, "Get up and come over here, or I swear I'll shoot!"

And he would have, it was plain in his voice. I got to my feet, hesitant, and walked trembling to the window, squinting against the glare.

"Look out there," he ordered. "Look!"

I looked.

IV

Terror. Horror. Dizziness and nausea.

Far and away and far, nothing and nothing. Only the glare, and the high blue, and the far far horizon, and the broken gray slag stretching out, way down below.

"Do you see?" he demanded. "Look down there! We're so high up, it's hard to see, but *look* for it. Do you see it? Do you see the green? Do you know what that means? There are green things growing again Outside! Not much yet. It's only just started back, but it's begun. The radiation is down. Plants are growing again."

The power of suggestion. And, of course, the heightened sensitivity caused by the double threat of a man beside me carrying a gun and that yawning aching expanse of nothing beyond the window. I nearly fancied that I did see faint specks of green.

"Do you see it?" he asked me.

"Wait," I said. I leaned closer to the window, though every nerve in me wanted to leap the other way. "Yes!" I said. "Yes, I see it! Green!"

He sighed, a long painful sigh of thanksgiving. "Then now you know," he said. "I've been telling the truth. It *is* safe Outside."

And my lie worked. For the first time, his guard was completely down.

I moved like a whirlwind. I leaped, and twisted his arm in a hard hammerlock, which caused him to cry out and drop the gun. That was wrestling. Then I turned and twisted and dipped, causing him to fly over my head and crash to the floor. That was judo. Then I jabbed one rigid forefinger against a certain spot on the side of his neck, causing the blood in his veins to forever stop its motion. That was karate.

Well, by the time the Army men had finished questioning me, it was three o'clock in the afternoon, and I was five hours late. The Army men corroborated my belief that the man had been a spy, who had apparently lost his mind when cornered in the elevator. Outside was still dangerous, of course, they assured me of that. And he'd been lying about having been here two months. He'd been in the Project less than two days. Not only that, the Army men told me they'd found the radiation-proof car he'd driven, and in which he had hoped to drive back to his own Project once he'd discovered all our defenses.

Despite the fact that I had the most legitimate excuse for tardiness under the roof, Linda refused to forgive me for not

44

making our ten o'clock meeting. When I asked her to marry me she refused, at length and descriptively.

But I was surprised and relieved to discover how rapidly I got over my heartbreak. This was aided by the fact that once the news of my exploit spread, there were any number of girls more than anxious to get to know me better, including the well-cleavaged young lady from the Transit Staff. After all, I was a hero.

They even gave me a medal.

The Risk Profession

Mr. Henderson called me into his office my third day back on Earth. That was a day and a half later than I'd expected. Roving claims investigators for Tangier Mutual Insurance Corporation don't usually get to spend more than thirty-six consecutive hours at home base.

Henderson was jovial but stern. That meant he was happy with the job I'd just completed, and that he was pretty sure I'd find some crooked shenanigans on this next assignment. That didn't please me. I'm basically a plain-living type, and I hate complications. I almost wished for a second that I was back on Fire and Theft in Greater New York. But I knew better than that. As a roving claims investigator, I avoided the more stultifying paperwork inherent in this line of work and had the additional luxury of an expense account nobody ever questioned.

It made working for a living almost worthwhile.

When I was settled in the chair beside his desk, Henderson

said, "That was good work you did on Luna, Ged. Saved the company a pretty pence."

I smiled modestly and said, "Thank you, sir." And reflected to myself for the thousandth time that the company could do worse than split that saving with the guy who'd made it possible. Me, in other words.

"Got a tricky one this time, Ged," said my boss. He had done his back-patting, now we got down to business. He peered keenly at me, or at least as keenly as a round-faced, tiny-eyed fat man *can* peer. "What do you know about the Risk Profession Retirement Plan?" he asked me.

"I've heard of it," I said truthfully. "That's about all."

He nodded. "Most of the policies are sold off-planet, of course. It's a form of insurance for non-insurables. Spaceship crews, asteroid prospectors, people like that."

"I see," I said unhappily. I knew right away this meant I was going to have to go off-Earth again. I'm a one-gee boy all the way. Gravity changes get me in the solar plexus. I get g-sick at the drop of an elevator.

"Here's the way it works," he went on, either not noticing my sad face or choosing to ignore it. "The client pays a monthly premium. He can be as far ahead or as far behind in his payments as he wants—the policy has no lapse clause— just so he's all paid up by the Target Date. The Target Date is a retirement age, forty-five or above, chosen by the client himself. After the Target Date he stops paying premiums, and we begin to pay him a monthly retirement check, the amount determined by the amount paid into the policy, his age at retiring, and so on. Clear?"

I nodded, looking for the gimmick that made this a paying proposition for good old Tangier Mutual.

"The Double R-P—that's what we call it around the office here—assures the client that he won't be reduced to panhandling in his old age, should his other retirement plans fall through. For Belt prospectors, of course, this means the big strike, which maybe one in a hundred find. For the man who never does make

47

that big strike, this is something to fall back on. He can come home to Earth and retire, with a guaranteed income for the rest of his life."

I nodded again, like a good company man.

"Of course," said Henderson, emphasizing this point with an upraised chubby finger, "these men are still uninsurables. This is a retirement plan only, not an insurance policy. There is no beneficiary other than the client himself."

And there was the gimmick. I knew a little something of the actuarial statistics concerning uninsurables, particularly Belt prospectors. Not many of them lived to be forty-five, and the few who would survive the Belt and come home to collect the retirement wouldn't last more than a year or two. A man who's spent the last twenty or thirty years on low-gee asteroids just shrivels up after a while when he tries to live on Earth.

It needed a company like Tangier Mutual to dream up a racket like that. The term "uninsurables" to most insurance companies means those people whose jobs or habitats make them too likely as prospects for obituaries. To Tangier Mutual, uninsurables are people who have money the company can't get at.

"Now," said Henderson importantly, "we come to the problem at hand." He ruffled his up-to-now-neat In-basket and finally found the folder he wanted. He studied the blank exterior of this folder for a few seconds, pursing his lips at it, and said, "One of our clients under the Double R-P was a man named Jafe McCann."

"Was?" I echoed.

He squinted at me, then nodded at my sharpness. "That's right, he's dead." He sighed heavily and tapped the folder with all those pudgy fingers. "Normally," he said, "that would be the end of it. File closed. However, this time there are complications."

Naturally. Otherwise, he wouldn't be telling *me* about it. But Henderson couldn't be rushed, and I knew it. I kept the alert look on my face and thought of other things, while waiting for him to get to the point.

"Two weeks after Jafe McCann's death," Henderson said, "we received a cash-return form on his policy."

"A cash-return form?" I'd never heard of such a thing. It didn't sound like anything Tangier Mutual would have anything to do with. We *never* return cash.

"It's something special in this case," he explained. "You see, this isn't an insurance policy, it's a retirement plan, and the client can withdraw from the retirement plan at any time, and have seventy-five per cent of his paid-up premiums returned to him. It's, uh, the law in plans such as this."

"Oh," I said. That explained it. A law that had snuck through the World Finance Code Commission while the insurance lobby wasn't looking.

"But you see the point," said Henderson. "This cash-return form arrived two weeks after the client's death."

"You said there weren't any beneficiaries," I pointed out.

"Of course. But the form was sent in by the man's partner, one Ab Karpin. McCann left a handwritten will bequeathing all his possessions to Karpin. Since, according to Karpin, this was done before McCann's death, the premium money cannot be considered part of the policy, but as part of McCann's cash-on-hand. And Karpin wants it."

"It can't be that much, can it?" Not enough, I was hoping, to make it worth the company's while to send me to the asteroids.

"McCann died," Henderson said ponderously, "at the age of fifty-six. He took out the policy at the age of thirty-four, with retirement at age sixty and monthly payments of fifty credits. Figure it out for yourself."

I did, and came up with a figure of thirteen thousand two hundred credits. Seventy-five per cent of that would be nine thousand nine hundred credits. Call it ten thousand.

I had to admit it; it was worth the trip.

"I see," I said sadly.

"Now," said Henderson, "the conditions—the circumstances—of McCann's death are somewhat suspicious. And so is the cash-return form itself."

49

"There's a chance it's a forgery?"

"One would think so. But our handwriting experts have worn themselves out with that form, comparing it with every other single scrap of McCann's writing they can find. And their conclusion is that not only is it genuinely McCann's handwriting, but it is McCann's handwriting at age fifty-six."

"So McCann must have written it," I said. "Under duress, do you think?"

"I have no idea," said Henderson complacently. "That's what you're supposed to find out. Oh, there's just one thing more."

I looked alert.

"McCann and Karpin," he said, "had been partners—unincorporated, of course—for the last fifteen years. They'd found small rare-metal deposits now and again, but never that one big strike all the Belt prospectors spend their lives looking for. Not until the day before McCann died."

"Ah hah," I said. "And McCann's death?"

"Accidental."

"Sure. What proof?"

"None. The body is lost in space. And law is rare that far out."

"So all we've got is Karpin's word for how McCann died, is that it?"

"That's all we have," Henderson agreed. "So far."

"And now you want me to go out there and find out what's cooking, and see if I can maybe save the company ten C's."

"Exactly," said Henderson.

The copter took me to the spaceport west of Cairo, and there I boarded the good ship *Demeter* for Luna City and points Out. By the time we got to Atronics City, in the asteroid belt, my insides and I had come to a shaky kind of agreement; as long as I didn't try to eat, my stomach would leave me alone.

Atronics City is as depressing as a Turkish bath with all the lights on. It stands on a chunk of rock a couple of miles thick and looks like nothing so much as a welder's practice range.

On the outside, Atronics City is a derby-shaped dome of

nickel-iron, black and dirty-looking, and on the inside it looks just as bad, four levels of Basic Life Maintenance. There's the top level, directly under the dome, with parking area for scooters and tuggers, plus office shacks for Assayer, Entry Authority, Industry Troopers, and so on. Below that, the levels have been burned into the bowels of the planetoid, level two being the Atronics plant, level three shopping and entertainment area, and level four housing. All of these levels have one thing in common: square corners, painted olive-drab. It's like being in the middle of a stack of jerry cans.

At any rate, this was as far as *Demeter* would take me. Now, while the ship went on to Ludlum City and Chemisant City and the other asteroid business towns, my two suitcases and I dribbled down by elevator to my hostelry on level four. And I do mean dribbled. An elevator ride on a low-gravity planetoid is well worth avoiding, if you ask me. The elevator manages to sink faster than you do, because rather than being lowered down it's being pulled down. Which means the suitcases have to be lashed down and the passengers have to hold tight to the hand-grips and all in all it's a bad experience.

But we did get down to level four, and off I went with my suitcases and the operator's directions. The suitcases weighed half an ounce each out here, and I felt not much heavier myself. Every time I raised a foot I was sure I was about to go sailing into a wall. Local citizens eased by me, their feet occasionally touching the iron pavement as they soared along, and I gave them all dirty looks.

Level four was nothing but walls and windows. The iron floor went among these walls and windows in a straight line, bisecting other "streets" at perfect right angles, and the iron ceiling sixteen feet up was lined with a double row of fluorescent tubes. I was beginning to feel claustrophobic already.

The Chalmers Hotel—named for an Atronics vice-president— had received my advance registration, which was nice. I was shown to a second-floor room—nothing on level four had more

51

than two stories—and was left to unpack my suitcases as best I could.

I had decided to spend a day or two at Atronics City before taking a scooter out to Ab Karpin's claim. Atronics City had been Karpin's and McCann's home base. All of McCann's premium payments had been mailed from here, and the normal mailing address for both of them was GPO Atronics City.

I wanted to know as much as possible about Ab Karpin before I went out to see him. And Atronics City seemed like the best place to get my information.

But not today. Today my stomach was very unhappy, and my head was on sympathy strike. Today I was going to spend my time exclusively in bed, trying not to float up to the ceiling.

The Mapping & Registry Office, it seemed to me the next day, was the best place to start. This was where prospectors filed their claims, but it was a lot more than that. The waiting room of M&R was the unofficial club of the asteroid prospectors. This was where they met with one another, talked together, and made and dissolved their transient partnerships.

In this way, Karpin and McCann were unusual. They had maintained their partnership for fifteen years. That was about sixty times longer than most such arrangements lasted.

Searching the asteroid chunks for rare and valuable metals is basically pretty lonely work, and it's inevitable that the prospectors will every once in a while get hungry for human company and decide to try a team operation. But at the same time work like this attracts people who don't get along very well with human company. So the partnerships come and go, and the hatreds flare and are forgotten, and the normal prospecting partnership lasts an average of three months.

The Mapping & Registry Office occupied a good-sized shack over near the dome wall on level one. I pushed open the door and went in, finding the waiting room cozy and surprisingly large, large enough comfortably to hold the six maroon sofas scattered here and there on the pale green carpet. There were only six prospectors here at the moment, chatting together in two groups of three, and they all looked alike. Grizzled, ageless, watery-eyed, their clothing clean but baggy. I passed them and went on to the desk at the far end, behind which sat a young man in official gray, slowly turning the crank of a microfilm reader.

He looked up at my approach. I flashed my company identification and asked to speak to the manager. He went away, came back, and ushered me into an office which managed to be Spartan and sumptuous at the same time. The walls had been plastic-painted in textured brown, the iron floor had been lushly carpeted in gray, and the desk had been covered with a simulated wood coating.

The manager—a man named Teaking—went well with the office. His face and hands were spare and lean, but his uniform was immaculate, covered with every curlicue the regulations allowed. He welcomed me politely but curiously, and I said, "I wonder if you know a prospector named Ab Karpin?"

"Karpin? Of course. He and old Jafe McCann—pity about McCann. I hear he got killed."

"Yes, he did."

"And that's what you're here for, eh? I didn't know the Belt boys could get insurance."

"It isn't exactly that," I said. "This concerns a retirement plan, and—well, the details don't matter. I was hoping you could give me some background on Karpin. And on McCann, too, for that matter."

He grinned a bit. "You saw the men sitting outside?"

I nodded.

"Then you've seen Karpin and McCann. Exactly the same. It doesn't matter if a man's thirty or sixty or what. It doesn't matter what he was like before he came out here. If he's been here a few years, he looks exactly like the bunch you saw outside there."

"That's appearance," I said. "What I was looking for was personality."

"Same thing," he said. "All of them. Close-mouthed, anti-social, fiercely independent, incurably romantic, always convinced that the big strike is just a piece of rock away. McCann, now, he was a bit more realistic than most. He'd be the one I'd expect to take out a retirement policy. A real pence-pincher, that one, though I shouldn't say it as he's dead. But that's the way he was. Brighter than most Belt boys when it came to money matters. I've seen him haggle over a new piece of equipment for their scooter, or some repair work, or some such thing, and he was a wonder to watch."

"And Karpin?" I asked him.

"A prospector," he said, as though that answered my question. "Same as everybody else. Not as sharp as McCann when it came to money. That's why all the money stuff in the partnership was handled by McCann. But Karpin was one of the sharpest boys in the business when it came to mineralogy. He knew rocks you and I never heard of, and most times he knew them by sight. Almost all of the Belt boys are college grads—you've got to know what you're looking for out here and what it looks like when you've found it—but Karpin has practically all of them beat. He's *sharp*."

"Sounds like a good team," I said.

"I guess that's why they stayed together so long," he said. "They complemented each other." He leaned forward, the inevitable prelude to a confidential remark. "I'll tell you something off the record, mister," he said. "Those two were smarter than they knew. Their partnership was never legalized, it was never anything more than a piece of paper. And there's a bunch of fellas around here mighty unhappy about that today. Jafe McCann is the one who handled all the money matters, like I said. He's got IOU's all over town."

"And they can't collect from Karpin?"

He nodded. "Jafe McCann died just a bit too soon. He was sharp and cheap, but he was honest. If he'd lived, he would have repaid all his debts, I'm sure of it. And if this strike they made is as good as I hear, he would have been able to repay them with no trouble at all."

I nodded, somewhat impatiently. I had the feeling by now that

I was talking to a man who was one of those who had a Jafe McCann IOU in his pocket. "How long has it been since you've seen Karpin?" I asked him, wondering what Karpin's attitude and expression were now that his partner was dead.

"Oh, Lord, not for a couple of months," he said. "Not since they went out together the last time and made that strike."

"Didn't Karpin come in to make his claim?"

"Not here. Over to Chemisant City. That was the nearest M&R to the strike."

"Oh." That was a pity. I would have liked to have known if there had been a change of any kind in Karpin since his partner's death. "I'll tell you what the situation is," I said with a false air of truthfulness. "We have some misgivings about McCann's death. Not suspicions, exactly, just misgivings. The timing is what bothers us."

"You mean, because it happened just after the strike?"

"That's it," I answered frankly.

He shook his head. "I wouldn't get too excited about that, if I were you," he said. "It wouldn't be the first time it's happened. A man makes the big strike after all, and he gets so excited he forgets himself for a minute and gets careless. And you only have to be careless once out here."

"That may be it," I said. I got to my feet, knowing I'd picked up all there was from this man. "Thanks a lot for your cooperation," I said.

"Anytime," he said. He stood and shook hands with me.

I went back out through the chatting prospectors and crossed the echoing cavern that was level one, aiming to rent myself a scooter.

I don't like rockets. They're noisy as the dickens, they steer hard and drive erratically, and you can never carry what *I* would consider a safe emergency excess of fuel. Nothing like the big steady-g interplanetary liners. On those I feel almost human.

The appearance of the scooter I was shown at the rental agency didn't do much to raise my opinion of this mode of transportation. The thing was a good ten years old, the paint scraped and scratched all over its egg-shaped, originally green-colored body, and the windshield—a silly term, really, for the front window of a craft that spends most of its time out where there isn't any wind—was scratched and pockmarked to the point of translucency by years of exposure to the asteroidal dust.

The rental agent was a sharp-nosed, thin-faced type who displayed this refugee from a melting vat without a blush, and still didn't blush when he told me the charges. Twenty credits a day, plus fuel.

I paid without a murmur—it was the company's money, not mine—and paid an additional ten credits for the rental of a suit to go with it. I worked my way awkwardly into the suit, and clambered into the driver's seat of the relic. I attached the suit to the ship in all necessary places, and the agent closed and spun the door.

Most of the black paint had worn off the handles of the controls, and insulation peeked through rips in the plastic siding here and there. I wondered if the thing had any slow leaks and supposed fatalistically that it had. The agent waved at me, stony-faced, the conveyor belt trundled me outside the dome, and I kicked the weary rocket into life.

The scooter had a tendency to roll to the right. If I hadn't kept fighting it back, it would have soon worked up a dandy little spin. I was spending so much time juggling with the controls that I practically missed a couple of my beacon rocks, and that would have been just too bad. If I'd gotten off the course I had carefully outlined for myself, I'd never have found my bearings again, and I would have just floated around amid the scenery until some passer-by took pity and towed me back home.

But I managed to avoid getting lost, which surprised me, and after four nerve-racking hours I finally spotted the yellow-painted X of a registered claim on a half-mile-thick chunk of rock dead ahead. As I got closer, I spied a scooter parked near the X, and beside it an inflated portable dome. The scooter was somewhat larger than mine, but no newer and probably even less safe. The dome was varicolored from repeated patching.

This is where I would find Karpin, sitting on his property while waiting for the sale to go through. Prospectors like Karpin are free-lance men, working for no particular company. They register their claims in their own names, and then sell the rights to whichever company shows up with the most attractive offer. There's a lot of paperwork to such a sale, and it's all handled by the company. While waiting, the smart prospector sits on his claim and makes sure nobody chips off a part of it for himself, a stunt that still happens now and again. It doesn't take too much concentrated explosive to make two rocks out of one rock, and a man's claim is only the rock with his X on it.

I set the scooter down next to the other one, and flicked the toggle for the air pumps, then put on the fishbowl and went about unattaching the suit from the ship. When the red light flashed on and off, I spun the door, opened it, and stepped out onto the rock, moving very cautiously.

I clumped across the crude X to Karpin's dome. The dome had no viewports at all, so I wasn't sure Karpin was aware of my presence. I rapped my metal glove on the metal outer door of the lock, and then I was sure.

But it took him long enough to open up. I had just about decided he'd joined his partner in the long sleep when the door cracked open an inch. I pushed it open and stepped into the lock, ducking my head.

When the red light high on the left-hand wall clicked off, I rapped on the inner door. It promptly opened, I stepped through and removed the fishbowl.

Karpin stood in the middle of the room, a small revolver in his hand. "Shut the door," he said.

I obeyed, moving slowly. I didn't want that gun to go off by mistake.

"Who are you?" Karpin demanded. The M&R man had been right. Ab Karpin was a dead ringer for all those other prospectors I'd seen back at Atronics City. Short and skinny and grizzled

57

and ageless. He could have been forty, and he could have been ninety, but he was probably somewhere the other side of fifty. His hair was black and limp and thinning, ruffled in little wisps across his wrinkled pate. His forehead and cheeks were lined like a plowed field, and were much the same color. His eyes were wide apart and small, so deep-set beneath shaggy brows that they seemed black. His mouth was thin, almost lipless. The hand holding the revolver was nothing but bones and blue veins covered with taut skin.

He was wearing a dirty undershirt and an old pair of trousers that had been cut off raggedly just above his knobby knees. Faded slippers were on his feet. He had good reason for dressing that way, the temperature inside the dome must have been nearly ninety degrees. The dome wasn't reflecting away the sun's heat as well as it had when it was young.

I looked at Karpin, and despite the revolver and the tense expression on his face, he was the least dangerous-looking man I'd ever run across. All at once, the idea that this anti-social old geezer had the drive or the imagination to murder his partner seemed ridiculous.

Apparently I spent too much time looking him over, because he said again, "Who are you?" And this time he motioned impatiently with the revolver.

"Stanton," I told him. "Ged Stanton, Tangier Mutual Insurance. I have identification, but it's in my pants pocket, down inside this suit."

"Get it," he said. "And move slow."

"Right you are."

I moved slow, as per directions, and peeled out of the suit, then reached into my trouser pocket and took out my ID clip. I flipped it open and showed him the card bearing my signature and picture and right thumbprint and the name of the company I represented, and he nodded, satisfied, and tossed the revolver over onto his bed. "I got to be careful," he said. "I got a big claim here."

"I know that," I told him. "Congratulations for it."

"Thanks," he said, but he still looked peevish. "You're here about Jafe's insurance, right?"

"That I am."

"Don't want to pay up, I suppose. That doesn't surprise me."

Blunt old men irritate me. "Well," I said, "we do have to investigate."

"Sure," he said. "You want some coffee?"

"Thank you."

"You can sit in that chair there. That was Jafe's."

I settled gingerly in the cloth-and-plastic foldaway chair he'd pointed at, and he went over to the kitchen area of the dome to start coffee. I took the opportunity to look the dome over. It was the first portable dome I'd ever been inside of.

It was all one room, roughly circular, with a diameter of about fifteen feet. The sides went straight up for the first seven feet, then curved gradually inward to form the roof. At the center of the dome, the ceiling was about twelve feet high.

The floor of the room was simply the asteroidal rock surface, not completely level and smooth. There were two chairs and a table to the right of the entry lock, two foldaway cots around the wall beyond them, the kitchen area next, and a cluttered storage area around on the other side. There was a heater standing alone in the center of the room, but it certainly wasn't needed now. Sweat was already trickling down the back of my neck and down my forehead into my eyebrows. I peeled off my shirt and used it to wipe sweat from my face. "Warm in here," I said.

"You get used to it," he muttered, which I found hard to believe.

He brought over the coffee, and I tasted it. It was rotten, as bitter as this old hermit's soul, but I said, "Good coffee. Thanks a lot."

"I like it strong," he said.

I looked around at the room again. "All the comforts of home, eh? Pretty ingenious arrangement."

"Sure," he said sourly. "How about getting to the point, mister?"

There's only one way to handle a blunt old man. Be blunt right back. "I'll tell you how it is," I said. "The company isn't accusing you of anything, but it has to be sure everything's on the up and up before it pays out any ten thousand credits. And your partner just happening to fill out the cash-return form just before he died—well, you've got to admit it is a funny kind of coincidence."

"How so?" He slurped coffee, and glowered at me over the cup. "We made this strike here," he said. "We knew it was the big one. Jafe had that insurance policy of his in case he never did make the big strike. As soon as we knew this was the big one, he said, 'I guess I don't need that retirement now,' and sat right down and wrote out the cash-return. Then we opened a bottle of liquor and celebrated, and he got himself killed."

The way Karpin said it, it sounded smooth and natural. *Too* smooth and natural. "How did this accident happen anyway?" I asked him.

"I'm not one hundred per cent sure of that myself," he said. "I was pretty well drunk by that time. But he put on his suit and said he was going out to paint the X. He was falling all over himself, and I tried to tell him it could wait till we'd had some sleep, but he wouldn't pay any attention to me."

"So he went out," I said.

He nodded. "He went out first. After a couple minutes I got lonesome in here, so I suited up and went out after him. It happened just as I was going out the lock, and I just barely got a glimpse of what happened."

He attacked the coffee again, noisily, and I prompted him, saying, "What did happen, Mr. Karpin?"

"Well, he was capering around out there, waving the paint tube and such. There's a lot of sharp rock sticking out around here. Just as I got outside, he lost his balance and kicked out, and scraped right into some of that rock and punctured his suit."

"I thought the body was lost," I said.

He nodded. "It was. The last thing in life Jafe ever did was try to shove himself away from those rocks. That, and the force of air coming out of that puncture for the first second or two, was enough to throw him up off the surface. It threw him up too high, and he never got back down."

My doubt must have showed in my face, because he added, "Mister, there isn't enough gravity on this place to shoot craps with."

He was right. As we talked, I kept finding myself holding unnecessarily tight to the arms of the chair. I kept having the feeling I was going to float out of the chair and hover around up at the top of the dome if I were to let go. It was silly of course—there was *some* gravity on that planetoid, after all—but I just don't seem to get used to low-gee.

Nevertheless, I still had some more questions. "Didn't you try to get his body back? Couldn't you have reached him?"

"I tried to, mister," he said. "Old Jafe McCann was my partner for fifteen years. But I was drunk, and that's a fact. And I was afraid to go jumping up in the air, for fear *I'd* go floating away, too."

"Frankly," I said, "I'm no expert on low gravity and asteroids. But wouldn't McCann's body just go into orbit around this rock? I mean, it wouldn't simply go floating off into space, would it?"

"It sure would," he said. "There's a lot of other rocks out here, too, mister, and a lot of them are bigger than this one and have a lot more gravity pull. I don't suppose there's a navigator in the business who could have computed Jafe's course in advance. He floated up, and then he floated back over the dome here and seemed to hover for a couple minutes, and then he just floated out and away. His isn't the only body circling around the sun with all these rocks, you know."

I chewed a lip and thought it all over. I didn't know enough about asteroid gravity or the conditions out here to be able to say for sure whether Karpin's story was true or not. Up to this point, I couldn't attack the problem on a fact basis. I had to depend on *feeling* now, the hunches and instincts of eight years in this job, hearing some people tell lies and other people tell the truth.

And my instinct said Ab Karpin was lying in his teeth. That

dramatic little touch about McCann's body hovering over the dome before disappearing into the void, that sounded more like the embellishment of fiction than the circumstance of truth. And the string of coincidences were just too much. McCann just coincidentally happens to die right after he and his partner make their big strike. He happens to write out the cash-return form just before dying. And his body just happens to float away, so nobody can look at it and check Karpin's story.

But no matter what my instinct said, the story was smooth. It was smooth as glass, and there was no place for me to get a grip on it.

What now? There wasn't any hole in Karpin's story, at least none that I could see. I had to break his story somehow, and in order to do that I had to do some nosing around on this planetoid. I couldn't know in advance what I was looking for, I could only look. I'd know it when I found it. It would be something that conflicted with Karpin's story.

And for that, I had to be sure the story was complete. "You said McCann had gone out to paint the X," I said. "Did he paint it?"

Karpin shook his head. "He never got a chance. He spent all his time dancing, up till he went and killed himself."

"So you painted it yourself."

He nodded.

"And then you went on into Atronics City and registered your claim, is that the story?"

"No. Chemisant City was closer than Atronics City right then, so I went there. Just after Jafe's death, and everything—I didn't feel like being alone any more than I had to."

"You said Chemisant City was closer to you *then*," I said. "Isn't it now?"

"Things move around a lot out here, mister," he said. "Right now Chemisant City's almost twice as far from here as Atronics City. In about three days it'll start swinging in closer again. Things keep shifting around out here."

"So I've noticed," I said. "When you took off to go to Chemisant City, didn't you make a try for your partner's body then?"

He shook his head. "He was long out of sight by then," he said. "That was ten, eleven hours later, when I took off."

"Why's that? All you had to do was paint the X and take off."

"Mister, I told you. I was drunk. I was falling down drunk, and when I saw I couldn't get at Jafe, and he was dead anyway, I came back in here and slept it off. Maybe if I'd been sober I would have taken the scooter and gone after him, but I was *drunk.*"

"I see." And there just weren't any more questions I could think of to ask, not right now. So I said, "I've just had a shaky four-hour ride coming out here. Mind if I stick around awhile before going back?"

"Help yourself," he said in a pretty poor attempt at genial hospitality. "You can sleep over, if you want."

"Fine," I said. "I think I'd like that."

"You wouldn't happen to play cribbage, would you?" he asked, with the first real sign of animation I'd seen in him yet.

"I learn fast," I told him.

"Okay," he said. "I'll teach you." And he produced a filthy deck of cards and taught me.

After losing nine straight games of cribbage I quit, and got to my feet. I was at my most casual as I stretched and said, "Okay if I wander around outside for a while? I've never been on an asteroid like this before. I mean, a little one like this. I've just been to the company cities up to now."

"Go right ahead," he said. "I've got some polishing and patching to do, anyway." He made his voice sound easy and innocent, but I noticed his eyes were alert and wary, watching me as I struggled back into my suit.

I didn't bother to put my shirt back on first, and that was a mistake. The temperature inside an atmosphere suit is a steady sixty-eight degrees. That had never seemed particularly chilly

63

before, but after the heat of that dome, it seemed cold as a blizzard inside the suit.

I went on out through the air-lock, and moved as briskly as possible in the cumbersome suit while the sweat chilled on my back and face, and I accepted the glum conviction that one thing I was going to get out of this trip for sure was a nasty head cold.

I went over to the X first, and stood looking at it. It was just an X, that's all, shakily scrawled in yellow paint, with the initials "J-A" scrawled much smaller beside it.

I left the X and clumped away. The horizon was practically at arm's length, so it didn't take long for the dome to be out of sight. And then I clumped more slowly, studying the surface of the asteroid.

What I was looking for was a grave. I believed that Karpin was lying, that he had murdered his partner. And I didn't believe that Jafe McCann's body had floated off into space. I was convinced that his body was still somewhere on this asteroid. Karpin had been forced to concoct a story about the body being lost because the appearance of the body would prove somehow that it had been murder and not an accident. I was convinced of that, and now all I had to do was prove it.

But that asteroid was a pretty unlikely place for a grave. That wasn't dirt I was walking on, it was rock, solid metallic rock. You don't dig a grave in solid rock, not with a shovel. You maybe can do it with dynamite, but that won't work too well if your object is to keep anybody from seeing that the hole has been made. Dirt can be patted down. Blown-up rock looks like blown-up rock, and that's all there is to it.

I considered crevices and fissures in the surface, some cranny large enough for Karpin to have stuffed the body into. But I didn't find any of these either as I plodded along, being sure to keep one magneted boot always in contact with the ground.

Karpin and McCann had set their dome up at just about the only really level spot on that entire planetoid. The rest of it was nothing but jagged rock, and it wasn't easy traveling at all, maneuvering around with magnets on my boots and a bulky atmosphere suit cramping my movements.

And then I stopped and looked out at space and cursed myself for a ring-tailed baboon. McCann's body might be anywhere in the Solar System, anywhere at all, but there was one place I could be sure it wasn't, and that place was this asteroid. No, Karpin had not blown a grave or stuffed the body into a fissure in the ground. Why not? Because this chunk of rock was valuable, that's why not. Because Karpin was in the process of selling it to one of the major companies, and that company would come along and chop this chunk of rock to pieces, getting the valuable metal out, and McCann's body would turn up in the first week of operations if Karpin were stupid enough to bury it here.

Ten hours between McCann's death and Karpin's departure for Chemisant City. He'd admitted that already. And I was willing to bet he'd spent at least part of that time carrying McCann's body to some other asteroid, one he was sure was nothing but worthless rock. If that were true, it meant the mortal remains of Jafe McCann were now somewhere—*anywhere*—in the Asteroid Belt. Even if I assumed that the body had been hidden on an asteroid somewhere between here and Chemisant City—which wasn't necessarily so—that wouldn't help at all. The relative positions of planetoids in the Belt just keep on shifting. A small chunk of rock that was between here and Chemisant City a few weeks ago—it could be almost anywhere in the Belt right now.

The body, that was the main item. I'd more or less counted on finding it somehow. At the moment I couldn't think of any other angle for attacking Karpin's story.

As I clopped morosely back to the dome, I nibbled at Karpin's story in my mind. For instance, why go to Chemisant City? It was closer, he said, but it couldn't have been closer by more than a couple of hours. The way I understood it, Karpin was well known back on Atronics City—it was the normal base of operations for him and his partner—and he didn't know a soul at

Chemisant City. Did it make sense for him to go somewhere he wasn't known after his partner's death, even if it *was* an hour closer? No, it made a lot more sense for a man in that situation to go where he's known, go someplace where he has friends who'll sympathize with him and help him over the shock of losing a partner of fifteen years' standing, even if going there does mean traveling an hour longer.

And there was always the cash-return form. That was what I was here about in the first place. It just didn't make sense for McCann to have held up his celebration while he filled out a form that he wouldn't be able to mail until he got back to Atronics City. And yet the company's handwriting experts were convinced that it wasn't a forgery, and I could pretty well take their word for it.

Mulling these things over as I tramped back toward the dome, I suddenly heard a distant bell ringing way back in my head. The glimmering of an idea, not an idea yet but just the hint of one. I wasn't sure where it led, or even if it led anywhere at all, but I was going to find out.

Karpin opened the doors for me. By the time I'd stripped off the suit he was back to work. He was cleaning the single unit which was his combination stove and refrigerator and sink and garbage disposal.

I looked around the dome again, and I had to admit that a lot of ingenuity had gone into the manufacture and design of this dome and its contents. The dome itself, when deflated, folded down into an oblong box three feet by one foot by one foot. The lock itself, of course, folded separately, into another box somewhat smaller than that.

As for the gear inside the dome, it was functional and collapsible, and there wasn't a single item there that wasn't needed. There were the two chairs and the two cots and the table, all of them foldaway. There was that fantastic combination job Karpin was cleaning right now, and that had dimensions of four feet by three feet by three feet. The clutter of gear over to the left wasn't as much of a clutter as it looked. There was a Geiger counter, an automatic spectrograph, two atmosphere suits, a torsion densiometer, a core-cutting drill, a few small hammers and picks, two spare air tanks, boxes of food concentrate, a paint tube, a doorless jimmy-john, and two small metal boxes about eight inches cube. These last were undoubtedly Karpin's and McCann's pouches, where they kept whatever letters, money, address books, or other small bits of possessions they owned. Back of this mound of gear, against the wall, stood the air reconditioner, humming quietly to itself.

In this small enclosed space there was everything a man needed to keep himself alive. Everything except human company. And if you didn't need human company, then you had everything. Just on the other side of that dome, there was a million miles of death, in a million possible ways. On this side of the dome, life was cozy, if somewhat Spartan and very hot.

I knew for sure I was going to get a head cold. My body had adjusted to the sixty-eight degrees inside the suit, finally, and now was very annoyed to find the temperature shooting up to ninety again.

Since Karpin didn't seem inclined to talk, and I would rather spend my time thinking than talking anyway, I took a hint from him and did some cleaning. I'd noticed a smeared spot about nose-level on the faceplate of my fishbowl, and now was as good a time as any to get rid of it. It had a tendency to make my eyes cross.

My shirt was sodden and wrinkled by this time anyway, having first been used to wipe sweat from my face and later been rolled into a ball and left on the chair when I went outside, so I used it for a cleaning rag, buffing like mad the silvered surface of the faceplate. Faceplates are silvered, not so the man inside can look out and no one else can look in, but in order to keep some of the more violent rays of the sun from getting through to the face.

I buffed for a while, and then I put the fishbowl on my head and looked through it. The spot was gone, so I went over and reattached it to the rest of the suit, and then settled back in my chair again and lit a cigarette.

Karpin spoke up. "Wish you wouldn't smoke. Makes it tough on the conditioner."

"Oh," I said. "Sorry." So I just sat, thinking morosely about nonforged cash-return forms, and coincidences, and likely spots to hide a body in the Asteroid Belt.

Where would one dispose of a body in the asteroids? I went back through my thinking on that topic, and I found holes big enough to drive Karpin's claim through. This idea of leaving the body on some worthless chunk of rock, for instance. If Karpin had killed his partner—and I was dead sure he had—he'd planned it carefully and he wouldn't be leaving anything to chance. Now, an asteroid isn't worthless to a prospector until that prospector has landed on it and tested it. *Karpin* might know that such-and-such an asteroid was nothing but worthless stone, but the guy who stops there and finds McCann's body might *not* know it.

No, Karpin wouldn't leave that to chance. He would get rid of that body, and he would do it in such a way that nobody would *ever* find it.

How? Not by leaving it on a worthless asteroid, and not by just pushing it off into space. The distance between asteroids is large, but so's the travel. McCann's body, floating around in the blackness, might just be found by somebody.

And that, so far as I could see, eliminated the possibilities. McCann's body was in the Belt. I'd eliminated both the asteroids themselves and the space around the asteroids as hiding places. What was left?

The sun, of course.

I thought that over for a while, rather surprised at myself for having noticed the possibility. Now, let's say Karpin attaches a small rocket to McCann's body, stuffed into its atmosphere suit. He sets the rocket going, and off goes McCann. Not that he aims it toward the sun, that wouldn't work well at all. Instead of falling into the sun, the body would simply take up a long elliptical orbit *around* the sun, and would come back to the asteroids every few hundred years. No, he would aim McCann *back*, in the direction opposite to the direction of rotation of the asteroids. He would, in essence, slow McCann's body down, make it practically stop in relation to the motion of the asteroids. And then it would simply *fall* into the sun.

None of my ideas, it seemed, were happy ones. If McCann's body were even at this moment falling toward the sun, it was just as useful to me as if it were on some other asteroid.

But wait a second. Karpin and McCann had worked with the minimum of equipment, I'd already noticed that. They didn't have extras of anything, and they certainly wouldn't have extra rockets. Except for one fast trip to Chemisant City—when he had neither the time nor the excuse to buy a jato rocket—Karpin had spent all of his time since McCann's death right here on this planetoid.

So that killed the idea.

While I was hunting around for some other idea, Karpin spoke up again, for the first time in maybe twenty minutes. "You think I killed him, don't you?" he said, not looking around from his cleaning job.

I considered my answer. There was no reason at all to be overly polite to this sour old buzzard, but at the same time I am naturally the soft-spoken type. "We aren't sure," I said. "We just think there are some odd items to be explained."

"Such as what?" he demanded.

"Such as the timing of McCann's cash-return form."

"I already explained that," he said.

"I know. You've explained everything."

"He wrote it out himself," the old man insisted. He put down his cleaning cloth and turned to face me. "I suppose your company checked the handwriting already, and Jafe McCann is the one who wrote that form."

He was so blasted sure of himself. "It would seem that way," I said.

"What other odd items you worried about?" he asked me, in a rusty attempt at sarcasm.

"Well," I said, "there's this business of going to Chemisant City. It would have made more sense for you to go to Atronics City, where you were known."

"Chemisant was closer," he said. He shook a finger at me. "That company of yours thinks it can cheat me out of my money," he said. "Well, it can't. I know my rights. That money belongs to me."

"I guess you're doing pretty well without McCann," I said.

His angry expression was replaced by one of bewilderment. "What do you mean?"

"They told me back at Atronics City," I explained, "that McCann was the money expert and you were the metals expert, and that's why McCann handled all your buying on credit and stuff like that. Looks as though you've got a pretty keen eye for money yourself."

"I know what's mine," he mumbled, and turned away. He went back to scrubbing the stove coils again.

I stared at his back. Something had happened just then, and I wasn't sure what. He'd just been starting to warm up to a tirade against the dirty insurance company, and all of a sudden he'd folded up and shut up like a clam.

And then I saw it. Or at least I saw part of it. I saw how that cash-return form fit in, and how it made perfect sense.

Now all I needed was proof of murder. Preferably a body. I had the rest of it. Then I could pack the old geezer back to Atronics City and get proof for the part I'd already figured out.

I'd like that. I'd like getting back to Atronics City, and having this all straightened out, and then taking the very next liner straight back to Earth. More immediately, I'd like getting out of this heat and back into the cool sixty-eight degrees of—

And then it hit me. The whole thing hit me, and I just sat there and stared. They did not carry extras, Karpin and McCann, they did not carry one item of equipment more than they needed.

70

I sat there and looked at the place where the dead body was hidden, and I said, "Well, I'll be a son of a gun!"

He turned and looked at me, and then he followed the direction of my gaze, and he saw what I was staring at, and he made a jump across the room at the revolver lying on the cot.

That's what saved me. He moved too fast, jerked his muscles too hard, and went sailing up and over the cot and ricocheted off the dome wall. And that gave me plenty of time to get up from the chair, moving more cautiously than he had, and get my hands on the revolver before he could get himself squared away again.

I straightened with the gun in my hand and looked into a face white with frustration and rage. "Okay, Mr. McCann," I said. "It's all over."

He knew I had him, but he tried not to show it. "What are you talking about? McCann's dead."

"Sure he is," I said. "Jafe McCann was the money-minded part of the team. He was the one who signed for all the loans and all the equipment bought on credit. With this big strike in, Jafe McCann was the one who'd have to pay all that money."

"You're babbling," he snapped, but the words were hollow.

"You weren't satisfied with half a loaf," I said. "You should have been. But you wanted every penny you could get your hands on, and you wanted to pay out just as little money as you possibly could. So when you killed Ab Karpin, you saw a way to kill your debts as well. You'd *become* Ab Karpin, and it would be Jafe McCann who was dead, and the debts dead with him."

"That's a lie," he said, his voice getting shrill. "*I'm* Ab Karpin, and I've got papers to prove it."

"Sure. Papers you stole from a dead man. And you might have gotten away with it, too. But you just couldn't leave well enough alone, could you? Not satisfied with having the whole claim to yourself, you switched identities with your victim to avoid your debts. And not satisfied with *that*, you filled out a cash-return form and tried to collect your money as your own heir. *That's* why you had to go to Chemisant City, where nobody would recognize Ab Karpin or Jafe McCann, rather than to Atronics City, where you were well known."

"You don't want to make too many wild accusations," he shouted, his voice shaking. "You don't want to go around accusing people of things you can't prove."

"I can't prove it," I told him. "I can't prove everything I've said. As to who you are, there's no problem. All I have to do is bring you back to Atronics City. There'll be plenty of people there to identify you. And as to proving you murdered Ab Karpin, I think his body will be proof enough, don't you?"

McCann watched me as I backed slowly around the room to the mound of gear. The partners had had no extra equipment, no extra equipment at all. I looked down at the two atmosphere suits lying side by side on the metallic rock floor.

Two atmosphere suits. The dead man was supposed to be in one of those, floating out in space somewhere. He was in the suit, right enough, I was sure of that, but he wasn't floating anywhere.

A space suit is a perfect place to hide a body, for as long as it has to be hid. The silvered faceplate keeps you from seeing inside, and the suit is, naturally, a sealed atmosphere. A body can rot away to ashes inside a space suit, and you'll never notice a thing on the outside.

I'd had the right idea after all. McCann had planned to get rid of Karpin's body by attaching a rocket to it, slowing it down, and letting it fall into the sun. But he hadn't had an opportunity yet to go buy a rocket. He couldn't go to Atronics City, where he could have bought the rocket on credit, and he couldn't go to Chemisant City until the claim sale went through and he had some money to spend. And in the meantime, Karpin's body was perfectly safe, sealed away inside his atmosphere suit.

And it would have been safe, too, if McCann hadn't been just a little bit too greedy. He could kill his partner and get away with it; policemen on the Belt are even farther apart than the asteroids. He could swindle his creditors and get away with it; they had no way of checking up and no reason to suspect a switch in identities. But when he tried to get his own money back from Tangier Mutual Insurance, *that's* when he made his mistake.

I studied the two atmosphere suits, at the same time managing to keep a wary eye on Jafe McCann, standing rigid and silent across the room. Which one of those suits contained the body of Ab Karpin?

The one with the new patch on the chest, of course. As I'd guessed, McCann had shot him, and that's why he had the problem of disposing of the body in the first place.

I prodded that suit with my toe. "He's in there, isn't he?"

"You're crazy."

"Think I should open it up and check? It's been almost a month, you know. I imagine he's pretty ripe by now."

I reached down to the neck-fastenings on the fishbowl, and McCann finally moved. His arms jerked up, and he cried, "Don't! He's in there, he's in there! For God's sake, don't open it up!"

I relaxed. Mission accomplished. "Crawl into your suit, little man," I said. "We've got ourselves a trip to make, the three of us."

Henderson, as usual, was jovial but stern. "You did a fine job up there, Ged," he said with false familiarity. "Really brilliant work."

"Thank you very much," I said. I was holding the last piece of news for a minute or two, relishing it.

"But you brought McCann in over a week ago. I don't see why you had to stay up at Atronics City at all after that, much less ten days."

I sat back in the chair and negligently crossed my legs. "I just thought I'd take a little vacation," I said carelessly, and lit a cigarette. I flicked ashes in the general direction of the ashtray on Henderson's desk. Some of them made it.

"A vacation?" he echoed, eyes widening. Henderson was a company man, a *real* company man. A vacation for him was purgatory, it was separation from a loved one. "I don't believe you have a vacation coming," he said frostily, "for at least six months."

"That's what you think, Henny," I said.

All he could do at that was blink.

I went on, enjoying myself hugely. "I don't like this company," I said. "And I don't like this job. And I don't like you. And from now on, I've decided, it's going to be vacation all the time."

"Ged," he said, his voice faint, "what's the matter with you? Don't you feel well?"

"I feel well," I told him. "I feel fine. Now I'll tell you why I spent an extra ten days at Atronics City. McCann made and registered the big strike, right?"

Henderson nodded blankly, apparently not trusting himself to speak.

"Wrong," I said cheerfully. "McCann went to Chemisant City and filled out all the forms required for registering a claim. But every place he was supposed to sign his name he wrote *Ab Karpin* instead. Jafe McCann *never did make a legal registration of his claim.*"

Henderson just looked fish-eyed.

"So," I went on, "as soon as I turned McCann over to the law at Atronics City, I went and registered that claim myself. And then I waited around for ten days until the company finished the paperwork involved in buying that claim from me. And then I came straight back here, just to say good-bye to you. Wasn't that nice?"

He didn't move.

"Goodbye," I said.

The Winner

Wordman stood at the window, looking out, and saw Revell walk away from the compound. "Come here," he said to the interviewer. "You'll see the Guardian in action."

The interviewer came around the desk and stood beside Wordman at the window. He said, "That's one of them?"

"Right." Wordman smiled, feeling pleasure. "You're lucky," he said. "It's rare when one of them even makes the attempt. Maybe he's doing it for your benefit."

The interviewer looked troubled. He said, "Doesn't he know what it will do?"

"Of course. Some of them don't believe it, not till they've tried it once. Watch."

They both watched. Revell walked without apparent haste, directly across the field toward the woods on the other side. After he'd gone about two hundred yards from the edge of the compound he began to bend forward slightly at the middle, and a few yards farther on he folded his arms across his stomach as though it ached him. He tottered, but kept moving forward, staggering more and more, appearing to be in great pain. He managed to stay on his feet nearly all the way to the trees, but finally crumpled to the ground, where he lay unmoving.

Wordman no longer felt pleasure. He liked the theory of the Guardian better than its application. Turning to his desk, he called the infirmary and said, "Send a stretcher out to the east, near the woods. Revell's out there."

The interviewer turned at the sound of the name, saying, "Revell? Is that who that is? The poet?"

"If you can call it poetry." Wordman's lips curled in disgust. He'd read some of Revell's so-called poems; garbage, garbage.

The interviewer looked back out the window. "I'd heard he was arrested," he said thoughtfully.

Looking over the interviewer's shoulder, Wordman saw that Revell had managed to get back up onto hands and knees, was now crawling slowly and painfully toward the woods. But a stretcher team was already trotting toward him and Wordman watched as they reached him, picked up the pain-weakened body, strapped it to the stretcher, and carried it back to the compound.

As they moved out of sight, the interviewer said, "Will he be all right?"

"After a few days in the infirmary. He'll have strained some muscles."

The interviewer turned away from the window. "That was very graphic," he said carefully.

"You're the first outsider to see it," Wordman told him, and smiled, feeling good again. "What do they call that? A scoop?"

"Yes," agreed the interviewer, sitting back down in his chair. "A scoop."

They returned to the interview, just the most recent of dozens Wordman had given in the year since this pilot project of the Guardian had been set up. For perhaps the fiftieth time he explained what the Guardian did and how it was of value to society.

The essence of the Guardian was the miniature black box, actually a tiny radio receiver, which was surgically inserted into the body of every prisoner. In the center of this prison compound was the Guardian transmitter, perpetually sending its message to these receivers. As long as a prisoner stayed within the hundred-and-fifty-yard range of that transmitter, all was well. Should he move beyond that range, the black box inside his skin would begin to send messages of pain throughout his nervous system. This pain increased as the prisoner moved farther from the transmitter, until at its peak it was totally immobilizing.

"The prisoner can't hide, you see," Wordman explained. "Even if Revell had reached the woods, we'd have found him. His screams would have led us to him."

The Guardian had been initially suggested by Wordman himself, at that time serving as assistant warden at a more ordinary penitentiary in the Federal system. Objections, mostly from sentimentalists, had delayed its acceptance for several years, but now at last this pilot project had been established, with a guaranteed five-year trial period, and Wordman had been placed in charge.

"If the results are as good as I'm sure they will be," Wordman said, "all prisons in the Federal system will be converted to the Guardian method."

The Guardian method had made jailbreaks impossible, riots easy to quell—by merely turning off the transmitter for a minute or two—and prisons simplicity to guard. "We have no guards here as such," Wordman pointed out. "Service employees only are needed here, people for the mess hall, infirmary and so on."

For the pilot project, prisoners were only those who had committed crimes against the State rather than against individuals. "You might say," Wordman said, smiling, "that here are gathered the Disloyal Opposition."

"You mean, political prisoners," suggested the interviewer.

"We don't like that phrase here," Wordman said, his manner suddenly icy. "It sounds Commie."

The interviewer apologized for his sloppy use of terminology, ended the interview shortly afterward, and Wordman, once again in a good mood, escorted him out of the building. "You see," he said, gesturing. "No walls. No machine guns in towers. Here at last is the model prison."

The interviewer thanked him again for his time, and went away to his car. Wordman watched him leave, then went over to the infirmary to see Revell. But he'd been given a shot, and was already asleep.

Revell lay flat on his back and stared at the ceiling. He kept thinking, over and over again, "I didn't know it would be as bad as that. I didn't know it would be as bad as that." Mentally, he took a big brush of black paint and wrote the words on the spotless white ceiling: *I didn't know it would be as bad as that.*

"Revell."

He turned his head slightly and saw Wordman standing beside the bed. He watched Wordman, but made no sign.

Wordman said, "They told me you were awake."

Revell waited.

"I tried to tell you when you first came," Wordman reminded him. "I told you there was no point trying to get away."

Revell opened his mouth and said, "It's all right, don't feel bad. You do what you have to do, I do what I have to do."

"Don't *feel* bad!" Wordman stared at him. "What have *I* got to feel bad about?"

Revell looked up at the ceiling, and the words he had painted there just a minute ago were gone already. He wished he had paper and pencil. Words were leaking out of him like water through a sieve. He needed paper and pencil to catch them in. He said, "May I have paper and pencil?"

"To write more obscenity? Of course not."

"Of course not," echoed Revell. He closed his eyes and watched the words leaking away. A man doesn't have time both to invent and memorize, he has to choose, and long ago Revell had chosen invention. But now there was no way to put the

78

inventions down on paper and they trickled through his mind like water and eroded away into the great outside world. "Twinkle, twinkle, little pain," Revell said softly, "in my groin and in my brain, down so low and up so high, will you live or will I die?"

"The pain goes away," said Wordman. "It's been three days, it should be gone already."

"It will come back," Revell said. He opened his eyes and wrote the words on the ceiling. "It will come back."

Wordman said, "Don't be silly. It's gone for good, unless you run away again."

Revell was silent.

Wordman waited, half-smiling, and then frowned. "You aren't," he said.

Revell looked at him in some surprise. "Of course I am," he said. "Didn't you know I would?"

"No one tries it twice."

"I'll never stop leaving. Don't you know that? I'll never stop leaving, I'll never stop being, I'll not stop believing I'm who I must be. You had to know that."

Wordman stared at him. "You'll go through it *again*?"

"Ever and ever," Revell said.

"It's a bluff." Wordman pointed an angry finger at Revell, saying, "If you want to die, I'll let you die. Do you know if we don't bring you back you'll die out there?"

"That's escape, too," Revell said.

"Is that what you want? All right. Go out there again, and I won't send anyone after you, that's a promise."

"Then you lose," Revell said. He looked at Wordman finally, seeing the blunt angry face. "They're your rules," Revell told him, "and by your own rules you're going to lose. You say your black box will make me stay, and that means the black box will make me stop being me. I say you're wrong. I say as long as I'm leaving you're losing, and if the black box kills me you've lost forever."

Spreading his arms, Wordman shouted, "Do you think this is a *game?*"

"Of course," said Revell. "That's why you invented it."

"You're insane," Wordman said. He started for the door. "You shouldn't be here, you should be in an asylum."

"That's losing, too," Revell shouted after him, but Wordman had slammed the door and gone.

Revell lay back on the pillow. Alone again, he could dwell once more on his terrors. He was afraid of the black box, much more now that he knew what it could do to him, afraid to the point where his fear made him sick to his stomach. But he was afraid of losing himself, too, this a more abstract and intellectual fear but just as strong. No, it was even stronger, because it was driving him to go out again.

"But I didn't know it would be as bad as that," he whispered. He painted it once more on the ceiling, this time in red.

Wordman had been told when Revell would be released from the infirmary, and he made a point of being at the door when Revell came out. Revell seemed somewhat leaner, perhaps a little older. He shielded his eyes from the sun with his hand, looked at Wordman, and said, "Good-bye, Wordman." He started walking east.

Wordman didn't believe it. He said, "You're bluffing, Revell."

Revell kept walking.

Wordman couldn't remember when he'd ever felt such anger. He wanted to run after Revell and kill him with his bare hands. He clenched his hands into fists and told himself he was a reasonable man, a rational man, a merciful man. As the Guardian was reasonable, was rational, was merciful. It required only obedience, and so did he. It punished only such purposeless defiance as Revell's, and so did he. Revell was antisocial, self-destructive, he had to learn. For his own sake, as well as for the sake of society, Revell had to be taught.

Wordman shouted, "What are you trying to *get* out of this?" He glared at Revell's moving back, listened to Revell's silence.

He shouted, "I won't send anyone after you! You'll crawl back *yourself!*"

He kept watching until Revell was far out from the compound, staggering across the field toward the trees, his arms folded across his stomach, his legs stumbling, his head bent forward. Wordman watched, and then gritted his teeth, and turned his back, and returned to his office to work on the monthly report. Only two attempted escapes last month.

Two or three times in the course of the afternoon he looked out the window. The first time, he saw Revell far across the field, on hands and knees, crawling toward the trees. The last time, Revell was out of sight, but he could be heard screaming. Wordman had a great deal of trouble concentrating his attention on the report.

Toward evening he went outside again. Revell's screams sounded from the woods, faint but continuous. Wordman stood listening, his fists clenching and relaxing at his sides. Grimly he forced himself not to feel pity. For Revell's own good he had to be taught.

A staff doctor came to him a while later and said, "Mr. Wordman, we've got to bring him in."

Wordman nodded. "I know. But I want to be sure he's learned."

"For God's sake," said the doctor, "*listen* to him."

Wordman looked bleak. "All right, bring him in."

As the doctor started away, the screaming stopped. Wordman and the doctor both turned their heads, listened—silence. The doctor ran for the infirmary.

Revell lay screaming. All he could think of was the pain, and the need to scream. But sometimes, when he managed a scream of the very loudest, it was possible for him to have a fraction of a second for himself, and in those fractions of seconds he still kept moving away from the prison, inching along the ground, so that in the last hour he had moved approximately seven feet. His head and right arm were now visible from the country road that passed through these woods.

On one level, he was conscious of nothing but the pain and his own screaming. On another level, he was totally, even insistently, aware of everything around him, the blades of grass near his eyes, the stillness of the woods, the tree branches high overhead. And the small pickup truck, when it stopped on the road beyond him.

The man who came over from the truck and squatted beside Revell had a lined and weathered face and the rough clothing of a farmer. He touched Revell's shoulder and said, "You hurt, fella?"

"Eeeeast!" screamed Revell. "Eeeeast!"

"Is it okay to move you?" asked the man.

"Yesssss!" shrieked Revell. "Eeeeast!"

"I'd best take you to a doctor."

There was no change in the pain when the man lifted him and carried him to the truck and lay him down on the floor in back. He was already at optimum distance from the transmitter; the pain now was as bad as it could get.

The farmer tucked a rolled-up wad of cloth into Revell's open mouth. "Bite on this," he said. "It'll make it easier."

It made nothing easier, but it muffled his screams. He was grateful for that; the screams embarrassed him.

He was aware of it all, the drive through increasing darkness, the farmer carrying him into a building that was of colonial design on the outside but looked like the infirmary on the inside, and a doctor who looked down at him and touched his forehead and then went to one side to thank the farmer for bringing him. They spoke briefly over there, and then the farmer went away and the doctor came back to look at Revell again. He was young, dressed in laboratory white, with a pudgy face and red hair. He seemed sick and angry. He said, "You're from that prison, aren't you?"

Revell was still screaming through the cloth. He managed a head-spasm which he meant to be a nod. His armpits felt as

82

though they were being cut open with knives of ice. The sides of his neck were being scraped by sandpaper. All of his joints were being ground back and forth, back and forth, the way a man at dinner separates the bones of a chicken wing. The interior of his stomach was full of acid. His body was stuck with needles, sprayed with fire. His skin was being peeled off, his nerves cut with razor blades, his muscles pounded with hammers. Thumbs were pushing his eyes out from inside his head. And yet, the genius of this pain, the brilliance that had gone into its construction, it permitted his mind to work, to remain constantly aware. There was no unconsciousness for him, no oblivion.

The doctor said, "What beasts some men are. I'll try to get it out of you. I don't know what will happen, we aren't supposed to know how it works, but I'll try to take the box out of you."

He went away, and came back with a needle. "Here. This will put you to sleep."

Ahhhhh.

"He isn't there. He just isn't anywhere in the woods."

Wordman glared at the doctor, but knew he had to accept what the man reported. "All right," he said. "Someone took him away. He had a confederate out there, someone who helped him get away."

"No one would dare," said the doctor. "Anyone who helped him would wind up here themselves."

"Nevertheless," said Wordman. "I'll call the State Police," he said, and went on into his office.

Two hours later the State Police called back. They'd checked the normal users of that road, local people who might have seen or heard something, and had found a farmer who'd picked up an injured man near the prison and taken him to a Dr. Allyn in Boonetown. The State Police were convinced the farmer had acted innocently.

"But not the doctor," Wordman said grimly. "He'd have to know the truth almost immediately."

"Yes, sir, I should think so."

"And he hasn't reported Revell."

"No, sir."

"Have you gone to pick him up yet?"

"Not yet. We just got the report."

"I'll want to come with you. Wait for me."

"Yes, sir."

Wordman traveled in the ambulance in which they'd bring Revell back. They arrived without siren at Dr. Allyn's with two cars of state troopers, marched into the tiny operating room, and found Allyn washing instruments at the sink.

Allyn looked at them all calmly and said, "I thought you might be along."

Wordman pointed at the man who lay, unconscious, on the table in the middle of the room. "There's Revell," he said.

Allyn glanced at the operating table in surprise. "Revell? The poet?"

"You didn't know? Then why help him?"

Instead of answering, Allyn studied his face and said, "Would you be Wordman himself?"

Wordman said, "Yes, I am."

"Then I believe this is yours," Allyn said, and put into Wordman's hands a small and bloody black box.

The ceiling was persistently bare. Revell's eyes wrote on it words that should have singed the paint away, but nothing ever happened. He shut his eyes against the white at last and wrote in spidery letters on the inside of his lids the single word *oblivion*.

He heard someone come into the room, but the effort of making a change was so great that for a moment longer he permitted his eyes to remain closed. When he did open them he saw Wordman there, standing grim and mundane at the foot of the bed.

Wordman said, "How are you, Revell?"

"I was thinking about oblivion," Revell told him. "Writing a poem on the subject." He looked up at the ceiling, but it was empty.

Wordman said, "You asked, one time, you asked for pencil and paper. We've decided you can have them."

Revell looked at him in sudden hope, but then understood. "Oh," he said. "Oh, *that*."

Wordman frowned and said, "What's wrong? I said you can have pencil and paper."

"If I promise not to leave anymore."

Wordman's hands gripped the foot of the bed. He said, "What's the matter with you? You can't get away, you have to know that by now."

"You mean I can't win. But I won't lose. It's your game, your rules, your home ground, your equipment; if I can manage a stalemate, that's pretty good."

Wordman said, "You still think it's a game. You think none of it matters. Do you want to see what you've done?" He stepped back to the door, opened it, made a motion, and Dr. Allyn was led in. Wordman said to Revell, "You remember this man?"

"I remember," said Revell.

Wordman said, "He just arrived. They'll be putting the Guardian in him in about an hour. Does it make you proud, Revell?"

Looking at Allyn, Revell said, "I'm sorry."

Allyn smiled and shook his head. "Don't be. I had the idea the publicity of a trial might help rid the world of things like the Guardian." His smile turned sour. "There wasn't very much publicity."

Wordman said, "You two are cut out of the same cloth. The emotions of the mob, that's all you can think of. Revell in those so-called poems of his, and you in that speech you made in court."

Revell, smiling, said, "Oh? You made a speech? I'm sorry I didn't get to hear it."

"It wasn't very good," Allyn said. "I hadn't known the trial would only be one day long, so I didn't have much time to prepare it."

Wordman said, "All right, that's enough. You two can talk later, you'll have years."

At the door Allyn turned back and said, "Don't go anywhere till I'm up and around, will you? After my operation."

Revell said, "You want to come along next time?"

"Naturally," said Allyn.

Dream a Dream

I'm dreaming, Nora thought, and she was right, but it didn't matter.

The dream was very realistic, even to the glitter on the knife in the hand of the tall Mayan priest. He faced Nora in a small chamber she knew to be at the base of the temple, and even while her attention was on the stone knife she was aware of the rightness of every detail, both in his costume and the room itself, a narrow stone-walled space with a dry-smelling thatch roof. Stylized hummingbirds and vultures flowed on the priest's robes as he gestured, saying, "Well? Are you ready?"

Of course he isn't speaking English, and of course I understand him. "Ready for what?"

"After the rains," the priest said, "we must sacrifice a virgin to ensure fertility in the new fields."

Astonished, almost offended, not yet scared, Nora said, *"I'm not a virgin!"*

His free hand extended toward her, "Come, you keep everybody waiting."

A great crowd could be faintly heard outside. Nora shrank away, feeling the rough wall against her back through the thin white cotton tunic. "I'm a married woman," she said. Safe in that other world, beyond the edge of the dream, Ray was now asleep in the cot next to hers, the two of them peaceful and at rest in the Central American night. "I'm twenty-seven years old," Nora said. "I've been married nearly three years. I am *not* a virgin!"

"Of course you are." His impatience made him draw quick cutting motions in the air with the blade. "There is no passion in your life," he said, "—not for anything with juice in it. You married your husband not for love of him but of *archaeology*," the word dripping with contempt. "You've never loved anything but dust. You're a virgin, no question. Come along." Eyes determined, his wiry hand closed around her arm.

"No!" She sat up straight in the dark, disturbing the mosquitoes, staring at the night. On the other cot, Ray turned heavily in his sleep, smacking his lips, a fiftyish man who slept profoundly after the hard physical days in the field.

"I'm not," she whispered. The pressure of that bony hand could still be felt, a tight band around her upper arm. The glassless screened rectangle of the window let in air and the tiny night sounds of the jungle. Nora slowly lay back, hands holding the sheet under her chin, eyes very wide in the dark.

During breakfast, at one of the long tables in the dining shed, Nora pensively picked at her eggs and beans while Ray talked with the oil company man. His name was Stafford, and he had come to this remote jungle camp five days ago for a stay of about a month. By day he wandered the high land to the west, and in the evenings after dinner he sat here in the dining shed in the circle of light, where he drew his tiny maps and made notes in a small, neat hand. Now he was saying something about tall mounds he had seen in the jungle, similar to those concealing the structures here in the main part of Actun Ek, the Mayan city whose excavation Ray was directing, "Thanks, Bill," Ray said. "We'll have a look."

Nora was relieved when breakfast was done and they could tramp on out to the site, where the workers already crawled over the high-stepped sides of Building B-1, the primary temple of Actun Ek. *I was here last night*, Nora thought.

The workers, Indian tribesmen who made their living from archaeological sites, had nearly finished the first task, clearing away the centuries of growth and decay, the earth and brush and trees that covered the cunningly nested old stones, the steep lines of stairs. Unlike the Egyptian pyramids, Mayan temples were built solid, without rooms or corridors, just the steps and walls and sculptures reaching upward. Only at the base had there originally been the small thatch-roofed rooms built out from the temple's side.

Nora and Ray worked behind the Indians, collecting shards, filling in site maps. This was Nora's third year at Actun Ek, her eighth year since she had fallen in love with the dignity, strength, and confidence of the Mayan civilization, the impervious mystery of their individual persons. Who had they been? When they awoke in the morning, what had they thought of themselves and the jungle around them and the high temples to which they devoted their lives?

Human sacrifice: yes, that was part of it but hardly everything. Something was known of their agriculture, their trade, their religion, even their sports, but never very much. Never enough to hamper Nora's imagination.

Every day, in her mind, as she gleaned her way across the uneven steps, Nora was a Mayan priestess. Not even Ray knew of this game, this fantasy she had lived and elaborated for eight years. She imagined her clothing, her food, the understated drama of her days. Little was known of the place of women among the Mayan upper class, so her invention could float unimpeded.

At dinner, Bill Stafford showed them, on his neat maps, the location of the mounds he'd seen. This earnest geologist seemed even younger than Nora, which from the beginning had pleased her. She'd married a man much older than herself, was mostly around people of his generation, and resented their usual assumption that she was too young to be serious. Stafford was barely out of engineering college, but there could be no doubt of *his* seriousness. He had a square-jawed, handsome face, softened by a faint vagueness of expression. His eyeglasses were square-lensed, with plastic frames just a bit darker than his tanned skin. His hair was blond but already very thin, sunlight reflecting from his scalp through his widow's peak. He wore hiking shoes, khaki slacks, a short-sleeved white dress shirt; in a white hard-plastic pouch in the shirt pocket, his pens and pencils were neatly arrayed. He shaved every day.

She didn't dream that night, but she barely slept either. Every time she dozed off, the fear of the dream startled her awake. She spent the night remembering her life, seeing herself as Dr. Helm's promising student, then as Mr. Helm's gifted graduate student, then as Raymond Helm's assistant, and now as Ray's wife. She had not slept with him until after his divorce from Joanna. He was Nora's first husband.

In another shed in the compound, Bill Stafford would be asleep. *This is terrible*, Nora told herself. *I must get over this. I must sleep.* Toward morning, she did.

"I'm just here to do the stuff on the ground," Bill Stafford was explaining to her. "Confirm or deny the technology's guesses."

"Does technology guess?" Nora asked, following him. She had volunteered at breakfast to go with him to see if the mounds he'd described did contain buried structures. Perspiration ran down behind her ears, between her breasts.

"It's all step by step," Stafford told her. "We've got satellite pictures to map the terrain, aerial survey using infrared, SLAR scanning. Now we have to walk the groun—"

"*What* kind of scanning? Help here, will you?"

They were crossing a gully. He held his hand back for her. His teeth glistened when he smiled. Sweat made gray islands on his shirt. He said, "SLAR—for Side-Looking Airborne Radar."

"Sounds very suggestive," she said, laughing, and released his hand. Then she had to clasp his arm to keep from slipping backward on a muddy stone.

His hand pressed to the small of her back. "Careful."

Not careful. "You're all wet," she said, showing her tongue, tracing with her fingertip a line of perspiration that ran from his throat down his chest and under the shirt.

Behind the glasses his eyes looked surprised, but when she kissed him he knew what it meant.

Before dinner, she used the primitive bucket-and-cistern-in-a-tree shower, the sun-warmed water splashing over her heated body. She lifted her right breast and, yes, his watchband had left a scratch. She smiled at it.

I wasn't wrong, she thought late that night, slipping silently through the sleeping camp, away from Bill's room, back toward her own cot. *I was right in college, right to follow my own needs and grow at my own pace. I wouldn't have been ready then for this. But now I'm right again!*

She was brand-new, tingling with rebirth. The dream had rescued her before she withered, using her Mayans as the symbol. Her stone passion had pointed the way to a richer, truer passion of the flesh.

Not that she would run off with Bill, nor leave Ray. There was no need to throw away the life she already had, the work she'd already accomplished. She would still admire Ray just as much, esteem and help him, serve him and the Mayans and the work, absorbed and satisfied; but now there would be more. A lifetime of Bill Staffords smiled in her mind, all young, all loving and giving, all a kind of delicious dessert. And no one need ever know, no one need ever be hurt. She could have it all.

Ray's breathing was long and regular. Nora slid between the cool, damp sheets.

*　*　*

The same cell. She stared, unbelieving. The same cell, the same rough thatch ceiling, square stone walls, tall imperious priest in all his finery, grasping the same rough-edged knife. "Now," he said, "what we do with adulteresses . . ."

In at the Death

It's hard not to believe in ghosts when you are one. I hanged myself in a fit of truculence—stronger than pique, but not so dignified as despair—and regretted it before the thing was well begun. The instant I kicked the chair away I wanted it back, but gravity was turning my former wish to its present command; the chair would not right itself from where it lay on the floor, and my thirteen stone eleven would not cease to urge downward from the rope thick around my neck.

There was pain, of course, quite horrible pain centered in my throat, but the most astounding thing was the way my cheeks seemed to swell. I could barely see over their round red hills, my eyes staring in agony at the door, *willing* someone to come in and rescue me, though I knew there was no one in the house, and in any event the door was carefully locked. My kicking legs caused me to twist and turn, so that sometimes I faced the door and sometimes the window, and my shivering hands struggled with the rope so deep in my flesh I could barely find it and most certainly could not pull loose.

I was frantic and terrified, yet at the same time my brain possessed a cold corner of aloof observation. I seemed now to be everywhere in the room at once, within my writhing body but also without, seeing my frenzied spasms, the thick rope, the heavy beam, the mismatched pair of lit bedside lamps throwing my convulsive double shadow on the walls, the closed locked door, the white-curtained window with its shade drawn all the way down. *This is death*, I thought, and I no longer wanted it, now that the choice was gone forever.

My name is—was—Edward Thornburn, and my dates are 1938-1977. I killed myself just a month before my fortieth birthday, though I don't believe the well-known pangs of that milestone had much if anything to do with my action. I blame it all (as I blamed most of the errors and failures of my life) on my sterility. Had I been able to father children my marriage would have remained strong, Emily would not have been unfaithful to me, and I would not have taken my own life in a final fit of truculence.

The setting was the guest room in our house in Barnstaple, Connecticut, and the time was just after seven PM; deep twilight, at this time of year. I had come home from the office—I was an estate agent, a fairly lucrative occupation in Connecticut, though my income had been falling off recently—shortly before six, to find the note on the kitchen table: "Antiquing with Greg. Afraid you'll have to make your own dinner. Sorry. Love, Emily."

Greg was the one; Emily's lover. He owned an antique shop out on the main road toward New York, and Emily filled a part of her days as his ill-paid assistant. I knew what they did together in the back of the shop on those long mid-week afternoons when there were no tourists, no antique collectors to disturb them. I knew, and I'd known for more than three years, but I had never decided how to deal with my knowledge. The fact was, I blamed myself, and therefore I had no way to *behave* if the ugly subject were ever to come into the open.

So I remained silent, but not content. I was discontent, unhappy, angry, resentful—truculent.

I'd tried to kill myself before. At first with the car, by steering it into an oncoming truck (I swerved at the last second, amid howling horns) and by driving it off a cliff into the Connecticut River (I slammed on the brakes at the very brink, and sat covered in perspiration for half an hour before backing away) and finally by stopping athwart one of the few level crossings left in this neighborhood. But no train came for twenty minutes, and my truculence wore off and I drove home.

Later I tried to slit my wrists, but found it impossible to push sharp metal into my own skin. Impossible. The vision of my naked wrist and that shining steel so close together washed my truculence completely out of my mind. Until the next time.

With the rope; and then I succeeded. Oh, totally, oh fully I succeeded. My legs kicked at air, my fingernails clawed at my throat, my bulging eyes stared out over my swollen purple cheeks, my tongue thickened and grew bulbous in my mouth, my body jigged and jangled like a toy at the end of a string, and the pain was excruciating, horrible, not to be endured. I can't endure it, I thought, it can't be endured. Much worse than knife slashings was the knotted strangled pain in my throat, and my head ballooned with pain, pressure outward, my face turning black, my eyes no longer human, the pressure in my head building and building as though I would explode. Endless horrible pain, not to be endured, but going on and on.

My legs kicked more feebly. My arms sagged, my hands dropped to my sides, my fingers twitched uselessly against my sopping trouser legs, my head hung at an angle from the rope, I turned more slowly in the air, like a broken windchime on a breezeless day. The pains lessened, in my throat and head, but never entirely stopped.

And now I saw that my distended eyes had become lusterless, grey. The moisture had dried on the eyeballs, they were as dead as stones. And yet I could see them, my own eyes, and when I widened my vision I could see my entire body, turning, hanging, no longer twitching, and with a dulled horror I realized I was dead.

But *present*. Dead, but still present, with the scraping ache still in my throat and the bulging pressure still in my head. Present, but no longer in that used-up clay, that hanging meat; I was suffused through the room, like indirect lighting, everywhere present but without a source. What happens now? I wondered, dulled by fear and strangeness and the continuing pains, and I waited, like a hovering mist, for whatever would happen next.

But nothing happened. I waited; the body became utterly still; the double shadow on the wall showed no vibration; the bedside lamps continued to burn; the door remained shut and the windowshade drawn; and nothing happened.

What *now*? I craved to scream the question aloud, but I could not. My throat ached, but I had no throat. My mouth burned, but I had no mouth. Every final strain and struggle of my body remained imprinted in my mind, but I had no body and no brain and no *self*, no substance. No power to speak, no power to move myself, no power to *re*move myself from this room and this suspended corpse. I could only wait here, and wonder, and go on waiting.

There was a digital clock on the dresser opposite the bed, and when it first occurred to me to look at it the numbers were 7:21—perhaps twenty minutes after I'd kicked the chair away, perhaps fifteen minutes since I'd died. Shouldn't something happen, shouldn't some *change* take place?

The clock read 9:11 when I heard Emily's Volkswagen drive around to the back of the house. I had left no note, having nothing I wanted to say to anyone and in any event believing my own dead body would be eloquent enough, but I hadn't thought I would be *present* when Emily found me. I was justified in my action, however much I now regretted having taken it, I was justified, I knew I was justified, but I didn't want to see her face when she came through that door. She had wronged me, she was the cause of it, she would have to know that as well as I, but I didn't want to see her face. I didn't want to see her face.

96

The pains increased, in what had been my throat, in what had been my head. I heard the back door slam, far away downstairs, and I stirred like air currents in the room, but I didn't leave. I couldn't leave.

"Ed? Ed? It's me, hon!"

I know it's you. I must go away now, I can't stay here, I must go away. Is there a God? Is this my soul, this hovering presence? *Hell* would be better than this, take me away to Hell or wherever I'm to go, don't leave me here!

She came up the stairs, calling again, walking past the closed guest room door. I heard her go into our bedroom, heard her call my name, heard the beginnings of apprehension in her voice. She went by again, out there in the hall, went downstairs, became quiet.

What was she doing? Searching for a note perhaps, some message from me. Looking out the window, seeing again my Chevrolet, knowing I must be home. Moving through the rooms of this old house, the original structure a barn nearly two hundred years old, converted by some previous owner just after the Second World War, bought by me twelve years ago, furnished by Emily—and Greg—from their interminable, damnable, awful antiques. Shaker furniture, Colonial furniture, hooked rugs and quilts, the old yellow pine tables, the faint sense always of being in some slightly shabby minor museum, this house that I had bought but never loved. I'd bought it for Emily, I did everything for Emily, because I knew I could never do the one thing for Emily that mattered. I could never give her a child.

She was good about it, of course. Emily *is* good, I never blamed her, never completely blamed *her* instead of myself. In the early days of our marriage she made a few wistful references, but I suppose she saw the effect they had on me, and for a long time she has said nothing. But I have known.

The beam from which I had hanged myself was a part of the original building, a thick hand-hewed length of aged timber eleven inches square, chevronned with the marks of the hatchet that shaped it. A strong beam, it would support my weight forever. It would support my weight until I was found, and cut down. Until I was found.

The clock read 9:23 and Emily had been in the house twelve minutes when she came upstairs again, her steps quick and light on the old wood, approaching, pausing, stopping. "Ed?"

The doorknob turned.

The door was locked, of course, with the key on the inside. She'd have to break it down, have to call someone else to break it down, perhaps she wouldn't be the one to find me after all. Hope rose in me, and the pains receded.

"Ed? Are you in there?" She knocked at the door, rattled the knob, called my name several times more, then abruptly turned and ran away downstairs again, and after a moment I heard her voice, murmuring and unclear. She had called someone, on the phone.

Greg, I thought, and the throat-rasp filled me, and I wanted this to be the end. I wanted to be taken away, dead body and living soul, taken away. I wanted everything to be finished.

She stayed downstairs, waiting for him, and I stayed upstairs, waiting for them both. Perhaps she already knew what she'd find up here, and that's why she waited below.

I didn't mind about Greg, about being present when he came in. I didn't mind about *him*. It was Emily I minded.

The clock read 9:44 when I heard tires on the gravel at the side of the house. He entered, I heard them talking down there, the deeper male voice slow and reassuring, the lighter female voice quick and frightened, and then they came up together, neither speaking. The doorknob turned, jiggled, rattled, and Greg's voice called, "Ed?"

After a little silence, Emily said, "He wouldn't—he wouldn't *do* anything, would he?"

"Do anything?" Greg sounded almost annoyed at the question. "What do you mean, do anything?"

"He's been so depressed, he's—Ed!" And forcibly the knob was rattled, the door was shaken in its frame.

"Emily, don't. Take it easy."

"I shouldn't have called you," she said. "Ed, *please!*"

"Why not? For Heaven's sake, Emily—"

"Ed, *please* come out, don't scare me like this!"

"Why *shouldn't* you call me, Emily?"

"Ed isn't stupid, Greg. He's—"

There was then a brief silence, pregnant with the hint of murmuring. They thought me still alive in here, they didn't want me to hear Emily say, "He *knows*, Greg, he knows about us."

The murmurings sifted and shifted, and then Greg spoke loudly: "That's ridiculous. Ed? Come out, Ed, let's talk this over." And the doorknob rattled and clattered, and he sounded merely annoyed when he said, "We must get in, that's all. Is there another key?"

"I think all the locks up here are the same. Just a minute."

They were. A simple skeleton key would open any interior door in the house. I waited, listening, knowing Emily had gone off to find another key, knowing they would soon come in together, and I felt such terror and revulsion for Emily's entrance that I could feel myself shimmer in the room, like a reflection in a warped mirror. Oh, can I at least stop seeing? In life I had eyes, but also eyelids, I could shut out the intolerable, but now I was only a presence, a total presence, I *could not* stop my awareness.

The rasp of key in lock was like rough metal edges in my throat; my memory of a throat. The pain flared in me, and through it I heard Emily asking what was wrong, and Greg answering, "The key's in it, on the other side."

"Oh, dear God! Oh, Greg, what has he done?"

"We'll have to take the door off its hinges," he told her. "Call Tony. Tell him to bring the toolbox."

"Can't you push the key through?"

Of course he could, but he said, quite determinedly, "Go *on*, Emily," and I realized then he had no intention of taking the door down. He simply wanted her away when the door was first opened. Oh, very good, *very* good!

"All right," she said doubtfully, and I heard her go away to phone Tony. A beetle-browed young man with great masses of black hair and an olive complexion, Tony lived in Greg's house and was a kind of handyman. He did work around the house and was also (according to Emily) very good at restoration of antique furniture; stripping paint, reassembling broken parts, that sort of thing.

There was now a renewed scraping and rasping at the lock, as Greg struggled to get the door open before Emily's return. I found myself feeling unexpected warmth and liking toward Greg. He wasn't a bad person; an opportunist with my wife, but not in general a bad person. Would he marry her now? They could live in this house, he'd had more to do with its furnishing than I. Or would this room hold too grim a memory, would Emily have to sell the house, live elsewhere? She might have to sell at a low price; as an estate agent, I knew the difficulty in selling a house where a suicide has taken place. No matter how much they may joke about it, people are still afraid of the supernatural. Many of them would believe this room was haunted.

It was then I finally realized the room *was* haunted. With me! *I'm a ghost*, I thought, thinking the word for the first time, in utter blank astonishment. I'm a ghost.

Oh, how dismal! To hover here, to be a boneless fleshless aching *presence* here, to be a kind of ectoplasmic mildew seeping through the days and nights, alone, unending, a stupid pain-racked misery-filled observer of the comings and goings of strangers—she *would* sell the house, she'd have to, I was sure of that—was this my punishment? The punishment of the suicide, the solitary Hell of him who takes his own life. To remain forever a sentient nothing, bound by a force greater than gravity itself to the place of one's finish.

I was distracted from this misery by a sudden agitation in the key on this side of the lock. I saw it quiver and jiggle like something alive, and then it popped out— it seemed to *leap* out, itself a suicide leaping from a cliff—and clattered to the floor, and an instant later the door was pushed open and Greg's ashen face stared at my own purple face, and after the astonishment and horror, his expression shifted to revulsion—and contempt?—and he backed out, slamming the door. Once more the key turned in the lock, and I heard him hurry away downstairs.

The clock read 9:58. *Now* he was telling her. *Now* he was giving her a drink to calm her. *Now* he was phoning the police. *Now* he was talking to her about whether or not to admit their affair to the police; what would they decide?

"NOOOO—OOOOO!"

The clock read 10:07. What had taken so long? Hadn't he even called the police yet?

She was coming up the stairs, stumbling and rushing, she was pounding at the door, screaming my name. I shrank into the corners of the room, I *felt* the thuds of her fists against the door, I cowered from her. She can't come in, dear God don't let her in! I don't care what she's done, I don't care about anything, just don't let her see me! *Don't let me see her!*

Greg joined her. She screamed at him, he persuaded her, she raved, he argued, she demanded, he denied. "Give me the key. Give me the key."

Surely he'll hold out, surely he'll take her away, surely he's stronger, more forceful.

He gave her the key.

No. *This* cannot be endured. *This* is the horror beyond all else. She came in, she walked into the room, and the sound she made will always live inside me. That cry wasn't human; it was the howl of every creature that has ever despaired. *Now* I know what despair is, and why I call my own state mere truculence.

Now that it was too late, Greg tried to restrain her, tried to hold her shoulders and draw her from the room, but she pulled away and crossed the room toward . . . not toward *me*. I was everywhere in the room, driven by pain and remorse, and Emily walked toward the carcass. She looked at it almost tenderly, she even reached up and touched its swollen cheek. "Oh, Ed," she murmured.

101

The pains were as violent now as in the moment before my death. The slashing torment in my throat, the awful distension in my head, they made me squirm in agony all over again; but I *could not* feel her hand on my cheek.

Greg followed her, touched her shoulder again, spoke her name, and immediately her face dissolved, she cried out once more and wrapped her arms around the corpse's legs and clung to it, weeping and gasping and jabbering words too quick and broken to understand. Thank *God* they were too quick and broken to understand!

Greg, that fool, did finally force her away, though he had great trouble breaking her clasp on the body. But he succeeded, and pulled her out of the room, and slammed the door, and for a little while the body swayed and turned, until it became still once more.

That was the worst. Nothing could be worse than that. The long days and nights here—how long must a stupid creature like myself *haunt* his death-place before release?—would be horrible, I knew that, but not so bad as this. Emily would survive, would sell the house, would slowly forget. (Even I would slowly forget.) She and Greg could marry now. She was only thirty-six, she could still be a mother.

For the rest of the night, I heard her wailing, elsewhere in the house. The police did come at last, and a pair of grim silent white-coated men from the morgue entered the room to cut me—it—down. They bundled it like a broken toy into a large oval wicker basket with long wooden handles, and they carried it away.

I had thought I might be forced to stay with the body, I had feared the possibility of being buried with it, of spending eternity as a thinking nothingness in the black dark of a casket, but the body left the room and I remained behind.

A doctor was called. When the body was carried away the room door was left open, and now I could plainly hear the voices from downstairs. Tony was among them now, his characteristic surly monosyllable occasionally rumbling, but the main thing for

102

a while was the doctor. He was trying to give Emily a sedative, but she kept wailing, she kept speaking high hurried frantic sentences as though she had too little time to say it all. "I did it!" she cried, over and over. "I did it! I'm to blame!"

Yes. That was the reaction I'd wanted, and expected, and here it was, and it was horrible. Everything I had desired in the last moments of my life had been granted to me, and they were all ghastly beyond belief. I *didn't* want to die! I *didn't* want to give Emily such misery! And more than all the rest, I didn't want to be here, seeing and hearing it all.

They did quiet her at last, and then a policeman in a rumpled blue suit came into the room with Greg, and listened while Greg described everything that had happened. While Greg talked, the policeman rather grumpily stared at the remaining length of rope still knotted around the beam, and when Greg had finished the policeman said, "You're a close friend of his?"

"More of his wife. She works for me, I own The Bibelot, an antique shop out on the New York Road."

"Mm. Why on earth did you let her in here?"

Greg smiled; a sheepish embarrassed expression. "She's stronger than I am," he said. "A more forceful personality. That's always been true."

It was with some surprise I realized it *was* true. Greg was something of a weakling, and Emily was very strong. (*I* had been something of a weakling, hadn't I? Emily was the strongest of us all.)

The policeman was saying, "Any idea why he'd do it?"

"I think he suspected his wife was having an affair with me." Clearly Greg had rehearsed this sentence, he'd much earlier come to the decision to say it and had braced himself for the moment. He blinked all the way through the statement, as though standing in a harsh glare.

The policeman gave him a quick shrewd look. "Were you?"

"Yes."

"She was getting a divorce?"

"No. She doesn't love me, she loved her husband."

"Then why sleep around?"

"Emily wasn't sleeping *around*," Greg said, showing offense only with that emphasized word. "From time to time, and not very often, she was sleeping with me."

"Why?"

"For comfort." Greg too looked at the rope around the beam, as though it had become me and he was awkward speaking in its presence. "Ed wasn't an easy man to get along with," he said carefully. "He was moody. It was getting worse."

"Cheerful people don't kill themselves," the policeman said.

"Exactly. Ed was depressed most of the time, obscurely angry now and then. It was affecting his business, costing him clients. He made Emily miserable but she wouldn't leave him, she loved him. I don't know what she'll do now."

"You two won't marry?"

"Oh, no." Greg smiled, a bit sadly. "Do you think we murdered him, made it look like suicide so we could marry?"

"Not at all," the policeman said. "But what's the problem? You already married?"

"I am homosexual."

The policeman was no more astonished than I. He said, "I don't get it."

"I live with my friend; that young man downstairs. I am—capable—of a wider range, but my preferences are set. I am very fond of Emily, I felt sorry for her, the life she had with Ed. I told you our physical relationship was infrequent. And often not very successful."

Oh, Emily. Oh, poor Emily.

The policeman said, "Did Thornburn know you were, uh, homosexual?"

"I have no idea. I don't make a public point of it."

"All right." The policeman gave one more half-angry look around the room, then said, "Let's go."

They left. The door remained open, and I heard them continue to talk as they went downstairs, first the policeman asking, "Is there somebody to stay the night? Mrs. Thornburn shouldn't be alone."

"She has relatives in Great Barrington. I phoned them earlier. Somebody should be arriving within the hour."

"You'll stay until then? The doctor says she'll probably sleep, but just in case—"

"Of course."

That was all I heard. Male voices murmured a while longer from below, and then stopped. I heard cars drive away.

How complicated men and women are. How stupid are simple actions. I had never understood anyone, least of all myself.

The room was visited once more that night, by Greg, shortly after the police left. He entered, looking as offended and repelled as though the body were still here, stood the chair up on its legs, climbed on it, and with some difficulty untied the remnant of rope. This he stuffed partway into his pocket as he stepped down again to the floor, then returned the chair to its usual spot in the corner of the room, picked the key off the floor and put it in the lock, switched off both bedside lamps and left the room, shutting the door behind him.

Now I was in darkness, except for the faint line of light around the door, and the illuminated numerals of the clock. How long one minute is! That clock was my enemy, it dragged out every minute, it paused and waited and paused and waited till I could stand it no more, and then it waited longer, and *then* the next number dropped into place. Sixty times an hour, hour after hour, all night long. I couldn't stand one night of this, how could I stand eternity?

And how could I stand the torment and torture inside my brain? That was much worse now than the physical pain, which never entirely left me. I had been right about Emily and Greg, but at the same time I had been hopelessly brainlessly wrong. I had been right about my life, but wrong; right about my death, but wrong. How *much* I wanted to make amends, and how impossible it was to do anything anymore, anything at all. My actions had all tended to this, and ended with this: black remorse, the most dreadful pain of all.

I had all night to think, and to feel the pains, and to wait without knowing what I was waiting for or when—or if—my waiting would ever end. Faintly I heard the arrival of Emily's sister and brother-in-law, the murmured conversation, then the departure of Tony and Greg. Not long afterward the guest room door opened, but almost immediately closed again, no one having entered, and a bit after that the hall light went out, and now only the illuminated clock broke the darkness.

When next would I see Emily? Would she ever enter this room again? It wouldn't be as horrible as the first time, but it would surely be horror enough.

Dawn greyed the windowshade, and gradually the room appeared out of the darkness, dim and silent and morose. Apparently it was a sunless day, which never got very bright. The day went on and on, featureless, each protracted minute marked by the clock. At times I dreaded someone's entering this room, at other times I prayed for something, anything—even the presence of Emily herself—to break this unending boring *absence*. But the day went on with no event, no sound, no activity anywhere—they must be keeping Emily sedated through this first day—and it wasn't until twilight, with the digital clock reading 6:52, that the door again opened and a person entered.

At first I didn't recognize him. An angry-looking man, blunt and determined, he came in with quick ragged steps, switched on both bedside lamps, then shut the door with rather more force than necessary, and turned the key in the lock. Truculent, his manner was, and when he turned from the door I saw with incredulity that he was *me*. Me! I wasn't dead, I was alive! But how could that be?

And what was that he was carrying? He picked up the chair from the corner, carried it to the middle of the room, stood on it—

No! No!

He tied the rope around the beam. The noose was already in

106

the other end, which he slipped over his head and tightened around his neck.

Good God, *don't!*

He kicked the chair away.

The instant I kicked the chair away I wanted it back, but gravity was turning my former wish to its present command; the chair would not right itself from where it lay on the floor, and my thirteen stone eleven would not cease to urge downward from the rope thick around my neck.

There was pain, of course, quite horrible pain centered in my throat, but the most astounding thing was the way my cheeks seemed to swell. I could barely see over their round red hills, my eyes staring in agony at the door, *willing* someone to come in and rescue me, though I knew there was no one in the house, and in any event the door was carefully locked. My kicking legs caused me to twist and turn, so that sometimes I faced the door and sometimes the window, and my shivering hands struggled with the rope so deep in my flesh I could barely find it and most certainly could not pull it loose.

I was frantic and terrified, yet at the same time my brain possessed a cold corner of aloof observation. I seemed now to be everywhere in the room at once, within my writhing body but also without, seeing my frenzied spasms, the thick rope, the heavy beam, the mismatched pair of lit bedside lamps throwing my convulsive double shadow on the walls, the closed locked door, the white-curtained window with its shade drawn all the way down. *This is death*, I thought.

Hydra

"**I**'m afraid that's the church again," Carrie Morton said. "Greg, push on."

"That's all right, I like it," Fay White told her, being polite, but Greg Morton had already pushed the bar on the slide projector—chip-*clock*—and after a brief interval of rectangular white, the wall reblossomed into yet another view of the same small concrete-block church roughly painted in pastels, glistening like a week-old wedding cake in the bright southern sun.

"Oh, dear," Carrie said. "Too many of the same picture. But I just *loved* that church."

"I'd be fascinated by those colors, too," Fay said, hating herself for her spineless politeness but helpless to change her manner. A dozen years ago in college it had been like this, Carrie blithe and uncaring while Fay smiled and said it was all right; and now here they were again, just the same.

Chip-chip-chip-chip—"The people are so *primitive*," Carrie said, as Greg struggled with the machine and they all stared at

108

the white-again wall. "They're *alleged* to be Christians, but what went on in that building seemed awfully jungle-jungle to *me*."

Then why not photograph that, Fay thought, sipping gamely at her pre-dinner drink. She and Carrie and Greg all held tiny glasses of a heavy, too-sweet South American liqueur the Mortons had brought back, while Fay's husband, Reed—no spineless politeness for *him*—sat contentedly with a glass of beer. I wish I were more like Reed, Fay thought. Self-confident and serene. I wish I liked my friends more.

Clock. Four smiling children shyly posed in that same harsh sunlight beside a rusted, springless, dark green American car. "So childlike," Carrie said, comfortably smiling.

"Well, they're children," Fay said, looking at the vulnerable little faces, the knobby brown knees.

"No, all of them, I mean." Carrie laughed. "Such sweet people, but so *naive!*"

"Ripe for agitators," Greg said.

The picture on the wall trembled, and Fay frowned at the children. A withered *arm*? And wasn't that— "Wait!" she said, but chip-*clock*, and they were looking now at a placid man walking down a dirt road, a large earthenware jug balanced on his shoulder. The road was dry and dusty, the land to both sides a sunbeaten brown. "Oh, it's *Hoo*-lee-oh!" Carrie said happily.

"Was that— Was one of those—" Fay looked across the projector's beam at Carrie, blond and sweet and recently maternal. "Was one of those children blind?"

But Reed was saying, "Agitators, Greg? Down there, too?"

"It's the same old story," Greg said, while Carrie turned her open smiling face to listen. "The big American company comes in, brings prosperity, jobs, consumer goods, education—*medical care*, for Christ's sake—and the first thing you know the locals think it's all theirs."

"Hoo-lee-oh was our houseboy," Carrie said, smiling at Fay. "I can't tell you what a pleasure it is, being where there's *no* servant problem."

"Hoo-lee-oh?"

Carrie spelled it out, and it turned out to be *Julio*. "He made the most delicious wine," Carrie said, "and used to bring us just *jugs* of the stuff. Not grape wine, from flowers or something. I never could understand how he grew anything at all—just *look* at the ground. When I think of my poor little kitchen garden; *hopeless*, tomatoes like acorns."

"Miserable soil," Greg said, "but naturally the politicals carried on all the time about pollution."

"It's the same up here," Reed said. "Love Canal, all that. Mountains out of molehills."

"Exactly," Greg said. "People make mistakes, we're all human, but you'd think it was *deliberate*. We aren't barbarians, for Christ's sake."

Fay twisted around to look at Greg. "I read about some valley in Brazil," she said, "where there's so much industry now, so much pollution, nothing grows anymore. And birth defects, and—"

Greg nodded, mouth expressing disapproval. "The dead valley, I know. Believe me, the politicals beat us over the head with *that* one, even though it isn't American companies, it's all multinationals, European, South American. But they did go too far there, no question, we all know there have to be *some* controls. But what *we* have to realize, every one of us right here in the U.S.A., the world is going to pass us by."

"I don't follow," Reed said.

Chip-*clock*. Julio and his jug became a very pregnant Carrie, in voluminous white top and pink slacks, blooming and beaming in front of their neat white modular company cottage. In the background, black lines like the smoke in a child's drawing squiggled upward from the tall metal stacks. "I wore pink the whole time," Carrie said, "so I'd have a girl."

"Vickie's such a little doll," Fay told her.

Greg was saying to Reed, "If it weren't for U.S. government regulations, PetChem wouldn't have *moved* down there back in the sixties. I'm all for the environment—I mean, for Christ's sake, we all breathe the same air—but you've got to weigh the

110

factors. These countries in the south, they *want* our business, they're ready to make an accommodation."

"How far along were you?" Fay asked.

"Six months." Carrie smiled dreamily, reminiscently, at the image of her pregnant self. "I carried so big, for a while I thought I was having triplets."

"Of course, *they* breed like rabbits," Greg said, "so they hardly show. The women. Walk along the road, you wouldn't know they were pregnant at all. Squat, and poof."

Laughing, Carrie said, "It's not quite *that* easy."

"Still," Fay said, "I don't suppose prenatal care is exactly up to our standards."

"One reason we're back," Greg said. Chip-*clock*. "Also, we wanted Vickie born in the U.S.A."

"That's the company lake," Carrie said.

The people along the shore were of no clearly defined types. "Even in bathing suits," Fay said, "Americans look like Americans."

Carrie said, "Remember the summer we both took cabins on Lake Monequois? Doesn't it look like that?"

"Except for the volcanoes."

"Maybe we can do the lake again next summer," Carrie said. "Now that we're back."

"You can't swim there anymore. They say it's algae or something."

"Oh, too bad." But Carrie's smile remained sunny, and she said, "Well, there's still the ocean."

Reed said, "Is that your Julio again? Are all those kids his?"

"I told you so," Greg said. "Like rabbits. Of course, we had to let the locals use the company lake, I mean we're *democratic*, for Christ's sake."

A child behind Julio was crawling toward the water. Fay said, "Where's his legs?"

Chip-*clock*. "What?" Greg said.

"Nothing. Never mind." Fay frowned at the white wall.

Carrie said, "That's the end of that box, honey."

111

Greg's watch was a masterpiece of several technologies. Consulting it, he said, "Seven fifty-three, dear. You wanted to know."

"Oh, my goodness." Carrie's long legs had been curled beneath her while they watched the slides; now she unlimbered and rose, saying, "Dinner's in five minutes. Later on, if we feel like it, we can look at the rest."

Greg said, "Maybe that's enough for tonight. One of the best things about being back, we've left all those hassles behind."

Fay said to Carrie, "Can I help?"

"Oh, no, just relax."

But of course Fay didn't. Leaving Greg and Reed to talk about government restrictions, she followed Carrie to the kitchen, where small red lights on various machines gave assurance that the meal was coming along. Carrie said, peering through the oven window, "Lord, this is *one* thing I'm glad to get back to. Modern appliances."

"Didn't the company housing have all that?"

"Microwave? Are you kidding?" Lifting a pot lid, releasing a pillow of vegetable-scented steam, Carrie said, "All you get there is the *basics*. A *tiny* Italian refrigerator, barely enough ice cubes for two people—Do you know, if you had friends over for dinner, they'd bring their own ice cube trays? Honestly."

"Other company people, you mean."

"Who else was there? Fay, I can't tell you how much we missed you and Reed."

"We're glad you're back," Fay said. And it was true. The uneasiness and discontent were all on Fay's side, and pointless. Carrie *was* her best friend, since college, since they'd been dating the boys who were now their husbands. "*Very* happy you're back," Fay said, and impulsively kissed Carrie's smooth, round cheek.

There really was nothing for Fay to do in the kitchen, and very little even for Carrie. The machines had everything under control. Having time, Fay went through the bedroom into the bath to refresh her makeup and wash her hands. Returning, she passed what had been Greg's den and was now the nursery, and movement caught her eye. Vickie was awake.

The baby had been asleep earlier, when they'd all come in to look at her. Now Fay stepped into the nursery, half-lit by a small table lamp, and leaned over the crib to smile down at Carrie's child.

Vickie was fair, like her mother, with wide-set eyes and pug nose. Her eyes were closed, but her pudgy hands and feet were moving, in that aimless way of infants learning their bodies. Light gleamed on her soft stretching throat.

Perhaps sensing Fay's presence, the baby abruptly opened her eyes and gazed upward with intense concentration. Beautiful green eyes, darker than jade. Then the wide mouth opened and the baby gave a gassy smile, complete with bubbles.

It's a trick of the light, Fay thought, but it wasn't. Holding tight to the side of the crib, she watched Vickie laugh. *We think we're safe*, she thought. *We move the danger far away where it can only hurt people we don't care about, and we stay here safe. But it's coming, anyway.*

In the doorway, Carrie said, "Fay? Dinner."

I can't let her guess I know, Fay thought, but when she turned the truth must have been plain in her eyes because Carrie, smiling with some irritation, said, "Oh, you noticed."

"Carrie."

"It's nothing, it's nothing." Taking Fay's arm, walking her out to the master bedroom, Carrie said, "There's a company doctor knows all about it, there's a little operation when Vickie's just a bit older, there won't be a *trace*."

"A *company* doctor? This has happened before?"

"And they're all just as healthy and happy as can be," Carrie said, smiling her contented smile. "Come along to dinner." She leaned close, the smile turning confidential. "But don't mention it to anyone, all right? I mean, it's going to be fixed."

"Oh, no, I wouldn't."

113

And she wouldn't. Following Carrie to the dining room, Fay knew she would never mention it to a soul. But she would remember. Clear in her mind's eye it would remain, the vision of Vickie, the wide-set deep green eyes, the little pug nose, the forked tongue.

Anarchaos

I

"Those who see by the light of Hell are blind to evil." Rohstock said that, in his *Voyages To Seven Planets*. As I rode the shuttle to Anarchaos his words circled and circled through my thoughts, the answer to a question I preferred not to ask.

The shuttle was nearly empty: myself, two other passengers, the steward. Up front were the two pilots, of course, but I never saw them, and so they don't count.

There is nothing more tedious than a shuttle flight between unimportant planets, even for someone like me, his first time away from home. On a shuttle there is nothing to do, nothing to see; one merely sits in an enclosed tube and is hurtled through hyperspace from here to here, without even the sensation of motion. The only difference between an elevator and such a shuttle is the distance covered. And, of course, the time spent in the voyage.

This one, from Cockaigne to Anarchaos, took four hours. It

was the last leg of my journey, and in objective time the shortest, but subjectively it was the longest of all.

I had left Earth five days before on a liner to Valhalla, a three-day trip filled with comfort and luxurious distraction. The customs inspection at Valhalla had taken me by surprise—after all, I was merely passing through their domain—and I had no chance adequately to hide my weapons. They were confiscated, and I was held overnight for questioning. My claim that I was simply a nervous tourist who had brought the weapons along for self-defense was, I suppose, absurd on the face of it; Anarchaos, my destination, was unlikely to attract even self-confident tourists, and the arsenal I'd been carrying was surely excessive for purposes of self-defense. Still, it was the only explanation I would give, and in any case I wasn't planning to visit Valhalla at all, so the next morning I was—without apologies—released. The weapons were not returned; I would have to get new ones on Anarchaos.

The trip from Valhalla to Cockaigne took seventeen hours. I was saved from boredom by a pleasant conversation with a fellow passenger in the first half of the trip, and by a long and dreamless sleep in the second half.

But now, on this final stage, boredom had me strongly in its grip. I occupied my mind with study of the steward and the other passengers as long as I could, but they were a dull trio, offering little to excite interest or speculation. The steward was male, fairly young, of medium height and weight, blank of face, given to that invisibility or lack of personality common among those in the service occupations. The two passengers, both male, were almost equally invisible; the young, pale, nervously smiling one in the clerical collar was obviously a missionary on his way to his first post, and the older one, with his briefcase and his threadbare dignity, was surely a governmental or industrial functionary of a minor sort, traveling on his employer's business.

There was only one brief conversation the whole trip, and that between the steward and the missionary. The latter, asking how

116

much longer till we reached Anarchaos, stumbled over the name, smiled apologetically, and said, "It's a hard word to say."

"There's a way to make it easy," the steward told him. "Start to say *anarchy*, and midway through switch and say *chaos*."

The missionary tried it: "Anarchaos." The apologetic smile flared again, and he thanked the steward, saying, "It certainly is a name to give one pause."

"I suppose they meant it that way," said the steward.

"And their sun," said the missionary. "Do they really call it Hell?"

"It *is* Hell," said the steward.

II

The hatch was opened, and we three passengers stepped out onto the mesh-sided elevator which would lower us to the ground. Beside me, the missionary blinked and whispered, "Oh, dear! Oh, dear me!"

He was right to be awed. It would take the most intrepid of missionaries not to be awed by his first sight of Anarchaos.

Above us, Hell stood at its perpetual zenith, a swollen red sun, huge and ancient, in the flushed fury of its long decline. Its light was red, rust-red, tingeing everything it touched: the shuttle ship we'd just departed, this elevator and its mesh housing, the flat and nearly empty expanse of the landing pad, the customs and administration shacks across the way, and the distant towers of the city of Ni. So long as Hell stood in the sky, there would be no color here but the shades of red.

The elevator descended, and we were met at the bottom by a slender young man in the uniform of the Union Commission; Anarchaos having no government of its own, the UC maintained a staff at the landing pad here for the assistance and advice of visitors.

"Come this way, please," he said, without that facile smile of impersonal good fellowship for which the UC is famous; Anarchaos, I suppose, made even official smiles impossible to retain.

We followed him toward the shacks. Behind us, our luggage was being unloaded by other UC men and piled onto a mechanized cart, which buzzed by us before we reached the edge of the pad.

How dreary this world was; walking along with the others I felt weighted down, morose, lethargic. Only with the greatest difficulty could I keep my sense of urgency and feeling of purpose. Already, it seemed, Anarchaos was draining me, sapping my strength.

Our guide led us to a small wooden building, marked on its door ORIENTATION, and motioned us inside, where we found several rows of seats facing a raised platform at the far end.

"Sit anywhere, gentlemen," he said, and walked down the room and onto the platform. Facing us there he said, "My task, gentlemen, is to acquaint you with some few of the facts of Anarchaos." And he proceeded to tell us several things which I for one already knew.

That Anarchaos was the only planet circling its sun. That it always showed the same face to its sun, as Earth's moon shows ever the same face to Earth, so that here there was no night or day in the Earthly sense that I was used to; the city of Ni, for instance, lived in perpetual noon, Hell motionless and unchanging directly overhead. That the planet's orbit was almost precisely circular, so that there were no seasons here. That humans had colonized it eighty-seven years ago and were to be found only along a narrow band north and south along the sunward face, with Moro-Geth the city farthest to the west and Ulik farthest to the east; at Moro-Geth, Hell stood forever in the attitude of mid-morning, while at Ulik the day was frozen at mid-afternoon. That the night side of the planet was dead and cold and no place for men. That the planet had a deep atmosphere, which constantly drained Hell's heat to east and west, dissipating most of it on the frigid night side, leaving the day side temperatures well within man's capacity; at Ni it was Fahrenheit eighty-five degrees and at Moro-Geth and Ulik approximately sixty degrees.

118

And more, about the humans here; their "society," if that's the word for it.

That they had no native government but were maintained entirely by the Union Commission. That they were total anarchists, and yet managed to maintain cities. That they were idealists of nihilism, and yet pragmatic and practical. That individuals should be approached with utmost caution, as nearly anything was liable to give offense. That as there were no laws there was statistically no crime, which merely meant that cheating, stealing, killing and so on were not considered crimes here, or even socially unacceptable.

"Finally," he said, "I wish to tell you gentlemen that the sun and planet here have been misnamed. It's the planet that should be called Hell, because its citizens are devils. You're safe from them here, on Commission territory, but once you go outside the gate you are totally on your own. Each major city has a Commission embassy where it is theoretically possible for off-worlders to take refuge in case of trouble, but I wouldn't depend upon it. According to the most recent report on the subject I've seen, seventy-two per cent of off-world visitors here in the last ten years disappeared without trace and are presumed to have been murdered. My urgent advice to all three of you is to get right back on that shuttle and return at once to Cockaigne. As I remember it, Cockaigne is a beautiful place, very friendly and completely safe. The tall blond girls of that world are noted throughout the Union. Will you go?"

He looked at each of us in turn. The missionary blinked and gulped, but stood his ground. The functionary gave him the defiant glare of the petty authoritarian. I, when it came my turn, merely met his gaze and shook my head.

He shrugged. "Very well. It's my job to warn you, and you've been warned. Just remember; statistically, less than one visitor in three survives. It's possible one of you will live to get off this planet again, but extremely unlikely that more than one will."

There was a table behind him on the platform. He went to it now, picked up a needle mike, and said, "I'll ask each of you to give his name, home world, purpose in coming here, expected duration of stay, and name and address of whoever you want notified in the event of your death or disappearance. This is for the record, so please speak distinctly."

He extended the mike toward the missionary, who said, in a high and somewhat shaky voice, "My name is Brother Roderus, Capeline Order, and my home world is Vicon. I am here as a missionary, to bring converts to the true faith and to establish a Capeline monastery here. I am expected to stay for three years. In the event of . . . of anything happening to me, notification should go to the Abbot, Capeline Monastery, New Augustus, Wainwright, Vicon."

The functionary was next: "William zi Mandell, of Cockaigne, employed by Roth Brothers Data Corporation. One of our ZT series computers was leased by a certain Allied Furriers of Ulik, who are now over a year deficit in their rental payments. I have been assigned to go to Ulik and either collect the rental due or reclaim the machine. I expect to be here a week, perhaps two. Earth Standards Terms. In the unlikely event of my death or disappearance, my home office should be contacted: Roth Brothers Data Corporation, Scottsville, Sedalia, Cockaigne."

Then the needle was pointed at me. I said, "Rolf Malone, of Earth. I'm here as a tourist, for an indefinite period, probably no longer than six months. There's no one to notify in case anything happens to me."

He continued to point the needle at me a few seconds longer, as though unwilling to believe I was finished, then shook his head, put the mike back on the table, and said, "Now I'll try to talk specific sense to you. Brother Roderus, missionaries aren't wanted on Anarchaos, please believe me. You'll gain no converts. By your manner, I suppose it's unlikely you'll give offense to any of the locals, so you're safe in that respect, but you aren't safe from bullying, and on Anarchaos bullying frequently ends in bloodshed. Unless you're determined on martyrdom, I strongly advise you to go back to Vicon."

The missionary looked frightened but game; that is to say, foolish. "I'll stay," he said. "I've been sent. I'll stay."

The UC man shrugged fatalistically and turned to the computer renter saying, "Mr. Mandell, I assume this is the first time your company has had dealings with anyone on this planet."

Mandell nodded curtly. "It is."

"You can't rent or lease property here, Mr. Mandell; you can only sell it. Allied Furriers has stolen your computer. If you go to them and demand your fees, they'll laugh in your face. If you try to repossess the machine, they'll kill you. This isn't a possibility I'm telling you, this is a certainty."

Mandell didn't think so. "Kill me?" he asked. "You're being melodramatic."

"Mr. Mandell, please. We can put you up temporarily. Send a message to your home office; ask them to contact the Commission and get the legal and economic situation here. Once your company understands the peculiar problem of Anarchaos, I'm sure they'll recall you."

"Nonsense." Mandell's spine was getting straighter and straighter, his voice stiffer and stiffer, his expression more and more severe. "I'm a businessman," he said, "and I'm here to discuss a business transaction."

"I can't stop you from leaving here," the UC man told him, "any more than I can protect you if you do."

"I'll need no protection. Is that all?"

The UC man spread his hands. "Yes, that's all. You and Brother Roderus can go to the customs shack across the way and pick up your luggage now. Mr. Malone, I'd like you to stay a moment longer, if you would."

The other two looked at me curiously as they left. Once the door was closed behind them I said, "You can't stop me either, you know."

"I know that. Mr. Malone, there are no tourists on Anarchaos."

"There's me. I'm a tourist."

"No. Customs at Valhalla reported you carrying a surprising

121

assortment of weapons, for which you had no believable explanation."

He waited for me to say something, but I had nothing to say. I sat there, and looked at him, and waited.

He grimaced, and half turned away, and then turned back to glare at me again; I was beginning to anger him. People get angry at what they don't understand; they always have.

"You can't beat these people, Malone. You're on their ground, playing by their rules."

"No rules," I said. "There aren't any rules here."

"You've been here before?"

"No. This is my first time off Earth."

"You won't tell me what it is? Unofficially. I give you my word not to use whatever you tell me."

"I have nothing to tell you. I'm a tourist."

He made a quick gesture: anger, bafflement, defeat. "Go on, then," he said. "Kill yourself."

"See you later," I said, as I started for the door.

"No you won't," he said after me. "You'll never make it back."

III

Mandell had been somewhat impressed by the UC man's warnings after all; he approached me in the customs shack to ask if I intended to go to Ulik. "If so, we could travel together. There's safety in numbers."

That's what all sheep believe. I *was* going to Ulik, as a matter of fact, but I told him I wasn't: "Moro-Geth is the city I want to see," I said. "I believe that's in the opposite direction."

"That fellow was right about you," he said. "You're no tourist."

There was no point arguing with him. I went on to see about my baggage.

My luggage consisted of three pieces: two large suitcases and a knapsack. The suitcases were actually unnecessary, merely full of extra clothing and whatnot, amid which I had hoped to hide my arsenal. Now that I was weaponless, there was no point carrying all that gear with me. I arranged with the UC customs men to store my suitcases with them, packed the few essentials into my knapsack, and went on to currency exchange.

Anarchaos, having no government, has no monetary system of its own, and therefore uses the same Union Commission paper money used in all new colonies until they're sufficiently established to set up their own monetary system. The basic unit of this UC money is the credit, with the credit value dependent upon local standard of living. That is, the assumption is that one hundred credits would be an average weekly income, so the value of the credit is higher or lower depending upon the cost of living, which is itself determined to a large extent by the cost of imported goods. On different planets, therefore, the credit will be worth different amounts. The Anarchaos credit turned out to be about the equivalent of two crowns on Earth. (A second monetary unit in this system is the token. Ten tokens equal one credit.)

I exchanged a part of my money—seven hundred credits worth—and left the rest with the UC representatives for safe-keeping. I took my time, wanting to be sure that Mandell was already gone before I went outside, and when I did go through the gate to the street neither he nor the missionary was anywhere in sight.

The ramshackle suburbs of Ni began here, stretching away toward the tall towers of the city itself in the distance. Those arches and spires, glinting ruby and saffron in the dull red glare of the sun, had a kind of feverish beauty to them, but the shacks and lean-tos in the foreground were merely scrubby, a junkyard in which people lived.

Awaiting me were two commercial groups eager to offer me their services: chauffeurs and prostitutes. They clamored and waved their arms, all of them, out-shouting and out-gesticulating one another and yet very carefully not bumping into one another, not standing in front of one another, not causing any direct offense to one another.

The prostitutes I had no use for, but the chauffeurs were potentially of interest. Each stood in front of his vehicle, showing it off, shouting its fine points at me, and I studied these vehicles and their drivers with a great deal of care.

There was just about every means of land locomotion imaginable there, most of them pulled by hairhorses, native Anarchaotic beasts whose shaggy hair and rough similarity to Earth's horses gave them their name. These I was not interested in; it was motorized transport I desired.

Motors were fewer in number, but varied in style. One contraption of wood, with large wooden wheels and no top, seemed to have been homemade, with an electric engine from some other kind of machine mounted on a platform at the rear. Another was a small truck, the sides and top of the body cut away and a fat lumpy sofa mounted sideways in the back for passengers. There were a few fairly ordinary automobiles, some with liquid fuel engines and others with electric engines, all imports from off-planet. There was some limited manufacture here, but not of anything as large and expensive as motorized transport. Those inter-system corporations which found it to their advantage to maintain offices here—and whose towers I could see in the center of Ni—brought any such large equipment here from off-planet, unassembled. These automobiles lined up with all the other conveyances were for the most part obsolete equipment sold by one or another corporation; or, perhaps, were simply stolen property.

In any case, they were what I was most interested in. I studied them, studied their clamoring drivers, and finally chose a small but rather clean auto with two sets of seats, one behind the other. The driver was short, narrow-faced, middle-aged, with nervous energetic movements and darting suspicious eyes; he looked right for my purposes.

I went to him and said, "You'll take me to Ulik?"

The shout went up all around me: "Here's another for Ulik! Ulik, Ulik! I live in Ulik, I'll take you to Ulik!"

124

My driver squinted at me. "Ulik? Of course. Climb aboard, climb aboard." He swept the door open.

"How much?" I said.

"The normal rate. Get in, get in."

"What's the normal rate?"

"We'll talk about it when we get there." And he kept motioning me anxiously to get in. He didn't quite dare pluck me by the sleeve.

The calls around us were dying down. Everyone wanted to see how the haggling would go, what I would like and what I would mistrust; they wanted to be ready to better this first man's offer if I should reject him.

I said, "We'll talk about it now. How much to Ulik?"

He studied me. He put the little finger of his right hand in the corner of his mouth, squinted up his face, squeezed his right eye shut, and with the left eye surveyed me for some clue to what the market would bear.

Another driver shouted, "Hurry it up! Make up your mind before sundown!" Everyone laughed at that, the whores across the street cackling the loudest of all, and I understood this to be a common and well-known joke; only natural, I suppose, on a world where the sun never moves from its place in the sky.

When the laughter died down, my little driver took his finger from his mouth and said, "Five credits an hour. You couldn't get a better price."

I shook my head. "No. You'll—"

"All right," he said. "Four credits fifty." He appealed to the others, saying, "Is that fair?"

They hooted him with what might have been good nature, and when they were done I said, "Give me a flat rate. Not by the hour."

"A flat rate? Nobody *ever* does that."

"No?" I turned as though to ask if anyone else would give me a flat rate.

Before I—or anyone—could say a word, my driver shouted, "Wait! Wait! A flat rate!"

"Name it."

"Mmm, two hundred credits."

"Forty," I said.

He turned his back on me.

The whole transaction took about another five minutes, and when we were done he had agreed to drive me to Ulik for ninety-eight credits and five tokens. I got into the back seat, he stationed himself behind the wheel, and we moved off. Behind us the crowd, knowing there'd be no more new-comers this time, separated and drifted aimlessly away.

We drove east across hard-packed dirt streets, through what seemed an endless succession of blocks of squalid huts, shacks, lean-tos and tents. Children flung rocks and other things at us as we passed, and the driver cursed them and shook his fist out his glassless side window. There was no glass in any of the windows, in fact, and a hot breeze blew in on us through the gaping windshield. The driver muttered and mumbled to himself and, hunched over his wheel, drove competently and with good speed down the endless dirt street.

Several blocks from the spaceport we passed a cluster of people, and I saw Brother Roderus standing in their midst. They'd ripped his clothing off him and he was now naked, his pale skin a wretched rose in the light of the sun, the tatters of his clothing around his feet. His suitcase had been ripped apart and its contents scattered over the ground. The crowd seemed to be in high spirits, and hadn't actually begun to kill him yet. His expression was very earnest, and I saw his lips move; I assume he was making a speech.

"That's a bad thing," my driver said, with natural hypocrisy. "No one ought to treat foreigners like that. But don't *you* worry. So long as you're with me, I'll see to it you're left alone. If you want a guide after we get to Ulik, someone to watch out for you, clear the way for you . . ."

"We'll see," I said. "What sort of engine do you have? Electric?"

"The finest. Molecular power source. Never run down, never." He was parroting something he himself knew nothing about.

126

A short while later we left Ni and got onto the narrow paved road to Ulik; the Union Commission had built this road, paying for it by assessing those off-world corporations with interests on Anarchaos.

For the first hour we crossed a vast grassy plain. Here and there, at great distances from the highway, I caught sight of the high walls of farms, but for the most part the plain was deserted, looking just as it had before man had first come here.

In this early part of the trip my driver attempted from time to time to pump me as to my purposes here, but I ignored him and after a while he gave it up. Then we drove in restful silence.

Adaptation comes quickly. Already I was taking the redness of everything for granted, and my body was feeling less irritated by the subtle increase in gravity. Still, I had to be careful, and not overestimate my adaptibility; I was still not as able in this environment as someone who had lived here all his life.

After the plain we came to hills, low but jagged, rocky and lifeless, one after the other for mile upon mile, the road curving back and forth among them, only rarely climbing to cross some stone-backed ridge. On one of these curves we met a hairhorse-drawn wagon coming the other way, and barely avoided an accident, which set the driver into another paroxysm of cursing. When it was done I asked him, "Is that the wagon the other traveler took?"

"Who? The one ahead of you? Not him. *He* took a car, the biggest one there."

"Car?"

"Like this," he said, motioning to indicate his own automobile.

"Oh," I said. "This is what you call a car. We call them autos, or automobiles."

He shrugged. Language meant nothing to him. Then he said, "You think something might happen to him? The man who took him maybe rob him, kill him, be coming back?"

"Something like that."

My driver shook his head. "Not him," he said. "Not that one.

127

He'll get where he's going, that one." Then, as an afterthought: "So will you. I can tell that sort of thing."

A while later we encountered our second vehicle since leaving Ni, another hairhorse and wagon, this one going the same direction as we. We overtook it amid the hills and curves and my driver passed it without hesitation, though he couldn't see ten feet ahead.

That second wagon was full of standing men, naked to the waist, in chains. They looked after us sullenly, and the wagon driver cracked his whip at us as we went by.

"Slaves," said my driver, and shuddered theatrically. "That's a bad business."

A while later we emerged from the hills to another plain, flat and grassy and featureless as the first. The road went straight, as far as the eye could see, and there was no traffic but ourselves.

I slipped off my belt, formed a loop by putting the other end through the buckle, slipped the loop over my driver's head from behind, pulled it tight, used the seat between us for leverage, and strangled him where he sat. The auto slowed, and continued straight down the road, until his flailing arms struck the steering wheel and we went jouncing off at an angle onto the grass and rolled to a stop.

I retrieved my belt and pushed the body out onto the ground. I searched the body and the auto and found what I'd hoped to find: I'd chosen this driver because he was small, physically unawesome, and therefore likelier to keep some sort of weaponry on his person. I needed new weapons.

I got them. From the body, a clasp knife and a good throwing knife, the latter in a neck sheath so the knife lies between the shoulder blades. From the auto, a pistol and extra supply of ammunition, a filled length of iron pipe, and a spray can of blinding gas.

On the body I also found over two hundred credits and several pornographic photos. I left the photos, took the money, got into the auto—*car* they call it here, I reminded myself— and drove on toward Ulik.

IV

On Earth, in the nineteenth century O.T., an obscure Russian nihilist named Mikhail Bakunin wrote in French a book called *Dieu et l'Etat*, in which he said such things as:

"Our first work must be the annihilation of everything as it now exists. The old world must be destroyed and replaced by a new one. When you have freed your mind from the fear of God, and that childish respect for the fiction of right, then all the remaining chains that bind you—property, marriage, morality, and justice—will snap asunder like threads."

Bakunin slept several centuries in well-earned oblivion, until resurrected by the founders of Anarchaos, who used his writings as the core of their social philosophy. If such a place as Anarchaos could be said to have a patron saint, Bakunin is it.

This re-emergence of the ancient nay-sayer was the direct, though unexpected, result of Union Commission law, in particular that law relating to the political structure of colonies. According to UC regulations, colonies receiving UC assistance—without which colonization is impossible—have total freedom for self-determination of their own style of government, within the limitations of precedence. That is, colonies are not permitted to invent whole new systems of government out of whole cloth, but are limited to those governments which have existed in the past, of any era, either in fact or in an extensive body of philosophical and socio-political literature. The framers of this regulation hoped thereby to save future colonies from half-digested or harebrained new political theories like those which, in the first wave of stellar colonization, caused such pain and bloodshed. Governmental theories which had never been tested in fact but which did boast a broad body of literature were

129

considered safe because it is a basic tenet of Union Commission faith that sooner or later discussion inevitably leads to reason.

The Commission had apparently never heard of anarchism. But the founders of Anarchaos had, and Bakunin was their chief prophet, assisted by such other anarchist, nihilist or syndicalist writers as William Godwin, Pierre Joseph Proudhon, Benjamin Tucker, Josiah Warren, Max Stirner, Prince Pyotr Kropotkin, Georges Sorel and Sergius Nachaev. The literature of anarchism is extensive and, in its way, distinguished, frequently—as in Turgenev and Tolstoy—calling upon the noblest elements of human nature as the bedrock of society, a call which is itself noble but not entirely realistic.

The UC disapproved, but was powerless to prevent the colony from going its own way. The Union Commission actually has few real teeth, and even those are kept carefully blunted by the member planets, each jealous of its own sovereignty. The Commission is the final—and only—authority in space, and has limited authority and responsibility in colonies. This latter authority the Commission itself has tried to expand from time to time but always without success. The greatest fear of every planetary government, it seems, is that some day the UC will succeed in usurping domestic planetary powers.

Which means there is nothing the UC can do about Anarchaos. The planet remains permanently on colony status, using UC money, with UC embassies in each city, with UC men staffing the spaceport. Only when a colony is ready for self-government does the UC depart, and Anarchaos, having no government and having no desire to form a government, will naturally never be ready.

The UC probably would do something about Anarchaos, even though it would be stretching legality, if there were no other factors to consider, but there is another factor; the businessmen, the corporations, the off-worlders who have money and prestige and political power and who profit hugely from Anarchaos as it now stands.

An adjunct of anarchist theory is syndicalism. Instead of

governments, men are to form voluntarily into syndicates which will run the factories and the farms, the schools and the transport systems, and goods and services will move by a barter system between the syndicates. The theory is naive now and must have always been naive, though a number of polysyllabic thinkers gave it weighty discussion in weighty tomes. Whatever its flaws, it was a part of the founding structure of Anarchaos, and for the first few years it apparently worked with some degree of success.

The first generation on Anarchaos, in fact, didn't do too badly at all, but of course they had been trained on other worlds and understood discipline and group effort, those two hallmarks of government. But the second generation, growing up with no influence but anarchism, followed their natural bent, atomized the society into its individual fragments, and the theoretical structure of Anarchaos collapsed in red dust.

At that point the off-worlders moved in. The syndicates founded by the first colonists were quietly and unofficially taken over by foreign corporations and soon the economic—if not the political—structure of Anarchaos was in the hands of profit-seekers who directed operations from grand offices light years away. Behind the facade of the syndicate towers in Ni, in Moro-Geth, in Ulik and the other cities, sat the corporations, fat and getting fatter.

For Anarchaos is a rich world, a storehouse of valuable minerals and a significant exporter of furs. Trapping and mining are the two primary occupations, the former done by rugged individualists out in the wilds, the latter done by slaves captured by roaming press gangs and sold to the mining syndicates.

Human occupancy of Anarchaos was in its eighty-seventh year when I arrived, making it the longest-running planet-wide madhouse in the history of the human race.

V

The sun inched minutely backwards across the sky as I drove eastward toward Ulik, so that I seemed gradually to be outdistancing it, until, when I first saw the city ahead of me, that red ball was in a position behind me that in my friendlier sun at home would indicate, in summer, approximately two o'clock in the afternoon. On Earth, of course, a distance of a thousand miles or more would separate sites two hours apart by the sun, but Anarchaos was in a much closer orbit to its Hell, so that Ni and Ulik were barely four hundred miles apart.

The last fifty miles or so had been across a high barren plateau, rocky and uninviting. Two men mounted on hairhorses had tried to stop me at one point, blocking my path, but I accelerated toward them, and fired a shot from my new pistol, and they whirled away in front of me, cursing and shaking their fists. They were bearded, and dressed in furs, and had heavy-looking swords at their waists. They were the last humans I saw before coming to Ulik.

Ulik was built in the center of a great flat brown valley, the dry bed of a onetime inland sea. The plateau ended here, the road sweeping down the bare eastern slope to the bottom, and then—a thin black line—arrowing straight across the dry sea-bed to the city.

Ulik, first seen from far away and high atop the eastern edge of the plateau, had a kind of frail grandeur to it, the only sign of man in all this emptiness. The syndicate towers were fewer here than at Ni, but just as tall and just as graceful and just as slender, reflecting blood-red glints of sunlight. Because Hell lay off the zenith there were shadows of the tallest rock formations, long pointing black fingers stretching toward the city across the valley floor. I drove quickly down the long decline.

It had been getting cold atop the plateau, but now as I moved down into the valley the air grew somewhat warmer again. I remembered that the UC man at the spaceport had said the temperature at Ulik was approximately sixty degrees.

Ulik was a fur center, where the trappers brought their pelts for sale, where they were cured and treated and prepared for transport off-world. This paved Union Commission road ended at the city itself, but on the other side broad dirt tracks moved off toward the evening line, showing the routes of the trappers and tradesmen, slavers and solitaries.

The junkyard hovels were all on that side, too, so that the western approach to the city, where I was coming in, was all beauty and shine, as modern as any city anywhere, all towers and spires and graceful arches, sweeping high walkways and gossamer webs of communications lines.

Now for the first time I was seeing the syndicate towers up close. At ground level they were surprisingly heavy and thick in appearance, all steel and concrete, massive and windowless, darkened by their own shadows. Armed guards patrolled in groups at their iron doorways, glowering at me in suspicion as I drove by, and here and there down the side streets raggedly dressed men and women slithered along the concrete walls on minor, urgent, and incomprehensible missions.

Although the off-world corporations owned these syndicates and their towers body and soul, nowhere did a corporate name or logo appear. Instead, above the heavy iron main doors of each structure was mounted the symbol of each syndicate: an inverted triangle containing the letter S, an X of crossed lightning bolts, a sledge hammer with a dog's head, a raised black grillwork on which was laid a silver stylization of a bird in flight.

Finally I saw the one I wanted: a cornucopia dripping ice. Originally a syndicate of those who made or repaired refrigeration machines—freezers, air conditioners, home refrigerators—it had been taken over long ago by the Wolmak Corporation, a chemical company with some connections to the local mining industry. In the first decade or so of the colony's existence, refrigeration units had actually been manufactured in this tower, and bartered with other syndicates, and later serviced and repaired by members of this syndicate, but all that was in the long dead past. The factory had long since been stripped bare, the original membership of the syndicate had died out, and the membership now was small, badly trained for repair work, and totally subservient to the Wolmak Corporation.

Each syndicate, in the beginning, had given itself a one

word—usually one syllable—name which implied the syndicate's purpose, and this one had called itself *Ice*. The old syndicate names were still used, although today when anyone on Anarchaos spoke of Ice he actually meant Wolmak. The names of the owner corporations were never seen and rarely heard.

I stopped my car in front of the Ice tower, saw to it that I had all my weapons on me, and stepped out onto the ground. The hunting knife was in its sheath against my back, the other knife in my left side pocket, the pistol in my right hip pocket, the gas spray can in my left hip pocket, and the piece of pipe tucked into my belt. I left my knapsack on the car seat.

There were half a dozen guards in front of the Ice tower door, dressed in silver uniforms with pale blue edgings. (Although everything was tinged with red by the light of Hell, the color red was never used by humans here. Blues and greens and yellows were in use everywhere, all mottled by the red light, but the shades of red itself were completely avoided.) These guards had watched me with as much suspicion as anyone else while I was driving toward them, but now that I had stopped and gotten out of the car their suspicion was doubled, tripled. They held automatic rifles in clenched fists and glowered at me in furious silence.

I didn't move toward them, suspecting their great tension might lead them to kill me without finding out who or what I was. I merely stood beside the car, showed them my hands to demonstrate that they were empty, and called, "Tell Whistler that Rolf Malone is here."

They looked at one another, consulting together with glances and expressions. Finally, one backed to the building, opened a small plate beside the door, and spoke into a phone. The rest of us waited, in our respective places.

Several minutes went by. The guard at the phone spoke, and waited, and then spoke again, and waited again. Finally he called to me, "You related to Gar Malone?"

"His brother."

The guard relayed this information, and listened, and nodded, and put the phone away. "Colonel Whistler will see you," he called. "Come forward."

I came forward. When I reached them I said, "You'll watch my car for me."

"Yes, of course. Leave weapons out here."

I gave him everything but the sheath knife. However, I was then frisked and the knife found. "This, too," said the guard, with neither humor nor indignation, and I took it off and gave it to him.

When they were sure I was weaponless, one of them rapped on the iron door. As we stood there, he said, "Who is Gar Malone?"

"My brother," I said.

He didn't like that answer, but before he could decide what to do about it the door slid open and I stepped inside.

VI

When I was getting out of prison, in with the other paperwork I put a request for a stellar passport. My counselor mentioned it in our last session, saying, "You plan to start life again on a new world, Rolf, is that it?"

"Something like that," I said.

"Why is that, Rolf?" He used my name a lot, to establish a personal relationship between us. I never used his name at all.

"My record here is pretty bad," I said. "I know that's not supposed to mean anything—an ex-convict is supposed to have the same rights as anybody else—but we both know it doesn't work that way."

"It does for some men, Rolf. Men who are willing to wait it out."

"A record doesn't travel with you to a new world," I said. "That's one good rule the UC's got."

He snapped at everything, like a piranha fish, saying now, "You have a grievance against the Union Commission, Rolf?"

"Not a bit," I said. "I've never been off Earth, never had

135

dealings with the Commission. But I know about that rule, and I think it's a good one."

"Do you know anyone out there, Rolf? Any friends or relations?"

"My brother's got a job on a place called Anarchaos."

"I don't believe I know the name."

"It's small, and way out. New, too."

"Rolf, you could do better on Earth."

"I could do worse, too. Waiting it out isn't a style that's natural with me."

"You mean your temper, Rolf? There hasn't been an outbreak from you in over three years. That's cured, Rolf, I'm convinced of it."

"It's not cured, it's controlled. And it's what got me in here, took seven years off my life. I don't want to push that control too far."

"You may be right at that, Rolf," he said. "I'll recommend approval."

"Thank you," I said. Because it was necessary.

He was right about my temper, but on the other hand he was dead wrong. There had been no outward demonstration of it in over three years, as he'd said, but it had existed, inside me, compressed, chained, stifled, almost every waking minute of all that time. A prison is full of petty irritations, and it is my nature to irritate easily.

But I had to learn to hold it in if I ever wanted to get out of that place, and what a man has to do he can do. And now, after seven years—I'd been given an indeterminate sentence for manslaughter, after I killed five people in an argument over a noisy party—the temper was in tight iron shackles and I at last was free.

I would never lose my temper again, this I knew. By now I was a little afraid of it myself; if once let out after being pent up so long, what would it be likely to do? No. It was the quiet way for me, from now on.

With Gar. My brother Gar, three years my senior, as near

136

enough like me to be my twin in all respects but one, and that one made all the difference. Gar had no temper at all. Nothing could enrage him, nothing aggravate him past endurance. Relatives—I've alienated myself from all of them by now, of course, parents included—used to say I had Gar's temper as well as my own. That was when we were both children, and my destructive frenzies could do comparatively little damage. Later, as I grew older and stronger, such pleasantries were not among the things my relatives said of me. Gar was their darling, and I—to the extent that they dared ignore me—had ceased to exist.

I suppose it would have been normal for me to grow up hating and envying Gar, but quite the reverse was true. He was the one person I never grew angry with, the only one in the world—in any world—whose opinion mattered to me. And he was fond of me, too, with a curious blend of normal brotherly affection combined with a goodhearted man's indulgence of a rambunctious pet. He kept me out of trouble when he could, calmed me when he could, made things right after my flare-ups when he could.

I finished my schooling at the minimum legal age, of course; school for me had been an endless succession of rows with teachers and fellow students. I had a number of jobs, none of them good, none of them for long. Then, at twenty-three, I went into prison, and stayed there till seven days past my thirtieth birthday.

Gar went on with school, became a mining engineer with additional degrees in allied fields, and went to work for one of the great alloy firms. His even disposition and absorption in his work made him an ideal explorer in virgin territories, either alone or with small parties. He changed jobs infrequently, but each change was a step upward. When he went to work for Wolmak Corporation, my fourth year in prison, he was the highest paid field man they had, could have had an administrative job at executive level if he'd wanted it, and was only thirty years old.

He wrote me from time to time, and less frequently I wrote

137

back. In his next to last letter he told me of his transfer to Anarchaos, exciting prospects, brand new and unrealized potential, and said that if I were to be released as soon as I expected he was authorized to offer me a job as his field assistant. I accepted at once, and in his final letter he said the job was mine.

After so many false starts, now at last I had found my place. I would be with Gar, the one man in all the world whose company I could tolerate, the two of us moving endlessly across empty landscapes where no human had ever been before, away from society, away from humankind, out where only nature could rasp my naked nerve-endings, and against nature in perfect safety I could howl my rage away.

The day I got out of prison, the message came from the Union Commission: Gar had been killed. He was dead.

Killed? By what? By whom?

I went to the UC embassy, and there I first heard something of the unique nature of Anarchaos. "It was the colony that killed your brother," a UC man told me; a statement I was to hear often.

But I wanted more. I read tape after tape at the library, soon exhausting all that had been written about that filthy little planet, and then I read the sources of its social structure— Bakunin and the rest. And Rohstock, in his *Voyages to Seven Planets*:

"Life on Anarchaos is itself sufficient punishment for any crimes its citizens may perform; there is, therefore, no other."

I was not satisfied. No one could tell me anything, no one could do anything. The identity of Gar's killer, his motive, even his method; I couldn't get a single fact. But I had my passport, and my traveling expenses had already been paid, and there was nothing to keep me on Earth, so I armed myself with an arsenal which was taken from me at Valhalla, and I went to Anarchaos.

When they took my weapons away at Valhalla, I knew I would have to kill. I required weapons on Anarchaos, for purposes both of protection and persuasion, and I knew from my reading that the only way to get weapons on Anarchaos was to take them from someone else. The realization that I would be

138

forced to kill at least one Anarchaotian did not bother me in the slightest, possibly because of my previous experience at the task but more probably because of the oft-repeated theory that, "The colony killed your brother."

Not that I was prepared to admit the theory as fact. Whatever guilt others might share—the colony, the founders, the UC, the corporations—finally it must come down to the one, or two, or three, who had in fact committed the one specific murder of Gar Malone.

Ultimately, I myself wasn't sure what I planned to do. Learn, to begin with, and once I knew I could decide. Deep inside me the fury coiled like a snake, like a mainspring, but I kept it in control. Mindless rage would get me nothing. I had to be cold, mind rather than emotion; I had to be a machine gathering data.

When the data was gathered, it itself would tell me what to do. What to do with the man who had killed Gar. Or, if it turned out that those were right who said the colony was his killer, I would again know what to do—then, not now. For now I knew only that I had questions to ask.

And the first man of whom I would ask them was Colonel Holbed Whistler, the Wolmak Corporation's manager at Anarchaos, the man who had been Gar's final employer.

VII

"This way, Mr. Malone."

I had stepped from the elevator into a wide, shallow, featureless, low-ceilinged tan room in which blank closed brown doors were spaced at regular intervals in every wall. The voice—feminine—had come from my right, where I saw a tall and slender blond woman holding a door open and smiling an invitation to me to enter.

I had been frisked a second time by the inside guards before being put into the elevator, so I now spread my arms out and said, "Don't you want to search me for weapons?"

She laughed gently, a musical political sound, and said, "No, I don't think so. They're very thorough downstairs."

"So they are."

I walked toward her, and she stepped aside to let me precede her through the doorway into a pale green corridor which curved away to the right. There were no windows here, nor in the tan room before it, so that nothing—the room, the corridor, the blond woman—was tinged with that unhealthy red light. The indirect lighting here was colorless; I could have been back home on Earth.

The corridor was wide enough for us to walk abreast, so I waited for her to close the door and join me, noticing that she had a kind of beauty I hadn't expected to find on Anarchaos, a smooth bland impersonal beauty that bespoke plastic surgery, social position or at least pretension, a background on Earth or on one of the oldest of civilized planets.

Her clothing encouraged the impression. The saying is that even the most advanced worlds are a year to three behind Earth fashions, and the outer worlds and more recent colonies are as much as a generation behind Earth styles of apparel, but the dress this woman wore would have been perfectly in style on the Earth I'd left five days ago. It was tailored to her body, emphasizing, as it was meant to, her best features, blending with her face, her hair style, her jewelry in a way that could be achieved nowhere other than Earth.

She turned, saw the attention I was giving her, and smiled companionably. "You like me?"

"Very much. I hadn't expected anyone as beautiful as you."

She was pleased, and honest enough to show it, saying, "Ah, you're as gallant as your brother."

"You knew Gar?"

"I thought of him as one of my dearest friends." The plastic face expressed regret. "It was terrible, what happened."

"What did happen?"

She became brisk. "Oh, the Colonel is the one to talk to. Come along, he's waiting for you."

140

We started together along the corridor, which continued to curve to the right and which appeared to be spiraling upward. I wasn't entirely sure whether we were going up a slight slope or that was merely the four per cent additional gravity I was feeling. I asked, and she said, "Oh, yes, we're going up. The elevator can't go any higher; the tower's too narrow for the housing up here. It's only a little distance."

I said, "What's your job here?"

"My job?" She seemed amused, I suppose at the bluntness of the question. "I'm sorry, I should have introduced myself. Jenna Guild, the Colonel's personal secretary."

"Rolf Malone," I said.

"Yes, I know."

I said, "Did you know Gar while he was here? Or from before?"

"Here. This is where I met him. At the elevator, in fact, where I just met you."

"How long have you been here?"

"Four years. Why?"

"I'm surprised at that dress."

Surprise made her laugh with a sound like a tinkling of small bells, much more pleasant than the political music of that first laugh I'd heard from her. "There are ways," she told me. "Ways to do anything. If you're connected with someone like the Colonel."

The spiraling corridor ended at last in closed double doors, against which Jenna Guild rapped just once. After the slightest of pauses, the doors slid apart into recesses in the walls, and we stepped through into a great luxurious room, all stuffed and carpeted, with furs everywhere and soft divans, different areas of the room at different levels; the whole was dominated by an incredibly broad curving window stretching around a full third of the wall space, through which could be seen a breathtaking view of the city, and of Hell at two o'clock in the sky.

But Hell, no longer Hell, had become the sun! This was no red globe suspended in the sky; no red tinge muddied the distant landscape or bloodied the other towers around us; there was no red anywhere. Except that the sun was too large, it was Earth, totally Earth, and I stood awestruck, staring at it.

A thin reedy voice said, "Are you impressed? It's only a trick, a special glass to filter out the red. A trick to convince me I'm not really here in this filthy place."

I turned toward the weary voice and, coming toward me, a drink in his bony hand, a twisted smile on his narrow face, figured crimson robe wrapped around his thin body, was the man who had to be Colonel Holbed Whistler.

VIII

We sat on facing divans near the long window, talking. Jenna Guild had brought me a drink at Colonel Whistler's request, and now was seated, composed and beautiful, on a low hassock a little away from us, ready to be called upon again.

The Colonel directed the conversation into meaningless channels. He asked me about my trip, and then briefly discussed his experiences with space travel. When I grew restive, he asked me about Earth, putting specific questions about specific cities, most of which I had never seen, and detailing for me his feelings of homesickness. He had been on Anarchaos, he said, seven years and had never ceased to hate it.

This talk, under other circumstances, might have been pleasant, but now it merely agitated my impatience. Still, I thought it best to let the Colonel have his head, at least until I got to know him better. As yet I wasn't even sure whether to consider him an enemy or a friend.

His manner and appearance I found not encouraging. There was a bony frailty to this man, an apparent weakness, everywhere but in his eyes, which, while his mouth produced pleasant banalities, studied me in cold calculation. Those eyes belied the brittleness of his body and the cordiality of his words. I felt emanating from him a great aura of coldness, of watchfulness, of secrecy and of caution.

He must have sensed my impatience, for at last he ended his monotonous pleasantries, studied me in silence a moment, and then said, "Frankly, Mr. Malone, I am surprised to see you here. You were informed of your brother's death before you left Earth, were you not?"

"Yes, I was."

"Jenna tells me"—he smiled briefly at her, and she smiled in acknowledgment—"your brother had arranged for you to be taken on by the company."

"That's right."

He smiled, and made a slight shrugging gesture. "Such details," he said, "are handled by the Department involved. I was not aware of your having been employed, or even of your existence, until just now. Your arrival is something of a surprise." He glanced at Jenna Guild again, and back at me, saying, "I'm told it was assumed you wouldn't be coming, under the circumstances. If you'd sent us notification, we would have arranged to have you picked up at Ni. Travel here is somewhat dangerous for a man alone."

"I was careful," I said.

"Yes, of course. Caution is always best." He offered me a blank, meaningless smile, sipped at his drink, and said, "But the point is, you are here. Jenna tells me you would have acted as your brother's field assistant, and that you appear to have no formal specialized education, that you went no further than junior college."

"That's right."

"Then I fear we have a rather embarrassing problem, Mr. Malone," he said. "I have no job for you. With your brother—"

"I'm not here for a job," I said.

"Oh?"

"I'm here to find out about my brother."

"Your brother?" He looked again at Jenna Guild, as though expecting her to step forward with an explanation, then said to me, "Your brother's dead. Gar Malone is dead."

143

"That's what I want to find out about," I said. "How he died and why. And by whose hand."

"On Anarchaos? My dear man, such questions are irrelevancies here. There are no answers."

"Still I mean to look for them."

"Why? What possible good can it do? You can't bring your brother back to life."

"I don't mean to try."

"What, then?"

"I want to know."

"For its own sake?"

"For my sake. Once I know what happened to Gar I'll know what to do about me."

He sat back, frowning, perplexed, even his eyes showing uncertainty. "I hardly know what to make of you," he said. "Or what to do with you."

"You could help me, if you would."

"How?"

"Tell me what is already known about Gar's death. Where he died, how he was killed, any other circumstances that are known. And where I might find his grave."

"Someone in the Department might know that," he said, ruminating, and asked Jenna Guild, "Which Department would that be? Development?"

"Special Projects, I think," she said.

He turned back to me. "You can talk to someone there in the morning, if you like. After that, we'll have to decide what's to be done about you."

"In the morning? Why not now?"

He seemed surprised. "Don't you know what time it is?"

I looked out the window, but then realized the fact of daylight meant nothing here. Hell stood always at two o'clock in the sky over Ulik. But I, used to the regularity of Sol around the Earth, had been assuming that daylight meant daytime as well. I said, "No, I don't. I hadn't thought about it."

"It's well after midnight," he said. "You have no watch?"

144

"No. I . . . haven't needed one."

"Jenna, get Mr. Malone a watch." Turning back to me he said, "A watch is indispensable here. So far as Anarchaos is concerned time does not exist."

"I'm sorry I came so late," I said, and got to my feet, leaving my untouched drink on the low table beside the divan.

"Perfectly all right," he assured me. He smiled, and remained seated. "Jenna and I were still up," he said. "Weren't we, Jenna?"

Jenna agreed silently, smiling, nodding at the Colonel. Was I wrong, or was there something strange in that smile she gave him, something secret that glittered there like fury or hate? I couldn't be sure.

The Colonel said, "Jenna will show you your room, and make arrangements for you to see the right people in the morning. Just place yourself in her hands."

"I will. Thank you for your time."

"Not at all. My only pleasure is speaking with new arrivals from home, even on such unhappy business."

All the way across the room my back itched, between the shoulderblades, where I could feel his eyes.

IX

The room I was to sleep in was small and windowless, but nevertheless extravagant. The walls were covered in a textured fabric of rich blue, complemented by a gray carpet on the floor. The furnishings continued the use of blues and grays, with the addition of dark polished wood tones. The lighting was soft, indirect, and a bit whiter than I was used to.

Jenna had led me here in silence, her face stern and expressionless. She was clearly angry about something and was trying unsuccessfully to keep that anger hidden. I supposed that the clues Colonel Whistler had managed to call to my attention concerning the relationship between himself and Jenna were what had caused the anger, but I couldn't understand why. Surely the implication of those clues was true; the services of a

Jenna would almost have to be among the fringe benefits offered executives sent to a remote place like Anarchaos. Why should she be angry that such an obvious role had been made clear to an unimportant stranger?

Looking at Jenna, reflecting on her para-secretarial duties, I began to think of myself in regard to those duties, and how long it had been since I had shared pleasure with a woman. There had been the years in prison, of course, and since then my attention had been focused exclusively on the death of my brother. Only when the subject was called to my attention, as it had been by the Colonel, did I remember my thirst, which then became feverish.

Jenna said, "If you're hungry, I could have food brought to you. Not much, of course; everything's shut down for the night." She was trying to be civil, but her voice was made of ice and her words had sharp edges.

I said, "Is it me you're mad at?"

She seemed surprised. "No, no," she said, and tried to smile which worked fairly well. "Don't mind me, I'm just tired."

"Do you have to go back to the Colonel now?"

Instantly, her face snapped shut again and coldly she said, "Why?"

"I wish you'd eat with me. I don't like to sit at a table alone."

Only slightly less hostile, she said, "It's late, Mr. Malone. I'm not very hungry, but I am tired."

Her coldness was helping me forget the thirst. "All right," I said. "I'll see you in the morning."

"I'll have some food sent to you."

"Thank you. My luggage is still outside, in the auto."

"I'll have it brought in." She hesitated, then said, somewhat contritely, "I'll try to be pleasanter in the morning."

"We all will be," I said, "after we've slept." It was meaningless politeness, and I was relieved when she accepted it as a goodbye and walked out, closing the door silently behind her. I sat down in a blue armchair, removed my shoes, and rubbed the bare soles of my feet back and forth across the carpet, giving myself over to the cat-pleasure of it while waiting for the food to be brought.

It came ten minutes later, and I wasn't entirely surprised when it was brought by Jenna herself, who smiled apologetically at me and said, "Is it too late to accept your invitation?"

"You're just in time." I glanced at the two servings on the tray she carried, and said, "I couldn't have eaten all that anyway."

She laughed, perhaps more than the joke warranted, and I helped her set the table for two. She kicked off her own shoes when she saw I was barefoot, spoke brightly and humorously about her troubles in getting this snack from the kitchen help, and all in all made every attempt to make up for her past behavior. I responded more than I wanted to, my thirst returning stronger than ever, and it being now in part a literal thirst, my mouth and throat as dry as the desert around the city. I drank down the glass of milk she'd brought me, plus several glasses of water, but my mouth remained dry, my skin somewhat feverish, my thoughts random and confused and explosive.

During the meal she led the conversation, talking to me as her employer had done of Earth, except that Jenna seemed more interested in Earth as I knew it than as she remembered it. She asked me questions, and I gave her the most harmless parts of my biography. She mentioned Gar once or twice, each time with sympathy and what seemed very like regret, but asked me nothing about him and volunteered nothing that she knew of his last months on Anarchaos.

A knock at the door interrupted us at one point. I went to it, and found a guard from downstairs, who had brought my knapsack. When I shut the door and turned back to the table, I saw that Jenna had left it and had moved to a part of the room which could not be seen by anyone standing in the doorway. She seemed to be quite interested in a small wooden chair there, and commented on how seldom one saw that style of furniture these days. I agreed, we both returned to the table, and we went on with our meal and our conversation.

She seemed interested in the auto, which she called in the local fashion—as I had done—a car. "You took a chance," she said, "driving alone all the way from Ni."

"I was armed," I said.

"But what if the car had broken down?"

"I would have been in trouble."

"Yes, indeed. Most people don't own cars here at all, and that's why. It's much safer to fly."

"I'm sure it is."

"I wouldn't even know how to go about buying a car," she said.

I shrugged. "Buying and selling are about the same anywhere."

"Did it cost much?"

"Not much. Excuse me, I need another glass of water."

She made a joking comment on the amount of water I was consuming, and I replied in kind. When I came back with the fresh glass we talked about other things, and neither of us mentioned the auto again.

Finishing the meal, she pushed her chair back and said, "It's getting late. We both need our sleep."

I said, "Will you stay here?"

She pretended to misunderstand me. "I'd love to talk some more, Rolf, but it's after two now."

I said, "I meant, *stay* here."

She studied me in silence for nearly a minute, and I read her every thought on her face. I knew when her curiosity about me was uppermost in her mind, and I knew when her dislike of being taken so bluntly for granted was strongest, and I knew when she was considering the possibility of using me to avenge her pique against the Colonel, and I knew when she decided that if she had the name she might as well have the game. I also knew when she was deciding not to answer me too quickly, in order not to appear eager or easy, and in my mind I counted to ten with her, missing by one beat, so that I had just finished thinking *nine* when she smiled with sex in it and said, "You're not very subtle, are you, Rolf?"

148

"I hoped you would think the invitation a compliment," I said, but didn't add that I was incapable at the moment of any greater subtlety. My mouth was dry again, but the glass was empty.

"I do think it a compliment," she said, her voice husky, "but I'm afraid I'm an incurable romantic. I like my compliments . . . sweeter."

I got to my feet, and went to her, and took her in my hands.

She spoke only twice more, the first time to whisper, "Turn out the light," which I did, though I would have preferred it on. The second time, just before I fell asleep, she ran her nails lightly over my chest, and laughed against my throat, and murmured pleasurably, "You act like a man just out of prison." I laughed too, and folded my arms around her, and fell asleep.

X

She was gone in the morning, when I was awakened by a knocking at the door. I was fully conscious at once, though baffled by where I was and by a sense that someone should be with me, though for a second I couldn't think who or why. But then the knock was repeated. I got out of bed, put on my trousers, and found at the door a short and sullen girl with greasy long hair, who wore a guard uniform exactly like those worn by the men outside the main door. She handed me a small package and said, "I'm supposed to show you to the diner. After you eat, I'm supposed to take you to see Miss Guild."

"Good," I said. "Wait there." I shut the door, leaving her outside.

The package contained a watch, which read eight-thirty. I washed and dressed, took the elevator with my sullen guide, and entered the diner at ten minutes to nine. The normal day had begun much earlier here, I saw, since all the tables in the diner—a room very similar to what we called the mess in prison—were empty. A sullen employee paced me along the servicing line, filling my tray with a stock breakfast, and as I ate at a table near the door I reflected on the reason for Jenna Guild's consideration in letting me sleep late, and I found a smile coming unbidden to my lips. How odd it felt. But then my memory stretched to include my reason for being here in the first place, and the smile dissolved, and I hurried through the rest of the meal.

At nine twenty-five my guide left me at the entrance to Jenna's office. I stepped in, wondering how I was going to behave on first seeing her, and she decided it for me, greeting me briskly with, "There you are. Had a good sleep? Does the watch fit?" She remained seated behind her desk.

Business hours, in other words, were exclusively for business. I said, "Yes to both questions. Now I get started."

"Certainly." Brisk, impersonal, friendly in the machined way she'd been when I'd first seen her by the elevator. "To begin with," she said, "I thought you might be interested in seeing your brother's file." She extended a folder across her desk toward me. "You could sit at that table over there while you look at it, if you like."

"Thank you."

The folder contained documents, and the documents reduced Gar to a blueprint. His height, his weight, his date of birth, the color of his hair and eyes and skin, the place of his birth, the names and current address of his parents, the GD address for me that hid my life in prison, his scholastic records, his work history; all things I already knew, all seeming false and out of focus and somehow incorrect when placed on paper within this folder.

There were other facts, too, which I hadn't known. His salary, which was large. His job title, which was Developmental Surveyor. His home address here at the tower of Ice, which was Suite 87. His last job assignment, which was Special Projects Department, working under SP Supervisor L. L. Goss.

And finally, there were job evaluations, six of them, the final one from the same L. L. Goss, the first three from V. Topher, four and five from G. D. zi Quinn. All six evaluations were full of praise; his supervisors had found Gar an excellent worker,

150

imaginative, self-reliant, capable of taking criticism, very pro-
ductive, cooperative, no trouble with co-workers, and so on and
so on.

But those weren't the final papers. There was one more: the
copy of a letter from Gar to Supervisor Goss recommending me
for the job as his Field Assistant. The description was not me.
Reading it, I saw that it too was a blueprint, like this folder,
except that this was a blueprint for Rolf Malone. A revised
blueprint. A loving description of who I might have been, if I
hadn't been who I am. Here and there in the revision glimpses of
the original could faintly be made out.

I closed the folder. I closed my eyes. I breathed as little as
possible, because breathing hurt my throat. After a while Jenna
came over and said, "What's wrong? Rolf? Is something wrong?"

"No," I said. I opened my eyes and handed her the folder.
"Thank you."

"You're pale," she said.

"I want to see where he lived."

"Where he lived?" As though she had no idea what I meant.
I pointed at the folder. "Suite 87. Gar."

"Oh." She shook her head. "That's all changed now," she said.

"I want to see it."

"But someone else lives there now. All your brother's personal
property was sent home to his parents. If we'd known you were
coming, if you'd wanted us to keep them and give them to you
here . . ." She trailed off.

"I just want to see the rooms," I said.

"I don't— " She stopped, and looked at the folder, and shook
her head. "I don't know. Let me see if I can get the key."

Of course she could get the key. She went away, and came
back almost immediately, and led me to Suite 87 herself.

No windows. Not in the halls, not in my room, not in the
diner, not in Jenna's office, and not here in Suite 87. Only the
Colonel, at the top of the tower, had a window, which told him
kindly lies. Windowless, Suite 87 had three rooms, each as small
as the one in which I had slept last night. The first was a sitting

151

room done in green and brown, with an entertainment center along one wall. I almost went over to look at the books and tapes, but then I remembered they wouldn't be Gar's, they'd be the new tenant's, and I turned away.

The second room was a dinette, in silver and yellow, the kitchen appliances grouped on one side and the meal area across the way. It was necessary to go through the dinette to get to the third room, a bedroom in yellow and green, continuing the two primary colors from the earlier part of the suite. (Just as there were no windows, there was no red anywhere. The only manmade red I'd seen since arrival was the Colonel's robe.) Finally, off the bedroom was a small silver and white bath.

There was nothing here. I could stand in any of the rooms and look around and know I was looking at the walls and floors and furnishings that Gar had looked at, but artifacts of the new tenant kept intruding, breaking into my communication. Suite 87 was barren.

At last I shook my head and said, "All right, I've had enough."

She looked at me with sympathy, and put her hand on my arm. I don't know why, but that look and that touch made me dislike her for the moment.

Out in the corridor again, I waited while Jenna relocked the door and then I said, "It's time for me to see L. L. Goss."

"Special Projects Supervisor. He'll help you, if anybody will."

We had to take the elevator, and came to the first really busy level I'd so far seen. Men and women in working jumpers sat at tables, carried papers from room to room, spoke into tape machines or discussed things together in low intense voices. Jenna led me to a door which took me away from all this activity into a brown room where a girl sat primly in a brown jumper at a brown desk. She was plain of face and very thin, and I saw a quick expression of something like bitter envy flash by her eyes when she looked up and saw Jenna. But her voice was bright and impersonal as she asked what we wanted.

Jenna answered: "Gar Malone's brother, to see Mr. Goss. He's expected."

152

"One moment."

When she left the room, going through another door into an inner office, Jenna turned to me and said, "Well, good luck, Rolf."

"You're going?"

"I have work to do. Goodbye."

"Will I see you later on?"

She smiled slightly, and shook her head. "I doubt you'll ever see me again, Rolf," she said.

"Why?"

"Because we both have work to do. And it takes us in different directions." Her smile twisted a little, and she said, "Besides, I don't think I like who you think I am."

"I don't even know you."

"What difference does that make?" Then she smiled more freely and said, "In some ways, you remind me of Gar. But in most ways you're very different."

I suddenly had to know. I said, "Did *he* ask you?"

"Of course not." Smiling, putting sex into it for just a second, she said, "I had to ask him."

It was an exit line, and she'd planned it that way, and she went out on it. Suddenly disliking her more than ever, I took a step toward the door, to follow her and spoil the exit, force her to give Gar and me and herself our individuality no matter what the pain, but the voice of the plain girl in brown stopped me, saying, "Mr. Goss will see you now."

XI

L. L. Goss was a short, stocky, rumpled man standing in the middle of a stuffed, square, rumpled room and trying to decide what expression he should have on his face while greeting the brother of a dead man he used to know. He seemed to be the compulsively friendly type, and a cheerful hail fellow sort of grin struggled on his face with a solemn and mournful funeral parlor wince. Since he'd been Gar's supervisor, a remote official detachment also strove for command of his features, but with little success.

"Mr. Malone," he said, and pumped my hand. "Your brother talked about you a lot. Talked about you a lot."

"Did he?"

"I was looking forward to meeting you," he assured me, talking all in a rush, continuing to hold my hand as though he'd forgotten it was there. "Expected big things from the Malone brothers, big things. Could hardly wait to see you walk in, but not under these conditions. No, not under these conditions."

"I feel the same way," I said.

"Of course you do. Of course you do." Still holding my hand, he led me deeper into the room and told me twice to sit down in one of two facing plastic chairs. When I had done so, and he had released my hand at last and sat facing me, he said, with solemnity now in charge of his face, "It was a really tragic thing, I assure you. Tragic. Gar had a brilliant mind. Yes, and a great future ahead of him. It's hard to believe a man so vibrant is gone, hard to believe."

"But he is gone," I said. I didn't want eulogies, with or without a second copy. I could supply myself all the eulogies I wanted concerning Gar.

The solemn face gave way for a while to the remote official face as he said, "Colonel Whistler tells me you understand there's no job opening for you at the moment, now that your brother is no longer with the corporation."

No longer with the corporation. What a phrase. I said, "I realize that."

"Certainly. Certainly."

"I'm not here for a job. I'm here to find out what happened."

Goss got to his feet, looking away from me, saying, "Yes, yes, perfectly natural. Under the circumstances, perfectly natural." He was roaming around the room, peering here and there on littered tables, not looking at me, saying, "I can understand how you feel, the shock of it—Ah, there it is!" He picked up a pipe and showed it to me, the hail fellow grin finally flashing out at me unrestrained. "Never find this thing," he said. "Never find it."

I said, "I want to know the details."

"Only to be expected," he muttered, busy now filling his pipe. "Only to be expected. Anything I can do to help, anything at all—"

"You can tell me about it."

He stopped fussing with the pipe, looked sharply at me with a wary look I hadn't seen in his face before, then went back to the pipe. "I'll be glad to, glad to. Whatever I know."

"Maybe it would be best," I said, "if I asked you questions about the parts that interest me."

"Excellent. Just the thing." He came back with his pipe, trailing a thread of smoke, and sat in front of me again. "Ask away," he invited me. "Ask away."

I could hardly think which question came first, and finally selected one at random: "Where was he killed?"

"Where? Yoroch Pass." He popped to his feet again, motioning at me with the pipe. "Come along, I'll show you the exact spot. Come along."

I followed him to one of the littered tables, and watched him clear it; stacks of papers went on another table, small lumpy specimen sacks went on the floor, pencils and rulers and compasses went anywhere they could fit. When the table top was at last clean, I could see inlaid in it a map of Anarchaos done in black and white.

"You see what this is," Goss said unnecessarily. "It's dayside of the planet. Here we are here, at Ulik. There's Ni, where you landed, the center of dayside. Here's Moro-Geth way over here to the west. And north of Ni, here's Prudence, here, the mining town."

"I see it," I said, to stop him tapping each spot and telling me each name legibly printed beside his pointing finger.

But he couldn't be stopped. He pointed to Chax, the city to the south, and told me he was pointing to Chax, and that it was to the south of Ni. He told me again that Ni was situated at dead center of dayside of the planet, where Hell stood permanently at zenith, and that the other four cities were at approximately equidistant locations from Ni, one to each of the four points of the compass, all of which I had already known and could plainly see for myself on the map. He went on to tell me that dayside was banded by a ring of twilight which, with few exceptions, was as far as man had explored the planet, and that this ring of twilight was for the most part contiguous with natural geographic boundaries of one sort or another. To the east of where we now stood reared the Evening Mountains, a north-south range, bleak and jagged and inhospitable, but dotted with important mining sites. To the west, past Moro-Geth, there stretched the broad cold Sea of Morning, the largest ocean on the planet, icebound on its farther coast. Northward, the barrier was the White Wall, a line of cliffs rearing upward, marking the polar plateau, and to the south the Black River wound from the Empty Ocean westward to empty into the Sea of Morning. All of this was described to me, all of this I could see for myself, and none of this was relevant.

But at last he got to it, bending over the map table, pointing to Ulik, moving his finger eastward from the city toward the mountains, saying, "You see this thin line here? This is the road, the main road to the mountains, the one most of the trappers use. You see here where it goes into the mountains. You see?"

"Yes," I said.

"That's Yoroch Pass," he said, and tapped the spot with his finger. "Right there, that's it."

"Was he going out or coming back?"

"What? Coming back. Yes, he'd been on a survey and he was coming back."

"Alone?"

"Of course not. No, no, naturally not. No one travels alone here, no one. He had a guide with him, an assistant. The post you would have had."

"Did this assistant know I was going to replace him?"

Goss looked at me in some surprise. "Did he know? You mean,

156

would he have—But no, not possibly. He didn't know, and it wouldn't have mattered anyway. He would simply have been transferred to other guard duties. Just transferred, that's all. He would have been anyway when your brother died, if he'd wanted."

"He didn't want to stay?"

"No. He said the killing had frightened him; he wanted no more such work."

I looked at the map, at Yoroch Pass. I said, "Where is he buried? Was the body brought back?"

"That would have been impossible. Unfortunately impossible."

"So he's still there. Is the grave marked?"

"I wouldn't know. The guard buried him, he'd know."

"How was he killed?"

"Shot. Shot from ambush."

"What about the guard? Where was he?"

"Right there. Oh, right there. He was shot too, wounded, left for dead. But the wound was slight, he was fortunate."

"Very fortunate."

"He radioed, told us what had happened. We sent a ship for him. He buried your brother, and when our men got to him they brought him back to the city."

"He buried my brother before the ship got to him?"

"You must understand the conditions," he said. "The ship couldn't go directly to Yoroch Pass. No air vehicle of any type could possible make a landing anywhere in the Evening Mountains or to the east of them. You can't imagine the jagged, broken conditions there, and never being sure which is solid rock and which is merely a flimsy superstructure of ice."

I said, "What about a helicopter?"

"Possibly. A one or two man vehicle, possible. But those mountains are full of Anarchaotians, trappers, press gangs, all sorts, and an aircraft would be an incredible prize for them. A two man helicopter would barely touch ground before it would be attacked. No, we sent a large plane to a landing field here, two

157

days' march from Yoroch Pass, and sent a party of five men in to get Lastus and bring him out."

"Is that the guard's name? Lastus?"

"Yes. Piekow Lastus." Suddenly he looked up and said, "Ah! Perhaps you've solved my problem."

"I don't understand."

"It has to do," he said, "with your brother's ring. His college ring."

"I remember it."

"It so happens your brother and I attended the same engineering university, though of course at different times. Just the other day I saw one of our door guards wearing a ring that looked very familiar, and which turned out to be your brother's. As I wormed the story out of him, Lastus had naturally robbed your brother's body before burying him, and that's standard practice here, and this guard, who had been one of the five sent to bring Lastus back, had seen the ring on Lastus' finger and had by threats and intimidation forced Lastus to give it to him. You understand, that's the way life works here. Outside the towers, of course, outside the towers."

"You've got the ring?"

"Yes, indeed. Yes. I've had it three days, and I haven't entirely known what to do with it. It should be sent to the next of kin, of course, in this case the parents, but how to explain its turning up so belatedly or its not having been buried with the body? The customs on Anarchaos are difficult to explain in a letter."

"I can see that," I said.

He said, "But now I can give the ring to you! Would you mind? You'd relieve me of quite a responsibility, quite a responsibility."

I said, "Mr. Goss, you are nothing more than you seem—a good man, fussy, a bit of a bureaucrat. Why were you wary when I first asked you to tell me about my brother's death?"

He blinked at me in amazement, and blushed with embarrassment, trying to start a dozen sentences at once, so that for half a minute or so he merely garbled at me. Finally he shut his mouth,

158

swallowed, licked his lips, and said, "I simply do my job, Mr. Malone; that's all I do, I simply do my job. I hate complications that aren't my concern, aren't my fault. I'm no good at this sort of thing, at conniving, at—at . . . Your brother's death was a tragedy, a tragedy, but it's done and over. Nothing can bring him back. And nothing can be done about it, not here, not on Anarchaos. Nothing."

"I'll take the ring," I said.

"Thank you," he said, trying for stiff formality. Then, more honestly, he said, "I considered your brother a friend of mine, Mr. Malone, despite the difference of our ages, our positions. I admired him, I expected some day that he would be my supervisor. I wish something could be done, and I'll help in any way open to me. I can say nothing more than that. I'll get you the ring."

It was in his desk drawer. He found it right away and gave it to me and I put it on the ring finger of my left hand, where it felt artificial but comforting, like responsibility.

I said, "Do you know where I can find Lastus?"

"I'm sorry, no. But one of the guards knows him well, and should be able to tell you. Lingo, his name is. He should be on duty at the main door right now."

"Is he the one who had the ring?"

"Yes."

"Lingo," I said.

Goss and I shook hands at his door, where he assured me again he would offer me assistance of any sort, "in any way open to me." He seemed ashamed of this escape clause even while he was saying it.

XII

Lingo looked like a shaved gorilla, wearing sunglasses and fondling an automatic rifle. At first he professed total ignorance of Lastus or anything else I might want to talk about, and then

he more openly stated his position: he wanted to trade information for money.

"I have money to give Lastus," I told him, "but nobody else.
If Lastus wants to split with you later, that's up to him."

"How much you got for him?"

"It depends."

"On what?"

"On things that aren't your business." I showed him impatience which wasn't entirely feigned, saying, "If you won't tell
me where to find him, I'll get the information somewhere else."

"Give me the money," he said, "and I'll see he gets it."

"Of course. Goodbye, Lingo."

"Wait a second," he said, as I turned away. When I faced him
again he said, "You're the brother of that surveyor who got
killed, the one Lastus was with."

"That's right."

"That's what you want to talk to him about, how your brother
got killed."

"Right again."

He glanced upward, toward the top of the tower. "And
nobody cares? They don't mind you asking questions?"

"No. Why should they?"

He shrugged heavy shoulders.

I said, "I might have some money for you after all. Who would
mind? Who do you think would mind, and why?"

He shook his head. "You give your money to Lastus. I'm no
part of it."

"You can tell me where to find him."

He considered, and then said, "Why not? It can't make any
difference."

Except for the center of the city where the towers were, the
streets of Ulik—all the streets of all the cities, in fact—were
nameless, mere dirt roads flanked by thrown together shacks and
huts and hovels. This namelessness made directions difficult to
give, and Lingo eventually had to draw a map, showing me how
many blocks to go in this direction, and then which way to turn,

and again how many blocks to go, until I should at last arrive at the place where Lastus was living. When we were both satisfied that I could find Lastus without too much trouble, I left Lingo and went out to the auto, still sitting where I'd left it yesterday.

I had made only one stop between leaving Goss and approaching Lingo, and that was at the guardroom on the first floor, near the elevator, where I reclaimed my weaponry, all of which was once again in place on my person. The throwing knife in its sheath was a pleasant presence between my shoulderblades, and the pistol, the gas can, the lead pipe and the other knife were comforting weights here and there in my clothing.

The auto started up at once, and I saw Lingo and the other guards watching me as I drove away, but what thoughts they had about me I couldn't read in their expressionless faces.

I was soon away from the city center, the towers behind me, the same slovenly filthy slum all around me as the one I'd first seen outside the spaceport at Ni. I was traveling east, the shadow of my auto preceding us along the dirt street, the towers of the city casting their shadows all about me, pointing long thin black fingers toward the mountains beyond the horizon.

After my night and morning in the normal lighting of the tower, I had to get used all over again to the blunt redness of everything out here. The shacks I passed looked rusted and scabrous, like wounds that had dried without healing.

No block was empty of people. They moved around as endlessly and purposelessly as wind-up toys on a sidewalk, a kind of defiant hopelessness to the curve of their shoulders, the set of their heads. Children ran after the auto, or flung stones at it, or shouted words at it. Men watched it pass with silent mouths and greedy eyes. Women for the most part pretended it didn't exist, though here and there one would with visual and verbal obscenity inform me of her commercial availability. I drove at a good pace, ignoring everyone, and keeping the pistol handy on the seat beside me.

Lastus lived in a sagging lean-to near the outer edges of this slum, far from the towers, several blocks south of the main road

161

to the east, the one that led eventually to Yoroch Pass. There were fewer people out here, and they showed less reaction to the presence of the auto, whether from jadedness or despair, I couldn't tell. I pulled off the road and stopped as close to the side of the lean-to as I could get.

When they saw the auto stop, several men and women in the general area began to take an obvious though furtive interest in me, and even began to sidle somewhat closer. I climbed from the auto and stood beside it while very ostentatiously I checked my pistol and then put it away. Interest in me abruptly ceased, and those who had been studying me now went back with renewed conviction to their own pointless preoccupations.

Lastus' lean-to was broad across the front, but shallow and not very high, the open front barely five feet from ground to roof. Going to the front, I saw that dirt had been piled up over most of the width to make a kind of wall closing the lean-to in, leaving only a narrow opening in which I could see rough steps cut into the ground, leading down and in. So some, maybe most, of Lastus' home was underground. It was dark down there, too dark to even make a guess of the dimensions of the place, though I doubted it was much more than a shallow hole in the ground with the lean-to roof erected over it.

I had noticed pervasive stenches in the air while driving out here, the stinks of too many people and too little sanitation, but the smell that now attacked my nostrils seemed twice as bad as anything from before. I supposed it was because I'd been in a moving auto until now, with a breeze of my own making to dilute the aromas and vary them. Now, standing still, I felt the almost physical impact of an odor that seemed to flow up from the dark hole of the lean-to like the exhalations of the minotaur.

But the impression, of course, was wrong. The stink was in the air, all around me, the smell of the neighborhood and not of this one hovel, though surely Lastus' home was contributing its share to the overall effect.

The other sensation I felt was the chill in the air. Why should it seem so much colder, so much damper, when I was standing

162

still than when I'm in motion in the auto? It was as though Hell, unlike any other sun, gave off cold instead of heat, so that standing in its red light I shivered and felt the air clammy against my skin.

I was impatient to be done here and back in the comfort of the Ice tower. "Lastus!" I called into the black hole. "Lastus! Come up here!"

There were faint rustlings from within, sounds you might hear from some rathole, but I still could see no movement in the blackness. After a minute a reedy voice called, "What is it? Who are you?"

"Come up here, I want to talk to you."

Now I saw him. He'd moved forward, was very nearly close enough for me to lean forward and touch him, and he blinked up at me like a mole. He was wearing only shorts, and dirt streaked his torso and arms and legs and face. He was short and thin but looked hard-sinewed, strong ropes of muscle defining his arms and legs, his chest strong looking, his stomach flat. His face looked wary, and belligerent, and afraid, as though too frequently in his life he'd tested his obvious strength against men who'd proved to be stronger.

He squinted and blinked at me and said, in his reedy voice, "I don't know you. What do you want of me? Who are you?"

"I want to hire you," I said.

He was interested. He wiped his lips with the back of a filthy hand, wiped the back of his hand on his leg. "To do what?"

"Guide me."

"Guide you where?"

"To Yoroch Pass."

He'd kept moving closer, was now barely three steps from the entrance. I backed away to permit him to feel safe about coming out the rest of the way, and he said, "Why do you want to go there?"

"I want to see my brother's grave," I said.

"Your brother's grave?" He came up the last three steps, and stood in the entrance. "What brother?"

163

"Gar Malone. I'm his brother, Rolf."

His eyes widened. At first I thought it was surprise at what I'd said, but then I saw he was staring beyond me, at something behind me, possibly out in the street. Before I could move, the shooting started.

I heard the first two shots. Number one caught Lastus in the right shoulder, spun him half around like a weathervane when the wind shifts. Number two plunged like an invisible spike into the back of his head, plummeting his corpse down the stairs he'd just come up.

I didn't hear the third shot, I felt it, in the middle of my back; a blunt punch from a hard metal fist. I opened my mouth, but I had no air. I tried to stand erect, but I had no will. The punch drove me forward and I saw myself hurtle down after Lastus into the darkness below. Then a greater darkness overtook me, and I ceased to know.

XIII

Violent pain in my right hand shocked me awake. I sat up, yelling, into dusty red semi-darkness, a powerful stink, a dirt floor, and a scrawny youth with the third finger of my right hand in his mouth. He hadn't been able to get Gar's ring off me any other way, so he'd decided to bite my finger off entirely and take it with him.

I hit him, reflexively, and he fell back, more surprised than hurt, but immediately leaped at me again, his hands going for my throat. The two of us scuffled in the dust.

There was sudden surprised movement in the darkness around us, and a man's amused shout: "Hey, Alfie! This one's alive!" And then laughter from the same voice, and, "Hold him, little one! Don't let him get away!"

But he did let me get away. I flung him off, and scrambled across the floor till I hit a dirt wall. I rolled onto my back—my body was an anthology of pains, too numerous to separate into individual aches—and saw the youth leaping for me again, his eyes wide, his face rigid with terror and determination. I kicked him away with both feet and clawed in my pockets for my weapons.

They were still there! The youth and his friends must have been sure I was dead, so they hadn't bothered to disarm me before going for my ring. I pulled the pistol from my pocket and fired it into the youth's face as he came leaping at me yet again. He died in mid-air and crumpled into my lap.

There was a yelp from across the room, and shouting: "He's got a gun! Alfie, he's got a gun!" It was the same voice as before, but no longer amused.

I looked toward the sound, and saw a tall rectangle of rusty light where the steps led up to the street. A bulky figure abruptly dashed into that rectangle, bent on escape: my shouter.

I fired at him and he yelped like a stray dog hit with a stone. He ran into the wall beside the door, half-turned, and sprawled backward onto the ground, yelping all the while. He lay there on his back, making a lot of noise and waving his arms around. He looked like a turtle flipped over onto its shell.

The dead youth was bleeding in my lap. I pushed him away and took stock of myself, trying to organize my thoughts and understand what had happened.

The finger that had been bitten was bleeding a little, but unless infection set in it shouldn't be anything to worry about. There was an abrasion on my forehead that stung to the touch, probably the result of my fall down the steps. The other aches and scrapes on my arms and legs were either from the same fall or from the scuffle with the youth.

But these were minor. The pain that drew my attention was in the middle of my back, between my shoulderblades, a wearying ache, a pressure on my back that dulled my movements and hampered my breathing. It was, so far as I knew, the result of a gunshot wound that should have killed me.

I didn't entirely have my wits about me yet, and was stupid enough to look at my chest to see if the bullet had passed all the way through and come out the other side, but of course it hadn't.

165

I was afraid to touch that spot behind me, both because it hurt more when I reached back there and because of what I might find, but it had to be done, and so very cautiously I put my left hand behind my back, and slid it up toward the ache, and felt the crumpled remains of my sheathed knife, still in what was left of the sheath.

That was why I was alive. The bullet had hit the knife, and so hadn't penetrated my back. But the knife had curled like the edges of a piece of paper at the impact, making sharp creases on the inner side, against my skin, and the force of the bullet had driven those creases into the flesh, cutting a random design into my back as though I'd been engraved. Or branded.

That whole area was bruised and battered, the flesh sensitive to the touch, the back of my shirt sticky with blood. From the pressure I felt when I breathed it seemed to me I might have broken a rib or two besides. If I wasn't careful how I moved, I was liable to puncture a lung.

Across the way, the turtle shape had begun to slacken, the arm and leg movements getting feebler, the yelps softer, but all at once he screamed, "Alfie! Alfie, come get me!"

We both waited. Nothing happened. The turtle shape began to groan, loud, windy, melodramatic sighs.

I began very cautiously to move, turning over at first onto my hands and knees, then moving my hands up onto the wall in front of me and slowly easing myself up the wall till I was on my feet. Then I tucked the pistol away in my pocket, undid the thong of the sheath around my neck, and carefully removed the knife that had saved me, slipping it up from inside my shirt. Moving it that way made quick stinging pains in my back, but I ignored them and looked instead in the dim red light at the knife.

It was a crumpled mess. The side of the sheath that had been against my back was cut and full of blood, and the other side had been almost completely sheared away by the bullet. The crater of the bullet's impact was there in the knife, plus a long groove where it had deflected and scratched its way up as far as the hilt.

The lip of the hilt was bent back where the scratch met it, but from that point bullet and knife had parted company.

I tossed the knife away and looked around, for the first time paying real attention to the room itself. It was sparsely furnished with a cot against one wall, a few ramshackle chairs, a battered trunk, a home-made table. Floor and walls were dirt. There were no decorations of any kind. Oh, brave new world!

There was a thin blanket on the cot. I took it and ripped off several strips, six inches wide, and wrapped two of the strips tightly around my chest, relieving the feeling of pressure and giving some support to my ribs. I thought I could dare to move more freely now.

Lastus lay on his side near the steps, not far from where the groaner lay on his back and made his noises. I went over and checked Lastus and he was dead, as I'd known he must be, his eyes wide open and full of surprise. I searched him, and then searched the room, and found nothing of interest.

The dead youth was dressed in rags so filthy I hardly searched his body at all. I hadn't expected to find anything noteworthy on him and I didn't.

I went over and squatted down beside the groaner and slapped his face, saying, "Shut up and listen to me."

He blinked several times, very rapidly, and stared at me in astonishment. I believe he'd forgotten about me. When he remembered, he shouted, "You killed my boy!" He waved his arms as though he wanted to get at me.

I took out the can of blinding gas and showed it to him and said, "Do you see what this is?"

He just kept waving his arms and glaring at me.

I slapped him again, to attract his attention. "I asked you, do you see what this is I'm holding in my hand?"

"I see it, you rotten thing. I know what it is."

"It will be the last thing you see," I told him, "if you don't tell me what I want to know."

"Rotter."

"It's a bad life in a place like this for a blind man," I said.

He understood me now. He blinked up at me; I saw him get frightened, and I knew when he was ready to listen to me.

I said, "You people didn't do the shooting, you don't have guns. You came down afterward, to pick the bodies."

"Why not?" he cried. "Somebody would."

"It's a fine system you've got," I said. "You saw who did do the shooting, though."

He shook his head emphatically. "It was all over when we got there!"

I tapped his nose gently with the can. "Be careful," I said. "Don't tell foolish lies."

"It was all over!"

"No," I said.

"Why not? Why not?"

"One, you wouldn't have known there were bodies down here to be picked if you hadn't seen them drop. Two, if you'd come along later you would have been too late because some other scavengers would have beaten you to it." I tapped him with the can again. "You're not very good at lying," I said. "Better not try it anymore, you'll just make me impatient."

"I didn't know them," he said.

"Which means you did know them. Who were they?"

"I swear—"

I hit him a little harder. "Don't waste my time."

"I'll tell you what I know!" he shouted. "There were two of them. They came out and shot you."

"Came out? Came out of where?"

"A place across the street, a house over there."

"Is that where they live?"

"No. Nobody's lived there for a long while."

"They're both men?"

"Oh, yes."

"They were already here, eh? Waiting for me. What did they do afterward, go back into the house?"

"No. They took your car and drove away."

"Did they come down here?"

"No."

"What are their names?"

"I don't know," he said stubbornly.

I started to hit him, then changed my mind. I said, reasonably, "What are they to you? Why protect them? Why get blinded instead of giving me a chance to get near them again? Maybe they'll kill me after all."

"They will," he said. "If you go after them they'll finish the job on you. I'll do them a favor, telling you."

"That's the way to think."

"Malik and Rose," he said.

I repeated the names, and said, "That's all the names they have?"

"That's all I know."

"Rose is a man?"

"Of course." He seemed surprised at the question.

"What do they look like?"

"Big, like you. Young, like Alfie, or like you. They shave their heads to keep the bugs away."

"Where do I find them?"

"I don't know. If I knew I'd tell you, because then you'd go there and they'd kill you, like you killed my boy."

He was telling the truth. I got to my feet and put the can away and said, "Goodbye."

He cursed.

I went to the steps, my pistol again in my hand, and went up them cautiously, pausing midway to let my eyes reaccustom themselves to the glare of daylight. I was stopped with my body still completely within the lean-to, my head at about street level. Looking out, the narrow strip of outside world I could see looked unnaturally empty and motionless, like the remains of lost colonies on the fic-films. Across the way was the corrugated metal shack which must be the "house" my assassins had been waiting in.

The stillness and emptiness continued unbroken as I stood

watching. The only sound was the heavy breathing of the wounded man down behind me. Of Alfie, to whom the wounded man had kept calling for help, there was no sign.

Yet I remained cautious. I crept out of that hole like a gopher in a desert of carnivores, moving one slow careful step at a time.

No one. I stood at last in the entranceway, one step down from ground level, peering this way and that, and still I saw no sign of life. The sound of shooting must have driven the locals into their own holes; here, curiosity was anti-survival.

I purposely made a noise, clinking the pistol against the spray can in my pocket, but nothing happened. I lifted one foot, slid it out onto the ground, waited. Nothing. I shifted my weight forward. I raised the other foot, brought it up beside the first.

The sun went out.

Confusion. Darkness. Stench. Coarse cloth scraping my face and neck. Soft heavy weights dropping on my shoulders and back, bending me, driving me to the ground.

I roared in rage and fright, but the noise was muffled even in my own ears. My arms were imprisoned, held against my sides. The pistol in my hand was useless and worse than useless. If it went off, I would be shooting myself in the leg.

I staggered, staggered, and toppled over. Out of my bewilderment came sprays of understanding.

The lean-to. Alfie—and others—had been atop it, *atop* it, waiting for me with a blanket in their hands. When I emerged the blanket was dropped on my head, and Alfie—and at least one other, there was more than one here—had jumped down on me, grappling me, knocking me off my feet.

Still I struggled, until someone kicked me on the side of the head. In the darkness inside the blanket I saw pinwheels of light, felt my awareness fading, tried to duck my head away, keep my consciousness, regain control.

I ducked into the path of the second kick.

XIV

"I think he's awake," said the woman.

"His eyes are closed," the old man told her.

"I don't care," said the woman. "I still think he's awake."

"So do I," said the young man. I heard his boots crunch on the ground as he walked over to me. He stopped with his feet very near my head. "He's faking," he said, and kicked me on the shoulder, painfully. "Open your eyes," he said.

I didn't respond, didn't move. The longer I could convince them I was still unconscious the better it was for me.

The old man said, "Take it easy, Alfie. Don't bust him up."

"You quit faking," said the young man. Alfie, he was the young one. He kicked me again. "Open your eyes and get up from there."

The old man said, "Alfie, don't! We won't get nothing for him if he's busted up."

"I'll bring him out of it," said Alfie. "Tina, go get a needle or something. Something with a point on it."

I heard the soft pad of the woman's feet as she hurried away. Then there was silence, while the old man and Alfie and I waited for her to return.

I was lying on my back, on bare ground, somewhere in the open; red sunlight illuminated my closed eyelids. I had been awake now for perhaps ten minutes, listening to the three of them talk.

They were taking no chances with me. They'd disarmed me this time, and tied my wrists together in front of me, and hobbled my ankles so I would be able to walk but only with small steps. From their conversation I understood they meant to sell me to the slavers.

They were a kind of family group. Tina, the woman, was the wife of the man I'd wounded and mother of the youth I'd killed. Alfie was some sort of cousin, and the leader of the group. The old man, whose name I hadn't yet heard, was the woman's

171

father. They lived nearby, had been on particularly hard times recently, and considered me—and my weapons—a real windfall. They were all more or less afraid some larger or stronger group would come and take this unexpected treasure away, though only the old man actually stated their fears. Alfie put up a good tough front, denying the possibility, and the woman preferred not to think or talk about it.

They'd checked the wounded man down in the lean-to, but none of them could guess whether he'd live or die, so they'd decided to leave him where he was until they'd taken care of me. Then they would come back and look the situation over. I had the impression they would prefer him to die, as being the simplest solution to the problem.

In the meantime they were only waiting for me to regain consciousness, and getting increasingly impatient. Now, as I heard the footsteps of Tina returning, I moved my head and groaned, as though just coming back to awareness, and blinked several times, and looked up at last into the disgusted eyes of Alfie.

He was very close to the mental picture I had formed on the basis of his voice; narrow and sleek, with a long thin face, shiny black hair brushed straight back and flat against his head, thin lips, a long thin nose, and eyes in which intelligence had been distorted into cunning. His clothing was old and mismatched, but worn with a certain flair.

"You've wasted our time, you," he said. "I ought to make you pay."

"Never mind, Alfie," said the old man nervously. "He's awake now, let's be off." He was a thin and shrunken old man with jittery birdlike movements. I'd heard a certain mushiness in his voice before this, and now I saw why; he had no teeth, his mouth was a collapsed double flap, his stubbly chin jutting out beneath his nose.

Alfie spat on the ground near my head and said, "All right, then. Up on your feet."

The woman, glaring at me, said, "The nasty thing. I ought to

172

stick him with this anyway." She waved something in her hand, something metallic that glinted. She was heavyset, fiftyish, as poorly dressed as the others, and with a round sullen face framed by stringy hair.

She made a move as though to attack me, but the old man clutched at her arm, saying, "Don't, Tina! Let's be off, let's be away from here!"

"He killed my boy," she cried, outraged, and shook the old man off.

Alfie, though, stopped her, saying, "Never mind that. He's right, we've got to get going." To me he said, "I told you to get up."

Laboriously, I rolled over onto my stomach and pushed myself up onto hands and knees. I was weak, and stiff, and shaken, but behaved as though I were much worse off than that. I was grasping at every advantage, however slight, and it seemed to me there was an advantage in being stronger than they knew.

When I finally got to my feet I saw that we were in the middle of the road between the lean-to and the metal shack across the way in which the assassins had lain in wait. I stood swaying, tottering, only half faking my dizziness and weakness, and Alfie approached me with a thick coarse rope, one end of which had been formed into a loop like a hangman's noose. As the older couple stood well out of the way, the woman pointing my own pistol at me, Alfie put the loop over my head and told me, "Now, you be good and give us no trouble. Don't make it no worse on yourself."

"I'll pay you," I said. "Take me to Ice, to the tower. I've got money there; I'll pay more than the slavers."

"You must think I'm simple," Alfie said, and smiled upon me, and backed away, letting the length of rope slide through his hands until he reached the other end of it. The rope was about ten feet long, connecting us. He looped the other end around his wrist.

"I give you my word," I said, though I knew it wouldn't do any good.

He didn't even bother to answer. "Follow them," he said. "Not too close. And watch yourself."

173

He meant Tina and the old man. They started off down the street now, looking back to see if I was coming. I hesitated, but I saw Alfie's face harden, and knew there was nothing to do but obey. I started off, stumbling, forced by the hobble to take short scuffling steps, and followed where Tina and the old man led. Behind me, at the far end of the rope around my neck, came Alfie.

My head drooped, from weariness and from frustration. I found myself looking at my hands, hanging useless from the ropes tying my wrists together, and I saw the dark red marks on my finger where the youth had bitten me. But I didn't see Gar's ring.

I raised my head, startled, and inadvertently took a longer step than the hobble would permit, and lost my balance. I thought I'd strangle when the rope around my neck grew taut, but when I hit the ground the tension lessened. I lay there gasping.

Alfie called, "Get up! Get up, you!" And tugged at the rope.

It was harder to get to my feet this time. I couldn't feign weakness greater than I actually felt. But I finally did attain my feet again, and the couple in front started off once more, and I followed them.

The ring? I could see it. It glinted in the light of Hell, ahead of me, on the hand of the woman, Tina. I ground my teeth at that, and very nearly gave in to a despairing fury.

But I held myself in check, as I had learned to do in the prison. I could see there was nothing to be done. They were all too far away, and I was bound too tightly. Besides, there was the weakness and stiffness all over my body. If I'd been stronger I might have tried attacking Alfie anyway, since I knew disabling him would stop or at least slow the other two, but not the way I was now. All I could do was scuff forward, led like a dog on a leash, and hope for a better chance later on.

As we moved away from the immediate area of the shooting we began to see people again, living their lives, moving about, traveling from here to there. None of them paid any attention to us as we passed in our slow parade, the woman and the old man ambling along in front and then me shuffling in their wake and at last Alfie bringing up the rear like the master of hounds. This

174

caravan, impossible anywhere else in civilization, was normal on Anarchaos. No one would come to my aid, no one would question my imprisonment, not here in the ultimate land of the rugged individualist. I was alone.

And I had lost.

XV

I cannot tell how much time went by. Weeks. Months.

If a man is treated like an animal, he will become an animal. There is something inside every human being that craves mindlessness, that aches to give up the nagging responsibility of being a creature with a rational brain, that yearns to be merely instinct and appetite and blindness. Those who join a rioting mob have given in to this animality within themselves; alcoholics and drug addicts are perpetually in search of it.

I became an animal. I became as stupid, as obedient, as unthinking, as placid as any plowhorse.

The early part of the transition is clear, but the last of the decline blends into unending sameness: the straw of my bed, the damp darkness of the mine, the looming mountains, Hell at perpetual evening on the western rim of the sky.

Alfie and the other two didn't keep me long. They walked me to a large wooden building, one story high but rambling, apparently a kind of meeting house or place for the bartering of goods. Here they sold me to two heavily bearded men in clothing made of furs, who bound me even more tightly than the others had and dumped me into the back of a rough-made wagon with two other new slaves. A fourth was tossed in after us later on, and then we rode out of Ulik, our two captors sitting together at the front of the wagon, calling to their hairhorses and talking together in guttural voices.

I passed out from time to time, and was probably unconscious for most of the trip. At the end of it, one of the two climbed into the back of the wagon, cut the ropes off us, and threw us one at a time out onto the ground, where we were all at first too weak

175

to move. But they forced us to stand up, kicking us and pulling our hair, until finally three of us were on our feet. The fourth turned out to be dead, which enraged them. One of them, in his fury, beat at the dead body with a rock until the other one told him he was wasting time. Then they marched us through rocks and granite and sharp projections to a wooden fence. A man in a green uniform gave them money there and they went away. I watched the transaction, though I was too dazed then to fully understand it.

The light was more Earthlike here, with Hell far away on the horizon, but the landscape was forbidding and unnatural. Jagged rocks and boulders were everywhere; shale rustled beneath one's feet; the sharp teeth of hills and mountains sprang up on all sides. Much of this had been cleared and flattened inside the compound, in the area circumscribed by that wooden fence. We were marched, the three of us, across the compound to a shed, where we were examined by a doctor.

I said to the doctor, "You aren't from this world." Because it was true, it could be seen in his face. But he acted as though I hadn't spoken.

I tried to observe everything, thinking of escape, but I saw nothing to give me hope. Only the compound, enclosed by the tall wooden fence everywhere except at the face of the mountain, where the mine entrance gaped like an open mouth. Inside the compound were several sheds, some for the administrators, the rest meant to house the slaves. The one I slept in had straw on a dirt floor, that was all. Fifteen of us slept in it. Because it was so cold here, at the edge of the Evening Mountains, we huddled together like cattle every sleep period, and our communal stench came to be precious to me, representing warmth and rest and our closest approximation to comfort. I don't know if any of the others were women, and it couldn't have mattered; brute exhaustion had desexed us.

Without the solar rhythm of day and night it was impossible to keep hold of the concept of the passage of time, so that we lived our lives to a pattern we could not comprehend. We were awakened by shouts, and the sun read evening. We ate gruel from a trough and then trotted into the mine, and behind us as we went the sun still read evening. We worked, scraping out a vein of some pale metal through the interior of the mountain, and at a shouted order we put down our tools and trotted back to the compound along the cold damp tunnels, and when we emerged the sun said evening still. We ate again at the trough, and crowded into our shed, and closed our eyes against the light of the evening sun, and slept.

At first I tried to keep hold of that within me which was rational and human, but it was impossible. My brain atrophied; in any realistic sense, I had ceased to exist.

I was brought out of this nothingness twice, the first time temporarily, in a brief incident that stands out in my memory like a single star in an otherwise black sky. I was at the trough with the others, and laughter made me raise my head. Some distance off, talking with a mine official, were two large muscular men with shaved bald heads. Seeing them, it came into my mind that I had been looking for these two, and I very nearly moved away from the trough in their direction, as though there was something I had to say to them. But then fear struck me, and my back twinged with pain, and I became very afraid—without knowing why—that they would see me. I ducked my head down again, and continued to eat, and kept my face hidden when a little while later we trotted past them on our way to work.

But the incident had driven me to self-awareness, and I remained nervous and upset for some time after that, until the monotonous routine of the work lulled me back to indifference.

The second incident was much stronger, and jolted me back to myself violently and permanently. That was when they cut off my hand.

Infection had set in where my finger had been bitten. Gradually the entire hand had become discolored and I felt increasing waves of pain. Apparently I had begun to howl, both while awake and in my sleep, until finally one of the guards took a look at my hand and I was taken to the doctor who had examined me back at the beginning.

It is possible the hand could have been saved by a doctor disposed to expend time and effort on the problem, but I think it more likely that the infection had been left to itself too long and there was by now nothing left to do but amputate. In any case, I was strapped into a chair, my left arm was tied to a kind of board, and a knife came down on my wrist.

I screamed myself back to life. First the knife, and then the cauterizing fire, and when the stony-faced doctor was done I was trembling and weak and half-mad with pain, but I was alive again, and I would know no more deaths until the last one.

XVI

They gave me a new job. Because of the amputation I could no longer work in the mine, so I was put to work on a machine in a small shed next to where the ore was loaded onto trucks and driven away. The machine did number problems, with my assistance. That is, slips of paper would be handed to me, with numbers on them. I would punch buttons showing the same numbers, and the machine would go on from there. The job required an ability to recognize numbers, and a right hand to push the buttons.

Now that I had been shocked back to myself, everything seemed to be working to help me keep my awareness. This job, though elementary, required at least a little brainwork, which the digging in the mine had not. And it was not continuous, as the mine work was; most of my time at the machine was idle, waiting for more carts to be wheeled out of the mine, more slips of paper to be handed in through the window to me. I still slept in the same shed with the same group, but the group identity was no longer strong with me, now that I was separated from them during all our working hours.

Still, a great deal of time went by before I had recovered sufficiently to start thinking in terms of escape. Simple awareness of my own identity was at first startling enough to occupy my full attention, and I spent work period after work period sitting slack-jawed in front of the machine, lost in contemplation of the wonders of my own brain, picking through the grand wealth of knowledge therein like a child delightedly investigating a trunk filled with bright-colored costume jewelry. I spent uncountable time, for instance, merely spelling words in my head, exalted at the vast store of words I knew and the unending diversity of their lettering.

(If, in speaking of the passage of time, I do not use the normal words—hours, days, weeks, minutes, seconds—it is because in this situation they had no real meaning. I lived to a pattern of sleeping and waking, with a communal meal at the trough at each transition; how long this pattern took to round itself out, in terms of hours and minutes, I have no idea. Nor could I guess how many of these cycles I lived through at each stage of my development; by the time I was capable of thinking in terms of record-keeping, I had more sophisticated thoughts of escape to hold my attention.)

At any rate, it was only after I had thoroughly explored myself that I could devote some attention to the world around me. And when at first I began to study the life of the compound I did so with no motive other than the use of my newly regained faculties of observation and memory. The possibility of finding a way to live any existence other than my present one had not as yet occurred to me.

The compound was a rather large area, containing twenty-six rough wooden sheds, none of them very big. They contained one of three classes of thing: slaves, officials, or machinery. The sheds containing machinery were the most carefully and soundly constructed; those containing slaves were the most ramshackle. I was glad to be working on the counting machine when the long cold rains came, as at odd intervals they did, because the roof of the shed housing that machine did not leak. None of the machine-holding sheds leaked, and all of them had stout wooden floors.

In my work, I sat at a tall black stool. The machine was to my right, with a counter where I could set the slips of paper. These were handed to me through a large open window directly to my left, out of which I could see a good view of almost the entire compound, including the main gate, which was just beside this shed.

The compound had been beaten out of ground so jagged and rocky and inhospitable that nothing at all lived here under normal conditions except a kind of tenacious moss. The rocky outcroppings had been pulverized by sledges and the resultant pebbly dust used to fill crannies and holes, until at last a large square of mostly flat ground had been torn out of the environment. One side of this square was against a rocky vertical mountain face, but the other three sides, naturally open, had been enclosed by high wooden walls.

I still don't know what mineral we were bringing out of that mountain. It was a pale gray stuff, lighter than the useless rock around it, and would sometimes chip off in layers, like shale. Picks were used to break this stuff free, and then it would be loaded by hand onto small deep carts with metal wheels. Slaves pushed these carts up the long tunnels to the compound, where officials added the slips of paper which eventually came to me. Other slaves emptied the carts by hand into large motorized trucks with treads rather than wheels, and the loaded trucks drove past my window and out the main gate and away.

Food and other material—and new slaves—arrived the same way, by truck or wagon, coming through the main gate and being unloaded very close to my window. The flow of traffic was really very light, but any movement at all was thrilling to a mind newly emerged from atrophy, so I watched the ore trucks and the supply trucks with fascination and a retentive memory. I came to know the pattern of the compound possibly better than anyone else within it.

Only once did anything break into that pattern, and that was the day the helicopter came. It was green and yellow, and it settled into the middle of the compound with a great whirling of

180

wings, blowing dust up and seeming to have been lowered into our midst on the end of an invisible rope. There was an insignia in outline on its side: a hammer with a dog's head. Hadn't I seen that symbol before?

Three men emerged from the helicopter, young and well-dressed, and I understood at once that they were also officials, but of much more importance than the officials who lived in the compound and who now clustered around the new arrivals the way we slaves clustered at feeding times around our trough.

It was a tour of inspection. The little group of officials moved off in a body, and for the next long while, very nearly until my work period ended, the ordinary routine of the compound was disrupted and almost halted, so much so that the flow of papers containing numbers for me to punch onto the machine slowed to the barest trickle. The officials still at their normal work were affected by this break in the pattern, being increasingly short-tempered and agitated, and the slaves felt it too, growing restive and sullen and unwilling to work, some of them having to be beaten with sticks.

The inspection was very thorough, including the sheds, the mine itself, everything. Near the end of it they came at last around to me and my machine. It was the machine, of course, which interested them; one of the compound officials hastily explained its function and methodology—an explanation I was incapable of following—while the three visitors listened carefully and observantly, nodding their heads.

As they were starting out, one of the visitors glanced in my direction for the first time, and stopped in his tracks, staring at me. "Malone?" he said, as though pointing out to himself the existence of an impossibility. He stepped closer to me, saying my name again: "Malone?" But this time it was a question directed at me, wanting an explanation.

I was terrified. No one had looked upon me as an individual for so long that I now couldn't possibly handle it. I stared at the compound officials, waiting for one of them to solve this problem for me.

The visitor called to one of his companions, "Elman, look! Could it be—"

The other one said, "Don't be silly. Malone's dead." Then he looked at me himself and said, "He's close, all right."

"It's uncanny," said the first one.

Elman said, "His head is broader, and his eyes are different. Besides, Malone is dead. You know it as well as I do."

I wanted to say that I wasn't dead, but I was unable to make any sound at all. I merely stood there and stared at the faces of the officials I knew, and hoped they would solve this for me soon.

It solved itself. Elman and the one who had seen me first and the one who had been no part of it at all, the three of them turned around and walked out of the shed. I had never seen any of them before, of that I was positive, and I was pleased when, a short while later, they got back into their helicopter and were drawn up once again into the sky.

Much later, after sleep periods and work periods, it occurred to me the particular mistake they had made. That was the day I found the note.

XVII

I no longer spent my sleep periods entirely in unconsciousness, but woke at intervals, to lie a while in thought amid the still limbs and soft breathings of the others, and then uneasily to drop off once again.

There were two reasons for this. Most obvious, I did not now spend my waking hours in exhaustive labor, but sat in comfort on the stool by the number machine. But there was also the constant pain in my left wrist, which refused to finish healing itself and which now and again twinged me out of slumber. The doctor kept the stump wrapped in cloth and when, from time to time, I was taken to him for the bandage to be changed, the same hot musky bloody smell always bloomed out as the cloth was removed. The doctor appeared to treat me with a competence unlit by interest, yet I had confidence in him and believed he would eventually make my wrist well again.

In the meantime, the pain was a constant background hum to my existence. It might be that it was this continuing pain which kept my brain awake and forced me back into being when I had already—like the other fourteen, snuffling and sleeping around me—ceased, in any way that matters, to be alive.

The periods of wakefulness in the shed, while all around me the others slept, seemed the worst parts of my life at that time, though ultimately they must have been the best for me. But they were so empty, so boring. During the work periods, though I had little myself to do, there was at least the activity outside my window with which to distract myself, while in the sleep periods there was just nothing at all. Around me lay the thin, white, wire-muscled bodies, all entwined together in the endless search for warmth. Under me was the straw, over me the wooden walls and roof of the shed, with long streaks of daylight showing the broad cracks where water came through when it rained.

It was in these restless periods that I did my most constructive thinking, the major part of the reconstruction of my personality and memory. And it was in such an interval that I connected at last the fact of my dead brother Gar with the incident of the visitor who had called me Malone and claimed that I was dead.

The visitor could not have meant me, even though he had used my last name, because he and I had never met before, of that I was certain. But if the last name were right, and if I looked quite similar to the person he'd been thinking of, and if the person he'd been thinking of was truly dead, the conclusion was belatedly obvious: He had mistaken me for Gar. And *that* meant he had known Gar! Might even know for certain what had happened to him, and why.

If only I'd thought it all out so clearly at the time, I could have asked him.

Usually I tried to keep perfectly still while awake in the shed, since movement disturbed the others and made them groan and twist about, but the agitation of this series of thoughts was too much for me. I shifted this way and that, disturbing them and not caring, and though they thrashed and muttered with their eyes squeezing shut I nevertheless still heard the sound of paper crackling just beneath my ear.

In my moving around, my head had come to rest directly atop the paper, which had been tucked down into the straw just barely below the surface. Turning my head, I could see it there, so close as to be out of focus. I picked it out and found it to be a small white scrap of notepaper, folded over once. Opening it, I read the three words shakily written on the inside:

WE MUST UNITE

Unite? The concept seemed to me then as mysterious as the sender. I looked around, trying to think who could have sent such a note and what he might have intended. Surely it had come from another slave, but what had he wanted, and why had he chosen such an unlikely method of communication? It would have been simpler merely to arrange to sleep beside me, and whisper his message to me while the others slept.

Of course, the problem was even more complex than that, because the note had clearly not been directed exclusively at me. The writer had tucked it away in the straw with the apparent hope that *someone* would see it. And, of course, someone had.

It had been left there recently, that was one thing I could know; we had had rain just two sleep periods ago, a very bad rain which would surely have left evidences of itself on the note. So it was recent, and it was an attempt at communication from someone who, like myself, was not entirely sunken into vacantness.

But there was no one like that among the fourteen. And where would a slave have found pencil and paper? And what did the note *mean*? Above all, what was I to do about it? (And there was still the revelation about the visitor and Gar to distract my mind.) I couldn't think. Clutching the paper, falling now and then into uneasy dozes, I spent the rest of that sleep period in frustrated attempts at concentration.

184

It was later, during the following work period, that I thought of the answer to a part of the problem. I was positive the note had been written by a slave, but just as positive he was none of the slaves with whom I slept in the shed, and while sitting at the number machine I finally thought of the explanation. The slave population was divided into three groups, or shifts, who slept in the same sheds one after the other; the note must have come from a member of one of the other groups!

As to the meaning of his message, that too came clear to me. There were better ways to live than as a slave at this mine, but the officials would not permit us to make any change. Still, there were more slaves than officials, so that if we were to unite together and *insist* on changing our way of life, possibly we would get what we wanted.

I could understand the theory, and even found myself excited by it, but I couldn't begin to visualize its application. The other fourteen in my shed were already united, to one another, bonded together in work, in exhaustion, in the search for warmth, in brute mindlessness. I had no desire to re-unite myself with them, nor could I see any way to get them to unite with me. It had taken the amputation of my hand to shock me back to self-awareness; an equivalent shock would be necessary for each of the other fourteen, and I could see no way to supply it.

Yet there might be a way. Perhaps he who had sent me this message also had some idea how to carry it out. For that reason, I kept his note with me all that work period, and used the back of it next sleep period to send him my reply. Out of dirt and saliva I made my ink, a blade of straw became my pen, and laboriously, slowly, one small line at a time, having to wait and wait for each stroke to dry before going on to the next, I wrote my one word answer:

HOW

I had intended to put a question mark at the end, but the process was so long and tiresome I decided the message would have to be comprehensible as it was, and I tucked it away into the straw as close as possible to where I had originally found it.

At the next sleep period, it was gone. I was elated; contact had been established! I couldn't sleep at all.

I never heard from the note writer again.

XVIII

This abortive communication left me very depressed and saddened at the time, but in many ways it was an excellent thing to have happened. In the first place, it got me to think in terms of change, of revolt, ultimately of escape. In the second place, it reminded me that I must depend upon nothing and no one other than myself.

Still, it was a hard lesson, and for some time after I had given up searching for another white slip of paper I sunk into an apathy very like the endless stupor of my companions. Except that, far inside me, I continued—against my will—to think.

There was no incident or event which drove me out of this apathy. It merely faded; slowly, my thinking grew steadily stronger and more purposeful, and a day came when I was looking at the compound outside my work-shed window with an eye escape-oriented for every detail that might be useful, and it occurred to me that my depression was gone and had been gone for quite some time. I smiled, and an official, arriving then with a sheet of numbers for me, said ironically, "What makes you so happy?" It was one of the few times in that place that anyone ever spoke directly to me.

I didn't answer, as I knew no answer was expected. I merely stopped smiling, took the sheet of paper, and turned at once to the machine. But even as I punched the buttons which told the machine these new numbers I continued to think about myself, and about the changes within me, and about my escape, which I now knew must be coming soon.

No one escaped from the compound, of course. Most of the slaves were so steeped in vacancy they no longer remembered themselves or their past lives or the possibility of a world outside the wooden walls. The only slaves not kept stunned by the grind of their labor were a few cripples like me. And because of this, because there was no such thing as escape and never had been any such thing as escape, the officials were very lax, very sloppy.

Still, there was the wall, very high, smooth on the inside, impossible to get over. The only way out was the gate near my workshed. The trucks came in there, on their treads, to be filled with ore from the mine. Trucks and wagons came in carrying food and other supplies or fresh slaves. From time to time someone on a hairhorse would come in, bearing papers of importance for the officials, and sometimes a group of officials would leave for a while in the back of a truck, looking happier than usual.

I intended to escape. In order to escape, it was necessary first to get on the other side of the compound wall. The only way to do that was to leave by the main gate. And the only way to leave by the main gate was somehow to become a part of the normal traffic which left by the main gate. A truck, or a wagon. Somehow, leave on a truck or a wagon.

I studied these vehicles from my window. The ore carriers I had the most opportunity to study, these being the most frequent arrivals, and finally I saw just how it could be done.

The ore carriers, as I said, were on treads. They had a large flat-faced cab in front, in which the driver and his assistant sat, and an ample high-sided metal open-topped storage area in the rear, where the ore was loaded. Between these two, there was a narrow empty space, no more than a foot wide, with the back wall of the cab on one side and the front wall of the storage area on the other. Tread mountings shielded it from view on the remaining two sides. A man inside there could not be seen.

Once the discovery was made, all that was left was timing. I understood by now the normal ebb and flow of my job, knew those points when a long stretch of time would go by before I was given any more numbers to punch. All I had to do was wait till such a time began just as an ore carrier was preparing to leave and at a moment when no official was looking directly toward my shed or the truck. I knew I would have only the one chance, so I permitted several possible opportunities to go by, and waited for that one perfect juxtaposition of factors.

It did come. I looked out my window, scanned this way and that, and saw that everything was perfect. Without hesitation, I performed the action I had rehearsed so often in my mind, raising both feet, sliding them out the window, leaping out onto the ground with both arms wide to help me keep my balance— the lack of a left hand bothered me there, made me tend to lean too heavily to the right—and running across the short stretch of open ground between the shed and the truck.

It was harder to climb over the treads than I'd anticipated also because of the lost hand, and when I reached the top and looked inside I saw what I couldn't possibly have known in advance, that this space between cab and trailer had no floor.

Of course not, of *course* not! Now that I saw it I could understand the reason for it. This truck was meant to be flexible, because of the rough country it was built to traverse, so only the treads—and a few cables underneath, down at the bottom— connected the two parts.

Could I do it anyway? If I could hold on to the top of the trailer front wall with my right hand, and stand on two of those cables which passed from underneath the cab to underneath the trailer, it was still possible. The cables were thick and looked rough-surfaced, but my bare feet were used to walking on the pulverized rock of the compound. As to the height, it seemed to me I would just be able to reach the top while standing on those cables.

In any case, I didn't have the choice. I dared not try to get back again to my workshed. Nor could I stay here, atop the treads in plain view. After only a second's hesitation, I went over the side of the treads, slid carefully down until I felt one of the cables beneath my left foot, and gradually inched myself into position.

It would work. I was extremely uncomfortable, and had to

stretch to my limit to reach the top of the trailer and hook my fingertips over it, but I was nevertheless fixed in place.

And just in time. Just behind my back, the truck engine started. I braced myself, waited, and after the longest five seconds I had ever lived the truck at last lurched forward. Out of the corner of my eye, above the treads, I caught a glimpse of the wall as we passed by.

I was free!

XIX

If I had known in advance what that journey was to be like, it is possible I would have chosen to remain a slave.

In the first place, one of the cables—the one on which I had my left foot—must have had something to do with the exhaust system from the engine, because it soon grew hot, and hotter, and quickly was too hot to touch. I had to keep my left knee bent, holding on only with my right foot on the cable and the fingertips of my right hand clutching the top of the trailer.

If I'd had two hands, it's possible I could have pulled myself up once we'd started, climbed out on top of the load of ore, and traveled in relative comfort. As it was, with only the one hand, I could do nothing but hold on and wait.

If only they'd stop. There were two drivers; sooner or later they'd have to stop while they switched places. But they wouldn't do it. I held on, and chewed my lower lip till it bled, and when I got weak and began to pass out my left foot sagged down onto the hot cable and snapped me awake again.

I considered hammering my elbow against the metal partition behind me, signaling the drivers. But if they found me they would only turn me in at the compound. And I wouldn't go back, not now, not after all I was going through to get out.

Still, I didn't want to die. And I would die, I knew that without doubt; I would die if I lost my grip and fell. Part of me would hit ground while part was still between cab and trailer; I would be torn to pieces.

I finally decided on a gamble, a bad gamble but the only thing I could think of to do. I would try to attract the attention of the drivers, and then I would try to avoid being discovered by them.

Accordingly, I hit my left elbow against the partition. And again. And again. And again.

My elbow was numb, and I was about ready to believe the partition was too thick for them to hear me pounding, when at long last I felt the brakes being applied. The truck ponderously slowed, and the great clattering treads on both sides of me came shuddering to a stop.

The instant the truck stopped, I let go my grip and dropped down onto the ground. I landed wrong, and painfully, on sharp stones, but immediately pushed farther down, squirming my legs under the trailer until I was sitting on the ground, then squirming more, hitting my head against the bottom edge of the cab body, forcing myself along the jagged ground until I was completely under the trailer, on my back, staring up at the pitted metal inches from my face, and waited to see what would happen.

The drivers both looked in the area I'd just vacated, and talked back and forth about what had been making the noise. Something obviously had come loose, but what? One of them got down on hands and knees in front of the cab and looked under; I heard him plainly as he said, "It's pitch black under there. I can't see a thing."

"We'll report it," the other one said. "Come on, let's get going."

They talked about it a minute or two more, then got back into the truck and drove away, the trailer sliding past above me and suddenly leaving clear sky, the violet color of evening on Anarchaos.

It was now necessary to get off the road. I was far too weak to walk by now, but I could still crawl. Slowly, heavily, I rolled myself over onto my stomach, bent my knees, stretched my right hand out ahead of me as far as it would go, and began to drag myself to the side of the road.

I crawled what seemed a considerable distance, over rough,

broken, rocky ground. When at last I could move no more, I was in darkness, in the shadow of a large boulder. I lay my face on the cold ground and closed my eyes.

I came to semi-consciousness some time later, aware of the cold. I could no longer feel my feet or fingers. I thought, "I must get up and walk, or I will freeze to death. I must get up and walk, or I will die."

I thought that. But I didn't move.

XX

I knew I was dreaming. I knew it, and yet everything that happened seemed real and urgent. I was loading an ore cart, down in the mine, and had to hurry, but instead of ore there was stacked a gray mound of severed hands. Both my own hands were missing, so I had to pick up each one between my forearms and raise it high and drop it over the side into the ore cart. Then Gar came and said, "You aren't doing very well. I expected better things of you. Jenna and I expected better things of you." Then Jenna was beside him, and he had an arm around her. She smiled as though to tell me it was all right that I was a failure, and a great river of water came washing down the tunnel, sweeping me away. Gar and Jenna just stood there, the water swirling around them and unable to move them. I wanted desperately to stay with them, but the water washed me down the long tunnel and out into an Arctic night, with icebergs floating by. I was freezing, and drowning, and I climbed out onto a block of ice and lay there, shivering and wet. Then a polar bear came along and stretched out on top of me. I grew warm, with the polar bear on top of me, but I was very frightened of it. My stumps began to sting and burn, and so did my feet. Then someone was cooking stew, and I was sitting at the kitchen table in the house where I'd lived as a boy, and I said to my mother, whose back was to me as she stood at the stove, "Where's Gar?" She turned, not saying anything, and it was the polar bear. Then it was a man with white hair and a white beard, dressed in a long

191

coat of gray fur, with heavy black boots on his feet. He had a spoon in his hand, with which he'd been stirring the stew, and he said, "So you're awake," and I realized I was.

I looked around. I was in a large, crowded wooden room figured by firelight. Flickering darkness and shadows hid the details of the ceiling. The walls were rough logs, the floor was logs planed smooth and the cracks filled with mud, and thick-haired animal skins hung everywhere, on the walls and from beams and draped over furniture. Almost everything in the room was wood, and rough-hewn, home-made: a table, some chairs, shelves on the walls, a trunk, a chest of drawers, a closet. The fireplace was of hand-fashioned tan bricks, with a great fire going inside, lighting the room and cooking the hanging pot of stew. How beautiful was the smell of stew.

I was lying on my back on something soft and deep, and over me were spread blankets of animal skins. I was very confused. I remembered being a slave, and I also remembered some sort of journey spent clinging to the side of a truck, and I remembered a jumble of details from my dream. But what was dream, and what was reality?

And what was this place where I now found myself? And who was the man who had spoken to me? I was sure of little, but of one thing I was certain: I had never seen him before in my life.

He came forward, little drops of liquid falling from the spoon, and he said, "Could you eat? You want some stew?" His voice was rough-grained, as though he seldom had a chance to use it.

My own was worse, when I said, "Please. Thank you."

"Good."

I closed my eyes, trying to restore order to my jumbled brain. The truck? Yes, now I remembered it, traveling on it and managing to leave it, and that I'd been escaping from the compound in which I had been held a slave. My mind ran backward, encompassing Anarchaos, Ulik, Jenna Guild and Colonel Whistler, Gar (dead), prison, fighting, being myself in all situations, everything. All back. All secure.

I was me again.

I opened my eyes, and he was approaching me with a wooden bowl from which steam was rising. I said, with my voice as rusty as unused track, "You found me out there. You brought me in."

"That's right," he said. He stood beside me, and somewhere inside his beard he was smiling, beaming at me.

"You saved my life."

"More than likely. Can you sit up?"

I could, but only with his help. I could now see that I was lying in his bed, a home-made affair like everything else here, built into one corner of the room. I sat with my back propped against the rough wall, feeling dizzy, my body stiff and aching, but not too badly, not much worse than after a normal work period inside the mine. My rags had been stripped off me and I was wearing a bulky fur coat like my rescuer's. Beneath it I was naked.

"Here," he said.

I held out my cupped hand, palm up, and he placed the bowl in it. It felt heavy. "Thank you," I said.

"Is it too hot?"

Acute heat drilled into my palm through the bottom of the bowl, but I welcomed it. "It's good," I said. "It's just right." I brought the bowl to my mouth, tipped it, tasted gravy and meat and vegetables. Gravy dribbled down my chin, making me smile with comfort, like a cat.

"You eat," he said, "and then sleep some more. I've got work to do outside."

I nodded, my mouth full of stew.

It was good food, and I think would have been good even if I hadn't been starving. But it was too rich, and I couldn't keep it down. I was alone in the cabin now, but I felt the roiling in my stomach and I refused to soil either the bed or the floor. I rolled out of the bed, my right hand clutching at everything for support, and somehow I staggered around the walls to the door and pushed it open and lurched outside.

Snow!

I fell face down into it, and emptied my stomach.

"What's this? What's this?"

I raised my head and saw him trotting toward me, bearlike in his heavy clothing, a large axe in his hand. He chopped the axe down into the snow and left it there, the handle angling upward for his return, and ran over to me, shouting, "What are you doing? You'll kill yourself!"

He picked me up, and cleaned my face with a handful of snow. Past him I could see black peaks, snow everywhere, pale moonlight. Moonlight! Where was I?

He carried me inside and put me back to bed. "I didn't want to make a mess in here," I said.

"Sure," he said. "But stay here now. Do you want to try biscuits?"

"Yes." I was very hungry now, hungrier than before I had eaten the stew.

He brought me three pale, hard, bumpy biscuits, and I lay on my back, covered by furs, the biscuits sitting on my chest. I nibbled at them, slowly, and they tasted of salt and soda. But they stayed down. I ate all three, and then I closed my eyes and slept.

XXI

I said, "Am I on Earth?"

He turned to look at me. "You're awake, eh?" He'd been sewing hides together, and he now put them down on the table, got to his feet and came over to look at me. "How do you feel?"

"Better. But weak."

"You want to try the stew again?"

"I think so. And a biscuit with it, to help it stay down."

"Just the thing."

I managed to sit up by myself this time, and prop myself against the wall, while he got a bowl of stew and two more biscuits and brought them over to me. I took the bowl in my cupped right hand again, but then there was no way for me to hold a biscuit. He saw my difficulty and said, "That's all right;

194

just a minute." He brought a chair over and sat down beside me and said, "When you want some biscuit, hand me the bowl."

"Thank you."

"We'll have to get you strong," he said, and smiled within his beard.

I chewed meat, and swallowed it, and said, "My name is Malone."

"Torgmund," he said. "That's me, Torgmund. Nobody ever gave me a name to go in front of it." He laughed, and took the bowl while I ate some biscuit. Watching me eat, he said, "Why'd you ask about Earth? You're on Anarchaos, where you've always been."

"Not always," I said.

He was surprised. "You came here from someplace else?"

"Earth."

"And that out there, that looked like Earth?"

"Because of the moon," I said. "I didn't know Anarchaos had a moon."

"A lot of them don't," he said. "Daysiders," he added, contemptuously. "They never see it, because they've got daylight all the time. But we on the rim, we see it." He chuckled, and gave me back the bowl. "Gives us a kind of day and night," he said. "You take a look out that door now, it's black as the bottom of a hole; you can't see your hand in front of your face." Then he glanced at my stump, and seemed embarrassed.

I said, "We must be farther east. A lot farther than where you found me."

"A full day," he said. "I was coming back from Ulik when I found you. I put you in the back of the wagon and took you home."

I said, "A full day? What sort of day?"

He laughed again, and pointed skyward, and said, "Rim sort. By the moon. Twenty-seven hours, fifteen minutes, Earth Standard. Little longer than an Earth day, isn't it?"

"Yes. You're a trapper."

"That's what I am. And you're a slave."

195

"Yes."

"Got away from one of those mines they have around there."

"Yes, I did."

"I never heard of one of you escaping," he said. "How'd you do it?"

Between mouthfuls of food I told him about working in the mine, and the loss of my hand, and the change of jobs, and how I'd found a way to escape and did it. He listened, bright-eyed, interested in what I had to tell him about a slave's life and enjoying the story of my escape and also, I think, pleased merely at the prospect of someone else in the cabin to talk to. Looking around, I could see that no thought had ever been given to more than one person occupying this place. His had to be a very lonely life.

When I was done eating and telling my story, he took the bowl away and then came back and said, "How's it sitting?"

"Better," I said. I felt warm and comfortable and totally at ease. My eyelids kept closing of their own weight.

"Go ahead and sleep," he said. "We'll talk more tomorrow."

"It's all right," I said. "I can talk now." But even as I said it my eyes shut themselves down and I felt sleep covering me like a net.

When I awoke, the cabin was empty. I rolled over and dozed some more, but lightly, so that I heard Torgmund when he came in. I rolled over again and saw him beating snow off his coat and out of his hair. He saw me looking at him and called, "Snow! A good one!"

"So I see."

"I'll make us something to eat," he said. "You watch me; you'll want to know where I keep things."

He fried eggs this time, and made up something hot that looked like coffee and tasted like charcoal. The eggs, too, were somewhat different in taste to what I remembered from Earth.

After we ate, Torgmund sat beside me again and said, "So you're not a local product, eh?"

"No, I'm from Earth."

"Funny place for a foreigner to come," he said.

196

"I wanted to study the social structure," I said. I hadn't mentioned Gar or my reasons for being here or anything that had happened before my enslavement, and I felt obscurely it was best to keep all of that to myself.

He accepted my answer at once, nodding and saying, "Student. You fellows think you're immune, nothing'll touch you. I guess you know different now."

"I guess I do," I said.

He got to his feet and pushed the chair against the wall, saying, "Time for me to get back to work."

"Outside?"

"Naturally. Got to get your room done."

I frowned at him. "My room?"

He pointed at the far wall. "Right there. When I get the roof on I'll put a door through there; you'll be able to come back and forth without going outside."

I said, "You think I'll be sick so very long?"

He laughed and said, "I sure hope not. I never had a slave before. I wouldn't want one that was sick all the time."

"Slave?"

"You," he said, pointing at me. "What's the matter with you? You addled in your wits?"

I said, "You want to keep me here?"

"You're my slave," he said. "I found you, you're mine."

"I'm *not* a slave."

"Don't lie to me," he said. "You already admitted it. Slave in a mine, ran away." He laughed again and said, "You won't want to run away from here; I'll treat you right. Besides, you'd never get back to dayside on foot." He went over to the door and called back, "You take it easy now, rest up. Two or three days you should be able to get up from there, start earning your keep." He went on out.

I lay in the bed for a long while after he left, staring into the fire across the way. He had been kind to me. More than kind; he had saved my life. And yet, and yet, I couldn't stay.

I knew what I had to do, knew it from the beginning, but I lay there anyway and stared into the fire as though no answer would come to me. Partly that was because I was still so physically weak and such a bad match for the obvious strength of Torgmund, but partly also it was because I did owe him my life, and he was operating out of a simple view of the world, doing nothing that seemed to him wrong. A trapper was a trapper. Daysiders were daysiders. And slaves were slaves. Forever.

Still there was what had to be done. I fell asleep knowing it.

When I awoke he was indoors again, making more stew. When he brought me my bowl he said, "How you coming?"

"Slow but steady," I said, although I was much improved.

During dinner and for a while afterward Torgmund spoke to me of trapping, and of skinning the hides, and of those other activities of his life in which he expected me from now on to take part. But eventually he stretched out on his makeshift bed—furs spread out on the floor—across the room, and I pretended at once to fall back asleep.

But I had never been more awake. My eyes were closed but my ears were open, listening to the sound of his breath going in and out of his body. When the unchanging evenness of that sound convinced me he was fully asleep I crept slowly from my bed.

I was still weak, very weak. Standing made me dizzy, and I wasn't entirely sure I had the strength to do what had to be done. If I were to wait till I was stronger . . .

No. In another two or three days he would know I was stronger and he would no longer expose himself so freely to me. He would most likely lock me away in the room he was building when it was time for him to sleep. So if it was going to be, it had to be now.

I made no noise. I inched around the room, hanging to the walls, my bare feet moving forward tentatively at every step, my hand clutching the wall. It had to be somewhere.

It was. The knife he used in skinning his catch, a long curving steel blade in a sheath hanging on a nail beside the door. Slowly

198

I grasped the hilt and drew the blade out of its sheath, and then I moved to Torgmund.

I had neither the time nor the strength for any sort of stroking cut. All I could do was drive the blade straight down into and through his throat.

It didn't kill him all at once, but the point of the knife was into the floor, pinning him there, and his thrashings finished the job, while I leaned spread-eagled against the wall, gasping and terrified, watching

When it was over, I pulled the knife free and dragged the body outside into the snow. Then I went back in and latched the door and staggered to my bed, too exhausted to do any more.

For hours, the firelight played nightmares around the room.

XXII

It was odd to think of moonlight as signifying day, but the period without moon was so utterly black that the time of moonglow by comparison took on a radiance as bright as day on any world in the cosmos. The moon itself was about half again as large as the moon of Earth, and much yellower in color, the result no doubt of the red sun it was reflecting. The light it produced on the ground was pale and luminescent, with perhaps a touch more of a swollen yellow than in moonlight on Earth.

This moon didn't exactly rise in the normal sense of the term. It appeared at first as a thin curving crescent low toward the horizon, thickened to half-moon shape by "midmorning," was a full moon when at its zenith in the sky, and reversed this process as it slid down the curve of sky toward the horizon again, ending as a crescent, thinner, thinner, then abruptly slicing out, as though a switch had been clicked in some massive control room in the sky.

The night, that time when the moon was blindly groping through the dayside sky, was almost utterly black. Hell stood lonely in a sparsely starred sector of space, as though ostracized for its sins from some civilized star cluster; only a few stray spots of light broke the blind blackness of the sky.

I never left the cabin at night. Once the afternoon moon had reached three-quarter I went inside for good, bolting the door and listening often for the sounds of my enemies approaching. I no longer slept in the bunk, but made for myself a mounded bed of skins and blankets by the door, and slept there with a pistol close by my hand. In the mornings I left the cabin cautiously, clutching Torgmund's rifle as I opened the door inch by inch, prepared to fight off those who might be skulking just out of sight against the outer wall. I felt a great and continuous fear during those days I spent at the cabin, believing the world to be full of faceless enemies out to capture me. I was never afraid that they might murder me, but only that they would capture me. I allowed my beard to grow, dressed myself in Torgmund's home-made clothing, and when walking about outside did my best to change my normal posture and manner—all to keep those unknown watching enemies from recognizing me. Because it was me I believed they were after, me personally, though I couldn't have said why.

I was full of strange thoughts then, like the business of Torgmund's body. Killing him had affected me badly, given me nightmares and worried my mind. I had returned now to a full awareness of what I had come to Anarchaos for in the first place, the vengeance of my dead brother, and it seemed to me that if I were to be worthy and capable of avenging him I would have to have a stronger and more impersonal attitude toward death, so for the first few days I wouldn't bury him. He kept well, lying in the cold and the snow, and I made a point of eating one meal each day outdoors, where I could see him, forcing myself to watch him as I downed a bowl of stew or gnawed at the hard biscuits. But after three days I could stand it no more, and decided to bury him anyway.

It was then I discovered that the cabin was not built on the ground but a thickness of permanent ice down under the snow. I chopped through it with Torgmund's pick, swinging it one-handed, and reached dirt about a foot down. My pick bounced back from that ground as though it were hitting iron. So Torgmund would have to do without burial.

Eventually I merely dragged him some distance away from the cabin and covered him with snow. In the night after that I heard the moaning and yapping of animals a little way off, but I never went to look and so I don't know precisely what happened.

I stayed at the cabin ten days, building my strength. Torgmund had left me almost endless provisions, including a separate unheated shack filled with smoked and frozen meat. Also there were sacks of flour, quantities of a root vegetable like a cross between a potato and a carrot, and commercial tins of powder which combined with hot water to make that coffee-like drink.

All in all, Torgmund had created a fine principality for himself, consisting of three and a half structures, the half being the slave quarters for me that he had never had a chance to finish. In addition to the cabin itself and the storage shed there was a kind of squat barn containing quantities of hay and two hairhorses, with his wagon sitting just out front. Also in the barn were a number of traps, mostly looking as though they'd been brought in for repairs.

I spent many of the moonlight hours in the barn, familiarizing myself with the hairhorses and them with me, since I would need them eventually to take me out of here and back to the Anarchaos version of civilization.

They never shied away from me at all, not even at first. Perhaps, with Torgmund's coat on, they thought I was their master. I doubt they had a much-developed sense of smell, since their own odor was quite strong and likely to blot out subtler aromas. The smell of them reminded me of rancid soup.

Before this I had seen hairhorses only at a certain distance and in passing. Now that I was close to them I saw they were somewhat larger than I'd thought, as powerfully built as a Terran plowhorse but somewhat taller, with long thick gray-black hair like that of a mountain goat back on Earth. Their heads were somewhat wider and shorter than a horse's, but

201

otherwise they were built very similarly indeed. Their eyes were large and brown and inevitably studied me with the calmness of a cow, lacking that nervousness always to be seen in the eyes of horses on Earth.

Since they were mostly like a horse I treated them like horses, patting their sides and speaking softly to them. They seemed totally unafraid, even disinterested, showing enthusiasm only when I daily kicked fodder down to them from the tiny loft above their heads. At such times they came very close to actually prancing.

I had never ridden a horse on Earth and knew next to nothing about them, but in a way I considered that possibly an advantage, since I couldn't make a mistake in handling these creatures based on their similarity in appearance to something they were not. I was learning from scratch and therefore moved with a caution I might not otherwise have shown.

There was a saddle in the barn, and by a process of trial and error I learned how to put it on. Beginning the fifth day, when I felt strong enough, I taught myself to mount, and then to sit astride the unmoving beast, and then to ride it at a slow and even walk, and ultimately how to ride it at a trot. I practiced with both of them, alternating with scrupulous fairness, wanting them both to get a full opportunity to become familiar with me. They would soon become vital to my progress, even to my life.

In all of this I had remarkably fine weather, losing only one day, the seventh, due to bad conditions. A snowstorm had blown up the night before, a whirling raging monster that lashed at the cabin as though enraged to find it poaching on the storm god's land, and though it was blown out by "morning" there was still full cloud cover, which lasted the full day. The moon, of course, had not the strength to cast illumination through cloud, and that day remained as blindly black as any night. Blacker; there were not even the dozen or so faint stars I was used to seeing in the sky.

I remained within the cabin all that day, sullen and pouting, angered at the moon for having deserted me. I left only once, lighting my way fearfully with a burning branch from the fire, going by necessity to the barn to feed the hairhorses. I couldn't carry both the torch and a weapon, so I had Torgmund's pistol tucked inside my belt and was prepared at any instant to hurl the torch into the snow, yank out the pistol, and fight my way back to safety. However, I was unmolested, fed the hairhorses successfully, and returned at once to the warm protection of the cabin, locking the door again behind me.

As to the wood—a heavy, almost smokeless, beautifully slow-burning variety—it was stacked against the cabin's rear wall. There were no trees, no vegetation of any kind growing within sight of the cabin, which meant that Torgmund must have had to make frequent trips in the direction of dayside for both fuel and fodder.

In the totally atomistic society of anarchists, Torgmund had chosen for himself perhaps the only sensible and viable form of life; absolute separation from and independence of all other human beings. And, of course, it was only when he forcibly introduced a second human being into his atomistic existence that he ran into trouble.

So here was another face of Anarchaos, the rugged individualist's heaven. So long, that is, as he never bent a fraction of an inch from the solitary implications of his principles.

There were no books in the cabin, no pictures, no films or music tapes. In many ways, Torgmund had been no more than an unusually clever animal, a sort of beaver combined with bear. His remote freehold, though it used a few of the most immediately practical of man's discoveries and inventions, was finally a refutation of and a turning away from all of man's history, all of his progress, all of his unending attempt at self-civilization.

After ten days, and though the outer world still frightened me, I was much relieved to be getting away from there.

I took both hairhorses. One I saddled, and would ride, while the other I loaded with Torgmund's provisions. His rifle and pistol and axe and knife I kept with me; spare furs and clothing

I added to the pack animal's load, and at moonrise on the eleventh day I was ready to leave.

There remained only one problem, but that one insoluble. I had no idea in which direction lay dayside. In deepest night I had gone outside—in terror, of course—to stare toward the horizon in all directions, but had seen not even the faintest glow anywhere. Torgmund had no compass, and even if he had it would have done me no good as I didn't know what an Anarchaotic compass would be oriented toward.

My only clue was Torgmund's statement that the moon did cross dayside, which meant that the spot where the moon first appeared above the horizon had to be either east or west and could not be north or south. I also knew that I was one day's ride from the evening zone in which Torgmund had found me, though I had no way of knowing what this meant in absolute terms, or how one day of Torgmund's travel would equate with one day of my own.

Still, one had to make a choice. I finally decided to travel toward the morning moon, giving three days to the trip, and if by the end of the third day I had not come within sight of the dayside horizon I would turn around and come back and try the other way. If I had guessed wrong it would mean a full week wasted, but there was nothing else to do. And, just in case, I brought along a number of thin branches from the woodpile in back, to leave as markers along the way, to guide me should I have to turn back. If my first guess was wrong, I would want to be able to find the cabin again, in order to restock myself with supplies.

I set off the first thing, on the morning of the eleventh day, with the moon barely a slit crescent—like a nearly closed eye—at the far horizon ahead of me. I rode the lead hairhorse, with the pack second beast trailing us, kept to us by a rope around its neck and tied at the other end around the pommel of the saddle.

We moved at a steady lope, the hairhorses trotting with easy muscularity across the snowy and icy ground. The rhythmic *chack-chack-chack* of their hoofs on the crust of snow and ice was the only sound.

We moved directly toward the thin crescent of moon, passing near to where I had left Torgmund's body. I did not look in that direction as we went by, though it was anyway probably still too dark for me to have seen anything.

When, a few minutes later, I looked back, the cabin was a tiny black smudge against the pale whiteness of the snow. I faced front again, folded my gloved hand around the pommel, felt the flex and flow of the animal's muscles against my knees, and rode onward toward the slowly opening luminous yellow eye.

XXIII

Although it was no colder at night than in the false moonday, it somehow seemed colder then. I assumed it was so because I was no longer in motion, but had to huddle fireless in one spot and wait for the moon to rise ahead of me once again. I would have preferred to travel constantly but of course could not; there was nothing but the moon itself to give me my direction.

Until the end of the third day, I saw nothing to indicate whether I was going in the right or wrong direction. It had seemed to me that the temperature must noticeably go either up or down, depending on whether or not I was moving toward dayside, but the biting cold, so far as I could tell, remained unchanged. That is, it seemed to be at one temperature when I was in motion and at a lower one when I was at rest, and these two temperatures did not seem to vary.

Toward evening of each day—the inaccuracy of these terms grates on me, but they are the only ones I can use—I would dismount, hobble the animals, and dig for myself a shallow sort of trench in the snow. In this I would lie, with furs beneath me and above me, and sleep or think the hours away until moonrise.

The cold affected my wrist badly, making it sting and burn. I kept it wrapped in furs, but to no effect, and the constant pain caused me to be irritable and impatient when there was no value in such feelings.

I don't know how long the faint light was visible before I noticed it. My attention was exclusively, vitally, almost balefully upon the black horizon ahead of me or—as we moved through the dark "afternoon"—in quick glances behind me to be sure I was still moving directly away from the declining moon. I was staring ahead more intently than ever as my self-imposed time limit neared its end; three days I had given myself and three days were just about up. The thought of having to retrace all that distance to the cabin, and then to have to begin the journey all over again in the opposite direction, both depressed and maddened me. If only, far out there across the snowy waste ahead of me, there would come some slight tinge of color on the horizon.

But it wasn't ahead of me that the light appeared. I had just about decided to stop for the night, and was looking around for a shallow dip in which to bed down—there was sometimes wind out here—when I saw that thin vague rosy line far far away, the line of light on a flat horizon.

Could it be man-made, some sort of city? No, that was impossible. It extended too far along the horizon, in the first place, and in the second place there was no city anywhere along the rim. The cities of Anarchaos were five; Ulik, Moro-Geth, Prudence and Chax at the four points of a diamond, and Ni at their center. The sun had to be off in that direction, to my left.

I turned at once, prodding the hairhorses to greater speed, riding along as though I expected to attain that horizon in half an hour. The moon, low to my left, winked out in its abrupt manner, and all about me now the land was black as the bottom of death. But I kept going, with that thin rusty glowing line to guide me, pushing on past the time when the animals and I usually stopped for food and rest, pushing on until all at once the hairhorse I was riding seemed to stumble, and for just an instant to regain its balance, and then down it went, head foremost, somersaulting in the air and hurling me clear to land bruisingly out in front on the snow and ice.

206

I rolled and rolled, then staggered to my feet and limped back to them, guided by the sounds they were making; the fallen one had a constant, almost an apologetic, cough, while the other was filling the night with ear-splitting whinny-shrieks, as though someone were torturing the mate of the missing link.

The next little while was a nightmare, as I tried in the darkness to regain control. The animal I'd been riding had stumbled in a hole or some such thing and had broken his leg, and was lying now on the ground, thrashing about and making that coughing sound. The other one was still attached to the hurt one by the rope that went from his own neck to the saddle of the other, and this nearness to a wounded member of his own species had him in a white panic of terror, causing him to rear and kick and try to run away, causing him to find the strength even to drag the hurt one for little distances this way and that through the snow. And I, fighting to restore order, was forced to work in blackness and haste and exhaustion, encumbered by the cold and my bulky clothing and a missing hand.

As much as possible, I kept them between me and the line of light at the horizon. That way, it was possible to get occasional quick glimpses of them in silhouette as they reared and fought, attached to one another by that taut stout rope.

At first I tried merely to calm the uninjured one, but with absolutely no success. He was so mad with terror that he wasn't even aware of my existence, and I ran every risk of being knocked over and trampled by him as he leaped and writhed at the end of the rope. After a while, it seemed to me that if only the hurt one would be quiet perhaps the other one would grow calm as well, but of course with his broken leg he wasn't ever going to be quiet. Unless he was dead.

I knew that I would have to kill him anyway, though I hated the thought. But my pistol had fallen out of my clothing when I'd taken the spill, and there was no way to find it in the blackness, and my rifle was still in its sheath, attached to the saddle on the wounded hairhorse.

The only thing to do was somehow get the rifle. The one on

the ground was thrashing, and the other one was yanking him around this way and that, but I did manage at last to get in close enough and then—lying on my stomach on the beast's heaving flank—I found the saddle with my hand, and then the sheath, and then the rifle. I was kicked several times in the attempt, but no matter. Holding for life to that rifle I jumped back out of the way of all those kicking legs and got ready to do the killing.

A rifle is a hard thing for a man with one hand to fire. I held it in my right hand, my left arm up and across my chest so the rifle barrel could rest on the forearm, and in that position I could fire with fair accuracy one time. But there was no way for me to control the recoil, so that with each firing the rifle barrel would leap into the air and then drop back again painfully on my left forearm.

It took three shots before I finally hit the silhouette of that streaming, thrashing, coughing head. Then it dropped to the snow as though yanked from beneath, and I fell down on my side on the snow and lay there panting as though I had run around the world.

Slowly the living one lost its panic and stopped making those terrible screams. When all was quiet I got again to my feet, dragging myself through all my movements, my limbs feeling as though weighted down with lead. I took fodder from the pack animal's back and fed it, dead grass in the snow beside the dead body. I took food out for myself as well, but I had no heart to eat it and so threw it away into the snow.

I looked at the light on the horizon, and took no pleasure in it.

I got my sleeping furs and dragged them a little off from where the living animal and the dead were tethered together. I scraped out a shallow pit for myself in the snow, made my bed, and settled into it sleeplessly to wait for the moon to rise.

XXIV

Seven days later I came at last to a city and it was not the right one.

After turning to the left from my original direction, I moved directly toward the red sun for four days, traveling gradually from a world of black and white into a world of fever and rust. The cold lessened, the horizon grew brighter, and the moon dimmed in a steadily reddening sky.

I felt one instant of naked primitive fear when the arc of Hell first crept up into sight above the horizon's edge ahead of me. I wanted fiercely at that moment to turn back, to flee again into the darkness, to cross the dead land once more and find Torgmund's cabin and stay there until I died. Out ahead of me, under the unmoving and baleful red sun, men crawled and cursed and preyed upon one another; when I rode among them they would surely fall upon me and gobble me up.

My mount felt it, too, the horror shimmering away out there under the red sun, or perhaps he merely sensed my own sudden disquiet. In any case, he grew restive, fidgety, and by his movements distracting my attention and breaking the spell. I soothed him, patting his long neck, and we moved on.

We traveled somewhat more rapidly now, as the light improved, even though my animal was more heavily loaded than before. I'd packed as much food as I could, leaving the remainder—and the extra furs—with the dead hairhorse back in the anonymous snow.

For the first two days of this stage of the journey it was still possible to tell time by the moon, seen ever more faintly in its passage across the sky from right to left. By the third day, however, Hell had crept upward until it was fully in view, a flaming red circle in the air just above the horizon, making it no longer possible to see the moon. From then on I counted the days by my own cycles: when I was hungry, when I was tired, when I was rested.

I came upon the road just as I was deciding to call the third day at its end. This road crossed my path at right angles, a broad bleak empty tan swath across the tundra-like plain. I halted at its edge, looking to left and right, seeing nothing. Since it was approximately time to stop in any case, I put off deciding which way to go until the following day. I turned about, retraced my steps until I found a shallow gully out of sight of the road, and bedded down there for the "night."

After I awoke, while feeding the hairhorse and myself, I considered the problem of where to go from here. Since I had turned left to come into dayside, it seemed to me that to turn left again would be to return to the rim. Still, this road had to lead from somewhere to somewhere, so that it was more sensible to take it than merely to cross it and keep going forward toward Hell. Although Hell's position didn't seem right for it, I finally made a guess that this was the road between Ulik and Yoroch Pass—where Gar was buried—and that if I turned right I would be moving toward Ulik and must eventually find it.

It was a wrong guess. As I worked it out later, I had been acting all along on certain wrong assumptions, such as that the mine was due east of Ulik when it was actually somewhat to the north-east. I had also assumed that Torgmund's cabin was east of the mine, but in fact it was almost straight north of there, with both mine and cabin to dayside of the Evening Mountains. (I should have realized my thinking was off when—besides the sun being in the wrong position—there was no mountain range to cross in my traveling, but my thoughts in that period were still none too clear.)

Again, the Anarchaotic moon did not travel from west to east, as I had supposed, but from north-west to south-east, so that *I* had been traveling north-west when I'd first left Torgmund's cabin, and all of my wandering since then had been based on false postulates.

It is as though, on a map of Anarchaos, one were to draw a square, with Ulik at the lower right corner, the central city of Ni at the lower left corner, the northerly city of Prudence at the upper left corner, and the point where I caught my first glimpse of dayside being at the upper right corner. When I turned and moved toward the light on the horizon I was traveling, although I didn't know it, along a diagonal from corner to corner, angling down into the civilized dayside Anarchaos like an arrow through a heart, on a line that would have taken me eventually to Ni, far far away at the noon center of man's settlement on this evil planet.

And the road I had come across was the equivalent diagonal the other way, a line drawn between Prudence at the north and Ulik at the east. I had stumbled on the Prudence-Ulik road, carefully but erroneously thought out what to do, and turned my back on Ulik, going off to the right, north-easterly again, toward distant Prudence.

I traveled this road for the next three days. In that time I occasionally caught glimpses of other travelers at a distance, but my uneasiness was so great that I invariably left the road and went into hiding until they had passed. Several times I considered approaching a party of travelers—I was the only solitary wayfarer to be seen on this road—in order to ask directions and be sure I was heading toward Ulik, but fear and caution and bad memories induced me to remain hidden.

Toward the end of the third day I began to see the towers of a city far ahead. The animal and I were both tired, both hungry, but I pressed on. I had no way of knowing how long I'd been gone—two months, six months—but all at once a great urgency came over me, I felt the full weight and impact of my purpose as I had not felt it since the day I'd been shot in the entrance of Piekow Lastus' hovel, and I found myself wanting to know *now* who had killed Gar, and why, and why they had thought it necessary to kill me also.

A short while later I reached the scrubby outskirts of the city, where the ramshackle huts and lean-tos were far apart, abandoned, most of them collapsing. It was as though the people who had once lived out here had decided to move closer to the center of town, like animals who huddle closer together on the coldest nights. In actual fact, it was not movement which had caused these shacks to be abandoned, it was shrinkage. The population of Anarchaos, which had gone steadily upward in its first fifty years or so, had then leveled off for a generation and was now on the decline. Anarchaos was moving slowly—too slowly—toward its inevitable dissolution. These empty shacks on the outskirts of the city would never be used again.

And the city was not Ulik. Looking at the towers, still far away, I could see that they were different, that this was some other city. I couldn't yet understand it, and pressed forward even faster, looking for someone to explain to me where I was.

The first person I saw was an old man hobbling along the road ahead of me, also heading inward. I hurried to catch up, but when he heard the hoofbeats behind him he cast one terrified glance over his shoulder and ran off to the right, behind a shack of corrugated metal. I rode after him, found him cowering in a corner with his arms over his head, and at length convinced him that I merely wanted to know the name of the city I was entering.

He blinked at me, watery and weak. Everything about him was watery and weak. He had lived so long, I guess, by constant playing of this one part: the rabbit.

"Prudence, sir," he quavered. "You're coming into Prudence, if you please, sir."

"Prudence."

"Prudence, sir. Yes, sir. Prudence, sir."

I turned away from the old man's bowings and waverings, urged the hairhorse back to the road and on in toward the heart of the city. The wrong city.

In my mind's eye I could see the map shown me by L. L. Goss back in Ice Tower, and seeing it I could begin to see some of the mistakes and wrong guesses I had made. Well, no matter. In Prudence there would be a Union Commission Embassy. There I would find sanctuary, where I might rest until I was ready to face Anarchaos on its own terms once more. And until I was strong enough to return to Ulik and enter the Ice Tower and obtain the answers I was denied the last time I was there. Ice Tower at Ulik, that was where the answers must be.

Riding, thinking, I heard the sound of whirling wings and looked up. Passing overhead, not very far from the ground, was

212

a helicopter of yellow and green, with a symbol clearly visible on its underside: A hammer with a dog's head.

"Yaaaahhhh!" I cried, hardly myself understanding why, and raised my empty wrist in challenge, and dug my heels into my hairhorse's ribs and gave furious and futile chase.

XXV

It was not easy to find the UC Embassy; no one on Anarchaos speaks unnecessarily to strangers. I could only roam back and forth through the center of the city amid the syndicate towers until eventually I did find the one with the silver UC in thin letters over the entrance.

Unlike all the other towers, there were no armed guards hanging around outside the entrance, although some watch apparently was kept; the door opened before I could knock, just as I was dismounting. The man who looked out at me wore the blue Union Commission uniform and his hand hovered near the weapon on his hip. He said, "What is it you're looking for?"

"Sanctuary. I'm an off-worlder."

He looked at my heavily bearded face, at my fur clothing, at the animal I'd been riding. "An off-worlder?"

"From Earth. I was captured and made a slave. I escaped."

He was still dubious, but he said, "Come in," and stepped to one side.

I said, "What about my hairhorse?"

"You can't take it to Earth with you," he said. "Leave it out there. Don't worry, someone will take it."

I felt uncomfortable to be leaving it, but of course he was right; I wouldn't be needing a hairhorse anymore. I dropped the reins, and followed him inside.

"Tell me," I said. "Is it day or night?"

"Evening." He glanced at his watch. "Twenty past seven." Then he smiled thinly at me, saying, "That was an Earthman's question. Come along, we'll get you food and shelter. You can do the paperwork in the morning."

213

The food and shelter he then offered me were both astonishing, recalling to me the kind of meal, the kind of room, the kind of bed I had at one time taken for granted but had now been without for so long that to an extent I had forgotten them. I slept that night like a dead man, and rose shortly before noon to eat the biggest breakfast of my life.

After breakfast came the paperwork I'd been promised, and there seemed to be endless amounts of it, administered by a slender ascetic young man in a barren and windowless office. He had a high-pitched voice with very little strength in it, so that even though we sat on opposite sides of the same desk I had from time to time to ask him to repeat a question. I answered all of his questions exactly, editing out only my desire to learn about the murder of my brother, and being unable to give him an exact answer only once, when he wanted to know how long I'd been a slave.

"It's just for the records," he said, in his reedy voice. "Make a guess."

"Three or four months," I said. "Maybe six months."

He wrote something, and went on.

When he was done with paper forms, there was another set to do, these the oral records. He produced a microphone from within the desk, asked me many of the same questions all over again, and at last announced that we were finished. I thanked him, left his office, and found outside in the corridor the man who had first met me at the door yesterday, a stolid quiet sort named Chafrey.

They still weren't sure about me, of course. There was the possibility I was a native trying to fob myself off as an off-worlder in order to wangle free transportation away from Anarchaos. Such attempts had been known to happen. Until they could be sure, Chafrey was never very far from me.

The next three days were a time of lazy waiting. I ate and slept and sat around and felt my battered body rebuilding itself. I shaved the beard away and was astonished at the face revealed beneath; it was unchanged. All over my body were the marks of

214

my recent existence, everywhere but on my face. Hidden away beneath all the hair, this face had survived intact, unscathed, looking now foolish and anachronistic, a lone toy forgotten and left behind in the room of a boy who had grown up.

The Embassy doctor looked me over and pronounced me in surprisingly good condition, considering my recent history. As to my wrist, he told me the amputation had been rough and ready but the wrist had healed well, the residual pain should soon end, and a prosthetic hand could be attached to the stump with little or no trouble.

"Not here, of course," he said. "On Earth. I doubt there's any prosthetic devices at all on this benighted planet."

The UC people I met within the Embassy were unanimous in their hatred and contempt of Anarchaos and the entirety of its population.

On the morning of the fourth day Chafrey came to me at breakfast and said, "We've got transportation for you to Ni. When you've had breakfast we'll go on up."

"I'm done now," I said.

I had wanted to ask for transit to Ulik, but it would have been hard to explain why I wanted to go back there without also explaining about Gar, so I'd agreed to the trip to Ni. The Embassy people assumed I would then take the next shuttle flight off-planet, and I said nothing to dissuade them. The fact was, I intended to pick up some more money and fresh clothing from my luggage checked at Ni, and then return to Ulik by surface transportation, as I had done the first time.

Chafrey and I went up in the elevator to the roof, where the helicopters landed. The elevator opened into a small bare room with a bench along one wall. Chafrey walked over to the door across the way, opened it, and said, "Here he is, Mr. Rose."

"Thank you." A youngish, smiling, burly man came in and looked at me. "You ran away," he said. His head was shaved.

Rose!

Chafrey said, as the second one came in, "Can you and Mr. Malik handle him all right?"

"Oh, I'm sure we can," said Rose. He produced a pistol and pointed it at me. "Don't be stupid now," he said.

I yelled, "Chafrey! What have you done?"

"You weren't even smart about it," Chafrey said to me, and I could hear in his voice the hatred and contempt these people all expressed when they spoke of Anarchaos or its inhabitants. "Didn't you know we'd check? No Rolf Malone arrived at Ni Spaceport within the last six months or the last year or the last *two* years!"

"But I did! I did!"

"The only Rolf Malone on their list down there is a man who came here over four years ago, went to work for Ice Syndicate, and was shot by robbers. Ice Syndicate reported his death. You're an escaped slave, all right, but everything else you said was hogwash. The Union Commission isn't interested in what you people do to one another; you can stew in your own juices. Your owners reported you missing, warned us you might come here, and asked for you back." He gave Malik and Rose a look of superiority and contempt. "We were happy to oblige," he said sarcastically, turned on his heels, entered the elevator, and the doors slid shut in my face as I tried desperately and uselessly to run after him.

Rose said, softly, "You surprised us, Rolf. So we missed you the first time, isn't that odd?"

Malik spoke for the first time, saying, "But we're lucky. We've got a second chance."

They wouldn't dare shoot me here, in the UC building. I fought them, but they pinned my arms and dragged me out onto the roof and across the windy flatness to the green and yellow helicopter with the symbol on its side: A hammer with a dog's head.

XXVI

Malik tapped my knee and pointed at the window. "Take a look," he said. "We're flying over Moro-Geth."

216

I looked, without interest. Below me was the familiar cluster of needle shapes surrounded by its sprawl of shacks, the whole scabbed over by the flushed light of Hell. "It's lovely," I said.

Malik laughed and said, "I love you, Rolf; I'll be sorry to say goodbye to you." Then, laughing and shaking his head, he went up front to tell Rose the funny thing I had said.

I had now lived two days longer than I had expected, and in these two days I had come to know Malik and Rose well enough to be bored by them. They were no more than large children, great hearty boys with blunt hearty senses of humor and easy hearty camaraderie, even in the company of someone they had once tried to murder. Even in the company of someone they would soon be trying to murder once again.

My lethargy and boredom was perhaps at least partially the result of terror, of not knowing when my last breath would come, of not knowing what lay in store for me before that last breath was drawn. I found myself somnolent, always half asleep, never able to really *care* about what was happening to me.

It wasn't that I was drugged, though I might have been, since I did eat whatever they fed me. But this lethargy struck me earlier than that, came over me the instant Malik and Rose put their hands on me and dragged me out to the waiting helicopter. My resistance, useless anyway, ceased entirely once they had me inside the copter. I sat between them, my eyes closed as the copter lifted from the roof, and waited for the bullet.

It didn't come. Instead, I was flown a short distance to another tower, taken down inside it to a plain but comfortable room, and kept there for two days. I was fed, but not talked to, not threatened, not *dealt with* at all. It seemed almost as though they had forgotten what they meant to do with me.

Until today. Malik and Rose abruptly entered my room, joked together as I dressed, and then took me up to the top of the tower and back into the helicopter. The helicopter then flew us to an airfield I took to be south-west of Prudence, and we transferred to the plane in which we now were riding. On the plane, on the hangars, on the backs of the ground crew's coveralls, everywhere was that same yellow and green symbol, the hammer with the dog's head.

I roused myself sufficiently as we entered the plane to ask Malik, "What is this syndicate called?"

"Sledge," he said.

"What corporation has it?"

He laughed in a jolly manner. "That would be telling," he said. Then we took our seats, the plane lifted, and we traveled south and west under the red sun.

On the trip, Malik and Rose joked together and with me, their voices and manner turning the interior of the plane into a locker room after a strenuous game of some sort. I didn't even pretend to be interested.

After we flew over Moro-Geth, their heartiness seemed to diminish. They glanced at one another and at me like men entering a situation they themselves didn't fully understand. The plane seemed to veer away into a more determinedly western direction, Hell receded down the sky behind us, and out ahead grew the darkness and cold of the rim.

In a way, I welcomed that onrushing black. It was like going home, like leaving an evil place and going to a place that was safe. But of course that was foolish; I was traveling with Malik and Rose, and no place that they were would be safe for me.

Rose was the wanderer of the two. While Malik spent most of his time sitting near me, watching me, Rose drifted back and forth, sometimes up front with the pilot, sometimes back with us, sometimes in the compartment behind us, sometimes merely pacing the aisle like an usher waiting for the show to begin.

One time, Rose came back from the pilot's compartment and said, "We'll land soon."

"Good," said Malik. "Fine." They had both lost much of their heartiness by now.

Rose went on back to the rear compartment and returned with heavy coats, boots, gloves and hats for all three of us. "Better put this stuff on," he told me. "It's going to be cold out there."

I didn't care. There was no reason to obey, but there was also no reason to disobey. I put on the extra clothing, and a short while later we landed. Malik and Rose took my arms and we marched together off the plane.

It was very late afternoon here, Hell an orange disc across the maroon plain. The airfield where we had landed looked primitive, makeshift, with small prefabricated huts near the runway. Snow was piled up all around, where it had been cleared away by motorized plows. Malik and Rose and I climbed into a small auto and, as behind us the plane taxied about and took off again, climbing abruptly into the sky as though it had been startled, we rode past the prefabricated huts and through a guarded gate in a high metal fence and along a snowy, silent, empty, anonymous road, straight down a channel between two high mounds of snow.

Although it was cold here, the temperature wasn't low enough to warrant the heavy clothing we'd put on. Our driver was dressed more lightly than we. I didn't understand this—even realize there was anything to understand—until our auto made a sharp right turn, drove down a bumpy white incline, and came to a stop beside the ocean.

It was like pictures I'd seen on Earth of Antarctica. The white snow leading down and down, and stopping, and then the black water stretching out away from us into the deeper blackness of the rim. The farther horizon couldn't be seen out there; it was too far away and too remote from the light of Hell.

There was a dock, a rickety-looking affair, all metal covered with a sheen of ice. Two shaky-seeming prefabricated shacks stood on shore next to where the dock began. Out at the farther end a small boat bobbed at the end of a black rope. A man stood out there, at the edge of the dock, looking this way. Waiting for us.

I said, "What is this?"

It was the driver who answered me: "Sea of Morning." It was said matter-of-fact, all the implications of beauty bleached out of it. The Sea of Morning, just a place, with black water, very cold. Out from shore there were whitecaps and a feeling of wind.

I shivered, and hunched farther within my heavy clothing.

Malik and Rose stepped down from the auto and brought me along with them, each holding one of my arms. They walked me out to the end of the dock, and the man there said, "Well, it took you long enough." He looked the same as them, only a few years older.

Rose said, "We weren't flying the plane."

"It doesn't matter. Get him aboard."

I yanked my arms free and went running. The footing was bad and I slipped and skidded with every step, my arms wheeling around as I ran.

Malik and Rose caught up with me just as I reached shore, but I fought them as much as I could. Once I was taken out across that water, I knew, there would be no way to come back.

But they were two to my one, and finally got me under control. They carried me back along the dock, Malik holding my arms and Rose my legs. I kicked and thrashed, but nothing I could do would make them lose their balance or their grip on me.

Panting, Rose said, "Why don't you give it up? It's all over, ride along with it, give it up."

The other man was still waiting for us near his little boat, showing a heavy impatience. "He should have been tranquilized," he said, as I was carried close.

"Phail wants him ready to talk," said Malik.

"If possible," said the other man.

Malik released my arms and stepped back, and they all three watched me, Malik and Rose warily, the other man wearily. So in the end I stepped down into the little boat with no more trouble.

The other three followed me, the new man taking a position by the engine in the back. Malik released the line holding us to the dock, the engine sputtered and started, and we curved out and away, toward the darkness.

Peering ahead, hoping to see, I tried to remember what I had once known about the Sea of Morning. That it was the largest body of water on the planet, forming the western edge of the rim, extending from the Black River in the south nearly all the way to the White Wall in the north. That its far shore, around on the night side of the planet, was permanently frozen. That the first colonists who'd stumbled on it, not realizing its magnitude, had called it West Lake, a name changed later on by some sentimentalist to Sea of Morning even though the quality of the light here seemed to me more like evening—approaching night.

My own night, it seemed.

Looking back, after a few minutes, I could no longer clearly distinguish the line of the shore. The black water merely faded away toward indistinguishable grayness. There seemed to be some sort of mist behind us, through which the light of Hell feebly burned, dissipating itself, turning the mist dusky rose above, gray below.

I faced front again. I had ceased to wonder why it was I was still alive, but I couldn't help the proddings of curiosity as to where I was being taken. Some island? Or all the way to the ice-shelf preceding the farther shore?

Neither.

When the ship loomed up before us, it was so sudden I ducked instinctively backward, thinking that the ship and this tiny boat had nothing to do with one another, were unaware of each other's existence, and would surely crash in an instant, hurling the four of us into water too cold to survive in, too far from shore, surrounded by a mist that hid movement and seemed to deaden sound.

But I was wrong; ship and boat were connected, both parts of the same incomprehensible nightmare. When, after the first shock, I looked up the cold wet black plates of the hull, there was the familiar hammer symbol on the prow, and the name, in white letters: SLEDGE.

Malik's hand closed on my shoulder. "Take it easy," he said, close against my ear. "Take it easy, now; don't get yourself excited."

A portion of the hull, at waterline, yawned open in front of us, like the mouth of a whale. We bobbed closer, a cork in a stream, our nose pointing this way and that but always moving steadily closer to the gaping hole, and then we were inside, and the hull shut down behind us again with a great shriek of rusted metal.

Inside, the water we floated on looked bilious. There were yellow lights high up in the metal ceiling, among the metal beams. There were metal walls painted yellow, reflecting the yellow light. There was a black metal platform sticking out of the wall just above the water, and a door in the wall by the platform. The door opened and two sailors in heavy workclothes came out and stood on the platform.

Malik moved forward to the prow of the boat. One of the sailors tossed him a line, the other end of which was knotted through a metal ring in the platform floor. Malik pulled us hand over hand along the line till the prow of the boat hit the platform. Then the two sailors held the boat, prow and stern, while we all four climbed out.

We stood around as the sailors tied the other end of the line through the ring in the nose of the boat. Then the sailors went back through the door and shut it behind them. They had not once looked at me or at any of the others with me.

The new man said to Malik and Rose, "Take his clothing off."

I fought them again, this time out of bewilderment, and lost again. They stripped my clothing away and held me shivering. The new man gestured with his head toward the bilious black water just below the platform, and Malik and Rose raised me and threw me out into the air over the water and I fell and the water closed over me.

It was freezing. It was so cold it was like falling into knives. It was so cold it was hot. It was so cold I could do nothing: not breathe, not move my arms, not try to surface nor dive, swim nor float, kill myself nor save myself. I fell into the water like a rubber statue, and sank, and returned to the surface, and bobbed there, shocked beyond reaction.

At the new man's command, they fished me out again, Malik and Rose. I was held up by their hands like a drowned cat, and the new man said to me, "It is cold."

I was trembling violently, nerves and muscles snapping in and out of tension. I couldn't have replied even if I'd had something to say.

He went on: "We are three miles from shore, and moving. We will never be less than three miles from shore, and usually we will be more than that. You couldn't survive it, I hope you understand that. You'd be dead inside five minutes, if you tried swimming to shore. Do you understand that?"

I tried to nod, tried desperately to nod. I didn't want him to think he needed to demonstrate his truth to me a second time.

He was satisfied. He said to Malik and Rose, "Take him away. Dry him. Dress him. I'll tell Phail he's here."

Malik and Rose turned me. They opened the door and led me into the ship.

XXVII

I thought: *I'll never be warm again.*

I was dry now, in heavy clothing, and sitting in a warm room, but down inside my skin, down in my veins and bones, in my stomach and my heart and my throat, I was trembling with the cold. I sat there and shivered endlessly, my arms wrapped around myself.

Malik said to me, "Oh, come on, Rolf, it isn't that bad," and the door behind him opened.

The man who came in was young, but bore himself with such arrogant irritation that it was obvious he had great authority. He said, "Is he ready for me?"

Malik and Rose were both suddenly nervous. "Yes, sir," said Malik, and motioned at me as though inviting this new one—this must be the Phail I'd heard mentioned—to help himself to me.

Phail came over and looked down at me, a crooked smile on his lips. "And to think I had you once," he said. "Had you and let you get away. You remember the last time we met?"

I raised my eyes and studied his face. The lines of arrogance were so deep, he must have been born with them. He had a cultured face, a face that showed breeding and education, but also betrayed degeneracy; the scion of a bloodline in decline. His hair was sandy, dry-looking, lying flat to his skull and brushed back from his forehead. His eyes were a peculiarly pale blue, snapping with impatience and contempt.

I said, "I don't know you." My voice and enunciation were both affected badly by the chill I felt, embarrassing me. I wanted to be equal to this man, superior to him. I felt instead like a cowering mongrel, waiting for a kick from his boot.

"You don't remember me?" he asked, and then I did.

The mine. He was one of the three young officials who had come on the tour of inspection. One had called me Malone, the second had reminded him that Malone was dead, and the third had said nothing. This was the third man, the silent one, watchful, keeping his own counsel.

He nodded now, smiling at me. "I can see you do," he said. "It comes back to you now, doesn't it?"

"Yes."

"Yes. Some day you must tell me how you escaped from that camp; you're the only one who ever has." His smile broadened. "You'll be pleased to know the camp personnel were appropriately punished for letting you go. They've taken your place, the lot of them."

"You made them slaves?"

"Doesn't that please you? They were your masters; I should think you'd be pleased to hear they now know what it was like."

I looked at my wrist; a shiny bluish glaze of skin had lately grown over the stump. I said, "The doctor, too?"

"Oh, the doctor especially. He was the one who said it was safe to put you on that job. And he cut your hand off, after all, when perhaps he could have saved it."

I looked at my wrist. Sometimes, when I was looking the other way, I seemed to feel the hand still there; I seemed to be able to flex the fingers, close them into a fist. I tried it now, looking, and saw useless muscles move in my forearm. "I'm sorry for him," I said.

Phail was as surprised as I was. "I should think you'd hate him."

"I don't," I said, not understanding why that should be true. Wasn't vengeance the fuel that kept me going?

"A remarkable attitude," said Phail, the contempt in his voice like a slap across the face. "But not what we're here to discuss." He turned toward Malik and Rose. "A chair."

Rose brought it, a heavy padded chair, carrying it over hurriedly and putting it down where Phail could sit directly in front of me, our knees almost touching. I watched this operation, distracted by odd questions about myself: Why didn't I hate the doctor and the other officials from the mine? Why wasn't I afraid of this vicious man Phail?

Phail sat down, leaned forward, tapped my knee, and smiled falsely at me. "You aren't going to be difficult, are you?"

"About what?"

"There are questions for you to answer."

I waited. I didn't know yet whether I would be difficult about answering his questions or not.

He seemed to want me to speak again, to give him some sort of assurance, but when I remained silent he shrugged, sat back, crossed his legs, and said, "Very well. I want to know where you've been since you left the mine. Everything."

There was no reason not to tell him. I said, "I got away in one of the ore trucks. I left it by—" But then my voice broke, and shivering controlled me for several seconds. When the spasm was over, I said, "Could I have something hot to drink? I'm so cold, it's hard to talk."

He frowned at me. "Cold? It isn't cold in here."

"I'm very cold," I said.

"Are you sick?"

Malik said, "Sir?"

Phail turned an impatient glare at Malik. "What?"

"Sir, Mister Davus made us throw him in the water."

"For what possible reason?"

"To show him he shouldn't try and swim for shore."

"Stupid," said Phail. He looked at me. "I apologize for Davus.

225

I don't believe in unnecessary cruelty." To Malik he said, "Get him something to drink."

We waited in silence till Malik returned, carrying a large mug of soup. It was a meat soup, steaming with heat, and it made me think of Torgmund. I found that I regretted Torgmund, that the thought of him saddened me and made me feel unworthy to be an instrument of vengeance. Everywhere I turned, it seemed, there were stray thoughts to take me away from my purpose. I could hardly remember myself as I was when first I'd come here: steel, sharp, singular, emotionless, machined. Now I was feeling as though all I wanted to do was confess.

Confess? Confess what?

I drank the soup, pouring it down my throat as though I were a cold and empty pitcher, hollow and white inside, and it did help to ease the chill. When I was done with it, Phail asked me again to recount my history since escaping from the mine, and this time I did. I told him everything, Torgmund and the cabin, the journey out of the darkness, the errors of direction, the death of the hairhorse, the three days in the UC Embassy, everything.

He listened intently, and when I was done he said, "Plausible. You had nothing on you, no papers, no maps, nothing to show—Still, it could be in your mind."

"What could?"

He peered at me. "Are you ignorant, or are you merely illustrating ignorance? An act, or reality?"

"I know nothing that I haven't told you."

"Patently false," he said briskly. "Whole areas of your life and knowledge haven't been touched upon at all."

"I meant, since I left the mine."

"Of course." He frowned, and tapped a knuckle against his chin. "It would be easier to believe you," he said thoughtfully, "but perhaps more dangerous as well. That you should disappear in precisely that direction, that you should return from that area, that you should have an animal and equipment you did not have before, all of this is suspicious. Even that you should be here on Anarchaos is itself suspicious. But your explanations are invariably plausible, for the hairhorse, for the clothing and equipment, for your whereabouts while not under surveillance."

"You might be able to find Torgmund's cabin," I said. "That would prove what I said."

"I am not interested in proof," he said. "Proof is secondary to judgment. I am interested solely in judging you, for truth or falsehood. Why did you come to Anarchaos?"

"To work for the Wolmak Corporation. For Ice."

"I believe you are lying now," he said. "But persuasively. If you can lie persuasively now, could you have been lying just as persuasively about the other things?"

"I was going to work with my brother," I said. "Wolmak paid my way from Earth; you can find out for yourself."

"Proof again. Only a liar needs proof. To prove details is simple, can be done no matter how complex the lie, but to judge overall veracity is much more difficult. It is the latter which is necessary. Why didn't you leave when you found out that your brother was dead?"

"There isn't any truth that I know that will hurt me if I tell you," I said. "I knew my brother was dead before I left Earth. I'd been offered the job, Gar got me the job, but just before I was supposed to leave the news came he'd been killed. I came anyway."

"To get the job?"

"No. I didn't care about the job. I came to find out what happened to my brother."

He smiled as though I'd just confessed a childishness, and said, "You wanted revenge?"

"I thought so."

"You *thought* so?"

"What I wanted," I said, being as truthful as I knew how, telling myself the way things were through this medium of apparently talking to Phail, "what I actually wanted was to understand."

"Why your brother was killed, you mean."

"Specifically that, yes."

He frowned again, saying, "Are you leading me away from the subject? These are strange answers. What do you mean, specifically?"

"I mean I wanted to understand. Everything. Myself, and everything around me in relation to myself. It seemed if I could understand about Gar's killing, it might be a clue, I could—" I hunted for the word.

"Extrapolate," he said.

"Yes. Extrapolate the general answer from the specific."

"And therefore understand."

"Yes."

"And have you been successful? *Do* you understand?"

"I'm no longer sure it was a thing that could be looked for."

"You *are* taking me away! The subject is not philosophy, the subject is money!"

I looked at him, saw the patrician face being angry, and said, "Money? What money?"

"You claim to know nothing," he said, enraged by me. "You claim to have come here on a philosophical quest. You say the word *money* and you look at me with an open guileless face, as though the existence of money had never before been pointed out to you. No one is that remote from money."

"I don't know what money you mean," I said.

He said, "Are you very stupid, or very clever? You present me with your mythic qualities, love and death, the slain brother, eternal questions, the unworldly view. You think if you show yourself to me as a saint you'll impress me and I'll stay away from you."

I didn't understand him, yet it did seem to be true that he was impressed by something. He was getting more and more nervous. I said, "I'm not stupid, but I'm not clever either. I came here, I came to this planet, I thought I was hard, I thought I was the strongest thing there was and it would all go my way, and nothing went my way. I lost every fight. I lost a hand. I learned nothing, and I'm sitting here a prisoner of a man I don't know, caught up in some sort of problem I don't understand. You're the one making the myths, the money myth, the golden fleece. I don't have what you want."

He glowered at me in surly indecision, and finally said, "I cannot believe in you. No one is a money virgin. What did you do on Earth? Where were you when you decided to come here?"

"In jail."

He sat up, looking hopeful. "For theft?"

"Manslaughter. I have—I used to have—a bad temper." I looked inside myself but couldn't tell, and said so: "I don't know if it's gone or not."

"Bad temper," he mimicked, in a sudden return to his angry contempt. He'd made up his mind about me, all at once. He pointed a finger at me and said, "You were at the site, I know you were. You'll tell us where it is, you'll lead us to it, you'll give us the whole thing. You'll either do it now, with no trouble, or you'll do it later on, after a great deal of trouble."

I said, "I don't want any trouble. I won't fight anybody, I won't hide anything. I don't want to be involved anymore. I'll answer anything you ask me, I swear I will."

"You'll take us to the site?"

There was nothing for me to say. I sat and looked at him, feeling helpless and very frightened.

He nodded cynically. "Ignorant again," he said. "Such touching innocence, such a blank expression. There is a drug called antizone, have you ever heard of it?"

"No."

"It is used with the hopelessly insane. One injection, and your brain empties itself through your mouth. You will speak your entire history, all your memories, every bit of your knowledge, the total of your conjectures, each of your hopes and expectations. You will state every item aloud, and in the act of stating it you will forget it. Sometimes this process takes days. When it is finished, your mind will be empty. You will then be retrained in those rudimentary skills necessary for survival, and you will be sent back to the mine. And this time, you won't escape."

Of course! A great light seemed to bloom in my mind, a

beautiful illumination, and with it a lovely sensation of peace. I had found *my* golden fleece!

I closed my eyes. I caressed the prospect he offered me.

He said, "Well? Is that what you want?"

I said, "Yes." I kept my eyes closed.

He slapped me stingingly across the face. My eyes popped open, and I saw him standing over me, glaring at me. "Don't play with me!"

"I want the drug," I said. "I am finished, but afraid to die. I didn't know about that drug, I would like it very much."

He backed away from me, stumbling against his chair but staying on his feet. "How clever are you? What game are you playing?"

There was no way to make him believe me, but surely he would do it anyway. I closed my eyes again. In the darkness inside I felt at peace.

I heard Phail moving around the room, prowling back and forth, muttering to himself. He asked himself what intricacies I might be plotting, if perhaps there were some drug he didn't know about which could be taken at some earlier date and leave the taker immune to antizone, if perhaps I were under some hypnotic protection which would allow him to empty my mind without getting the information he wanted, if I were perhaps merely trying a desperate bluff.

Finally he said, with abrupt decisiveness, "Very well. We'll fall back on proof. Malik, get all he can tell you about this alleged cabin where he spent so much of his time. Then see if you can find it, see if it exists."

I opened my eyes, hoping to see his face, but he had already turned away and was going out the door.

XXVIII

They fed me three meals, and I slept. Then they fed me three meals, and I slept. I counted five such cycles, then I stopped counting; a while later I counted again for another three cycles, then gave it up again, and between the second and third meals on

230

some subsequent cycle the door was unlocked and opened and Phail came in to see me.

We both stood. There was no furniture in this room other than the blanket-covered board on which I slept. The walls and ceiling and floor were all gray metal. There was no window. Each time the door was opened I caught a narrow glimpse of gray corridor. At all times there was the throb of the ship's engines; we were in insistent motion somewhere.

Phail gave me a hard look and checked off the points briskly on his fingers: "There was a trapper named Torgmund. He has disappeared. His cabin has been found and searched, and it matches your description. His two hairhorses are gone. A half-built addition to his cabin was noted." There were five points, adding up to the five fingers of his right hand. He closed this hand into a fist, lowered the fist to his side, and said, "It would appear you were telling the truth."

I said, "How long have I been here? In this room."

"That doesn't make any difference," he said. "The point is, you can still help us."

"All the time I've been here," I said, "I thought of nothing but antizone."

"I don't care," he said, with all of his arrogance and impatience.

"Nevertheless," I said carefully, "it is a fact. Antizone has been my only thought. I never believed, in all that darkness out there beyond the rim, you would find Torgmund's cabin, and so I thought eventually you would come back and give me the injection of antizone."

"There's no point in that now," he snapped.

"Nevertheless," I said again, "it is what I thought. And I want to tell you about it."

He said, "Why should I listen to you?"

"Because it's important," I said. "Important to me. You think I can help you. I don't know why you think that, I don't know if you're right or not, but you do think it. I will help you, if

231

you're right and it's possible for me to. But first you must listen to what I have to say."

He smiled thinly. "An odd bargain," he said. "All right, I'll listen."

"At first," I said, "I was impatient for the search to be given up. I couldn't think of anything lovelier than an end of self. Oblivion without death, who could ask for anything more? I expressed this attitude when you first mentioned antizone."

"Yes. I thought it was a bluff. Now I'm not so sure."

"I continued to think that way," I said, "for some time after being put into this room. But gradually my attitude began to change. I saw that I was being defeatist and cowardly. I cannot help yearning for antizone, but I began to see that the yearning was shameful, and I want you to know that I am ashamed. I am ashamed of the way I acted about antizone the last time. I want you to know that."

He studied me in some perplexity, and finally said, "Is that all?"

"Yes."

"You want me to know you're ashamed of wanting antizone."

"Yes."

He shook his head. "I don't know about you. I can't touch you anywhere; I can't relate you to anything I know. Could it simply be that you're insane?"

"I'm not sure," I said. "I've thought about it, but I don't know."

He waved a hand in sudden irritation, as though brushing away cobwebs. "You keep taking me away, leading me off the subject. The site, that's the important thing. I believe you now, you don't know where it is. But you might be able to help us find it."

"Then I will," I said.

"Good. Come along with me."

He turned and rapped on the door. The guard opened it, and we left the little gray room. I followed him down the corridor, feeling the ship move sluggishly beneath my feet, and through another door, and out on deck.

The deck was covered, with lights spaced along the roof. To our left as we walked along it was the metal skin of the ship. To our right was blackness, utter and complete. Small water sounds could be heard in the blackness. The impression was that this ship was flying with great speed through empty black space. It was very cold.

Phail led me through another door, inside the ship again, up a flight of stairs, and into a gorgeous room full of bright colors. Carpeting on the floor. Polished wood furniture. Gleaming brass fixtures. Ornate windows onto the outer blackness. Opulence and luxury. In the center, a large and beautiful wooden desk with a polished and empty top.

Phail motioned at this desk. "Sit down," he said. "You'll work there. You'll find pencils and paper in the center drawer."

Feeling that some mistake was being made, I went to the desk and sat down. I opened the center drawer, and pencils and paper were there, as Phail had said they would be. Since it seemed the proper thing to do, I removed them from the drawer and placed them on the desk. Then I leaned forward, and in the polished top I could see an unclear view of my own face.

In the meantime, Phail had gone to a safe in the corner, had pressed his palm to the scanner of the personnel lock, and had opened the safe door. As he took from the safe a package wrapped in brown paper, the room door burst open and a sailor came in, very excited. "Mister Phail!" I recognized this man as Davus, the one who had me thrown into the water.

Phail looked up at him with apparent annoyance. "What now?"

"General Ingor!"

Phail sprang to his feet. "The General! Where?"

"Coming here! They just radioed."

Phail glanced at the package in his hand, then at me, then back at Davus. "How long do we have?"

Davus pointed at the ceiling. "He's right up there! In a plane. They're landing now."

In a sudden fury, Phail cried, "How did he find us? Someone on board—" But he cut it abruptly off, spun around, tossed the package back into the safe and shut the safe door. He pointed at me and said to Davus, "Get him out of sight. Back in his room."

"Yes, sir." Davus came toward me.

Phail said to him, with cold authority, "Gently, Davus. He'll go with you, there won't be any trouble."

Davus pouted, as though he'd been scolded by a teacher. "Yes, sir," he said sullenly.

Phail said to me, "Go with him. We'll get back to this later."

I said, "Should I put the paper and pencils away?"

Phail made a crooked smile and said, "No, that won't be necessary. Just go with Davus."

"All right."

I followed Davus out of the room. He took me back the same way I had come. This time, as we walked along the deck, the ship was on our right and the empty dark on our left. There was suddenly light out there in the emptiness. I stopped and looked, my hand resting on the rail, and saw an airplane, outlined by its own lights, sail on a long diagonal across the black, from upper right to lower left, its landing lights suddenly picking out at the end of the diagonal the choppiness of black water in the black night. The plane landed on the water and made a long sweeping turn toward us, its lights creating choppy water wherever they touched.

Davus tugged at my arm. "You're supposed to come along peaceful," he said. "Don't get your hopes up about the General. He isn't here to save you from anybody."

I let him pull me away, and after that followed him without trouble back to my room.

XXIX

There was no third meal in that cycle. Being without it made me hungry, and this hunger made it difficult for me to go to sleep, but there was nothing else to do and so eventually sleep did come to me.

For the first time in a long while I was not permitted to sleep until I woke up of my own volition. Rough hands shaking me drove me out of sleep, and it seemed as though I'd barely closed my eyes. I sat up, bleary-eyed and fuzzy-minded, and saw that it was Davus who had awakened me.

Davus, speaking swiftly and softly, said to me, "The General wants you. He wants to see you. You awake?"

"I haven't been fed," I said. "The food was never brought to me."

"Don't be an idiot. Listen to me. If you're smart, you'll listen to me. Keep a close mouth when you talk to the General, you hear me?"

"A close mouth?"

"Nobody mistreated you," he said. "Mister Phail asked you some questions and you gave him the answers, and that's all. And nobody hit you or threw you in the water or anything like that."

"You had me thrown in the water," I said.

"Not if you know what's good for you," he said, still speaking low and fast. "Not if you don't want trouble later on. You just be careful and watch yourself." He straightened. "Come on."

I got up from the bed and followed him and he took me the same route back to the same room. We entered, and this time the room was full of people.

Back in the corner, near the safe, stood Phail, looking wary. In another corner, their arms folded over their chests and their faces carefully blank, stood Malik and Rose. Sitting at the desk was a big old man as gnarled and thick as an old tree. He had thick white hair, a heavy and strong-looking body, huge jagged hands resting on the desktop, and a weathered craggy face dominated by burning eyes of a pale pale blue. Standing behind him, one to either side, were the other two young officials who had been with Phail on the inspection tour of the mine.

The big old man at the desk said, "You're Malone?" His voice was hoarse and scattered, as though he'd had a very strong deep voice and had overworked it.

I said, "Yes. Rolf Malone."

He said, "Phail tells me you're willing to cooperate."

"Yes."

He said, "How much?"

"What?"

"How much do you want? What's your bargaining price? You want a percentage, I suppose."

I said, "Could I have antizone?"

Everyone reacted to that. Phail blanched, and looked frightened. All the others seemed surprised. Only Malik and Rose maintained their impassivity.

The old man said, "What do you mean, you want antizone?"

"I want to blot everything out," I said. "If I could have an injection of antizone, and then you could send me back to the mine."

The old man said, "Where did you hear about antizone?"

I pointed at Phail. "He told me about it."

Phail started shaking his head, but when the old man twisted around and glared at him he stopped. The old man said, "You threatened him."

"I had to do something," Phail said defensively. He motioned at me. "You see how he is. I had to try and reach him."

"You've got him doped?"

"No, sir. I swear I haven't."

The old man studied me, squinting at me with those burning eyes, and said, "He isn't normal. He behaves as though he's doped."

One of the other young officials, the one who had asked me if I was Malone back at the mine, said diffidently, "Excuse me, General?"

The General was the old man. He turned in the chair and said, "What is it?"

"Malone was at the mine four years, sir. I'm told that very

often has a permanent effect on a man, makes him more . . . placid. Almost like a vegetable sometimes."

The other young official said, "I've heard that too, sir. It's almost like giving a man a lobotomy."

The General turned back and studied me some more, and now I could see distaste in his expression and I felt ashamed of myself again. The good opinion of others meant much more to me now that I no longer deserved it than it ever had in the past.

The General said, "If that's what he's like, how do we know he'll be any use to us?"

Phail said, eagerly, "All we have to do is try, General. It can't cost us anything to try."

The General turned to glower at him once more, saying, "You've mishandled this affair from the beginning, Phail. It isn't over yet. Taking this man out from under my nose, hiding him down here, refusing to answer when I called—"

"Our radio was out," Phail said quickly. "We didn't realize it ourselves."

"A frail lie," the General said.

Phail said, "And we didn't come down here to hide from you, sir, that's the truth. Ice had found out about Malone, when the UC tracer went out. They were looking for him. I knew they'd look at Prudence, and at our installations to the east, because that's where the site is, so I thought if I took him down here, we'd be—"

"All right," said the General. "That's enough."

"Yes, sir."

"At least this time," the General said, grudging the point, "you weren't trigger-happy."

"I've learned from my mistakes, General," Phail assured him. It was odd for me to be watching how his arrogance turned itself into servility when he talked to the old man.

"I'm not sure there's time left for you to learn," the General said, with a heavy kind of thoughtfulness. "Time will tell." He turned back to look at me, distaste on his face again, and said, "As to you, you say you'll help us if you can."

"Yes, sir."

"If afterward we agree to give you an injection of antizone."

"Yes, sir."

He nodded briskly. "Agreed."

I smiled. I was ashamed of the smile as I felt it spread across my face, but I couldn't help it. I smiled.

The General made a face, and looked away from me. "Triss," he said. "You take over. Work with him."

Triss was the one who had called me Malone at the mine. He nodded and said, "Yes, sir."

"Elman," said the General, "you take charge of the ship. We'll put in at Cannemuss."

Elman, the third of the young officials, said, "Yes, sir."

The General said, "Phail, you will go to your rooms and stay there, until I decide what to do about you."

Phail bowed his head. "Yes, sir," he said.

"Go now."

"Yes, sir."

On his way out, Phail gave me a look that no one else could have seen. In the look, he promised me death.

XXX

I was alone with Triss, who said to me, "You might as well sit down at the desk."

I went over and sat, where the General had just been. I said, "Should I get out the paper and pencils?"

Triss seemed surprised. He said, "Well, I suppose so, yes. You know where they are?"

"Yes." I opened the drawer, and showed him.

Triss seemed younger than the other two, Phail and Elman, and looked at me always as though he were trying to understand me or connect himself with me, as though he wanted to feel things as I felt them in order to comprehend me. I could remember having seen the same thing in his eyes that time at the

238

mine, when he had looked at me and found my brother in my face and called me Malone.

Now, as Triss went to the safe and opened it, I found a vague and impersonal curiosity fretting in the corners of my mind. Under what circumstances had Triss and the others known Gar? Why had Malik and Rose tried to kill me the first time, if now I was being kept alive by their employers in order somehow to be of help? But the effort needed to obtain such knowledge was more than I could produce. I sat quietly at the desk, waiting to see what would be desired of me, and Triss came over to me carrying in his hands the package that Phail had been about to show me just before everyone else had arrived.

Triss said, "Before we get down to it, I want to say something. Will you listen to me?"

I was surprised at the question; it implied choice. But Triss seemed to require an answer, so I nodded and said, "Yes."

"I hope you'll change your mind about the antizone," he said. "It's a terrible thing to do to yourself. I know you've been through a great deal, but the future can be very much better for you, particularly if you solve this." He held up the brown paper package. Then he lowered it again and said, earnestly, "I'm sure the General would let you reconsider, change the agreement. Will you at least think about it?"

I could have explained it to him. I could have said, *While I live I have a responsibility and a purpose, and they require of me strengths I no longer possess. It is not permitted me to stop with the job undone, but I cannot go on. Antizone rescues me from this dilemma. I embrace antizone with the last of my will.*

But the explanation itself was too much for me. I merely nodded and said, "Yes. I will."

"Good," he said. He then placed the package on the desk and carefully unwrapped it.

Inside there was a notebook with a yellow cover. There were no words on the cover. Triss pushed the brown paper to one side, placed the notebook directly in front of me, and said, "This was your brother's. He kept personal notations of various kinds in here, some just written out and others in code. It was his own private code."

I said, touching the yellow cover with my fingertips, "This belonged to Gar?"

"Yes."

I wanted to ask how this notebook had come to be here, but I was afraid; to ask anything, to think about anything, was only to open it all again, drive me once more into the struggle. Beneath my fingertips the yellow cover seemed warm, as though Gar himself had just put it down and gone away. I took my hand back and put it in my lap.

Triss said, "Toward the back there is a passage in code, headed by the word 'strike.' We know that on his last trip beyond the rim your brother made an important mineral find. The details of that strike, and the location of the site, are given in that code section. So far, no one has been able to break the code; it apparently had some specific personal equivalents for your brother that no cryptographer could possibly know or guess at. But you are his brother; it is just possible you will be able to give us the equivalents. I know something about cryptography, and will be able to help you to an extent. When we get to Cannemuss tomorrow our crypto experts will be down from Ni, and they'll be able to help even more."

I said, "I don't know anything about codes."

"But you knew your brother, that's the important thing." He flipped the notebook open. It lay on the desk in front of me, and he stood leaning forward and flipping the pages. "It's toward the back," he said.

I sat and watched the pages as they turned. It was Gar's writing; I recognized that neat and economical hand. Some pages had lists, others had long notes, still others merely had sequences of numbers.

I put my hand out and placed it flat on the notebook and stopped the flipping of the pages. "Wait," I said. I had seen my own name on one sheet as it had gone by.

Triss said, "It's toward the back."

"Wait," I said. I turned the pages toward the front again, two pages, three pages, and there it was, a long paragraph with my name at the top of the page.

It read:

ROLF

I am going to have a second chance. This time, I have to do what is right with Rolf. I must *not* make believe nothing is wrong, I must *not* try to hide everything under the rug. He has just come from jail and we both know it. I know he'll be all right, but *I* must be strong. I wish I had Rolf's ability to face unpleasant facts. Maybe I can learn from him, and he can learn patience from me.

I still think it's best to tell Colonel Whistler the truth, even though that means Jenna will find out. But the question is, should I tell Rolf? It's ridiculous for me to think of protecting him, he's always been the one to protect me, but this time it might be better to keep silent, at least for a while. Let Rolf not have to put up that strong silent front he affects when he's embarrassed.

I *must* keep Rolf away from Jenna. She would push just to see him explode.

We're a couple of emotional cripples, Rolf and me. He's too involved with life, too volatile, too emotional, too caught up in everything, and I'm too bloodless, too remote, too bound up in my own inadequacies. Maybe this time Rolf and I can cure one another. God knows I owe him at least a good try, after all he's done for me.

I wish I hated Jenna.

Triss said, "We don't have time for all that now. You can keep the notebook when we're done, and read it cover to cover if you want."

Life will not leave us alone. Weariness draped itself on me like a blanket. Despite everything. I still must act.

I looked up at Triss. If I could have felt anger toward him, or his superiors, or anyone connected with him, it would have been so much easier. But I couldn't, there was no fury in me at all. There was only the responsibility.

I reached out and closed my hand around his throat. I said, "You will tell me about the notebook."

XXXI

It was difficult to get the story from him. Each time he recovered from my attentions he tried to scream for help, so that I finally had to adjust him and make it impossible for him to speak above a whisper. Then his recital was marred by general inconsistency and interrupted from time to time by faintings and bubblings up of blood. But I eventually did get the story and rearranged it into sensible and chronological order:

Behind the name Sledge was an inter-star corporation named Kemistek, an operation quite similar to the Wolmak Corporation and in fact in direct competition with Wolmak. Both Kemistek and Wolmak maintained spies in the other's employ, and two such Kemistek spies working for Wolmak were Lingo, the entrance guard at Ice Tower in Ulik, and Piekow Lastus, the man who had accompanied Gar on his last trip.

Lastus had no technical education whatever. Although he'd been with Gar when Gar made his last important strike, Lastus could not subsequently have described what the strike was nor how to get back to it. All Lastus could do was secretly radio to Sledge, which he did.

Phail and Triss and Elman were sent to intercept Gar at Yoroch Pass. Triss insisted they were not sent to kill Gar but merely to bribe him if possible, or if bribery failed to attempt intimidation. I believed him, since those three were not by nature or occupation killers. If Gar's death had been requested or anticipated, Malik and Rose would have been the ones sent.

But death should always be anticipated on Anarchaos, where all legal and social restraints on individual behavior have been

242

stripped away. Gar refused to be bribed, nor could this trio of puppies successfully intimidate him. Phail waved a gun around. Phail grew increasingly angry. It was surely significant that Phail had recently suffered personal problems, involving a woman on his home world whom he had not seen since coming to Anarchaos fifteen months before. All at once, Phail was shooting. Before anyone realized what was happening, Gar had been shot dead and Piekow Lastus himself was wounded and down on the ground.

At that point, Triss and Elman managed to disarm Phail and keep him from finishing the job on Lastus. Phail wanted Lastus dead because, in the shocked reaction to his deed, he wanted no witnesses. Triss and Elman, frightened of their companion by now, definitely wanted Lastus alive; so long as Lastus lived, surely Phail would not be thinking of killing Triss and Elman.

As to Lastus, he swore never to tell. And why should he tell? To do so, he would have had to admit his status as secret agent for Kemistek. Besides, Kemistek would not pay him a pension, in addition to the disability pension he would be eligible for from Wolmak.

Phail and Elman and Triss all helped bury Gar, and then took the notebook and left. General Ingor, the top Kemistek executive on Anarchaos, was furious when told what had happened, but chose to do nothing. A Kemistek executive, while acting for Kemistek, represented the company in anything he chose to do, so that the General was forced to support Phail's action at least to the extent of maintaining silence about it. This silence was made easier by the fact that Phail had apparently gotten away with it.

The only thing that did not appear to resolve itself satisfactorily was Gar's notebook. The code he'd used in it proved to be unbreakable. It was perhaps this as much as anything else that influenced the General to punish his three young executives by extending their stay on Anarchaos indefinitely. (In the normal course of events, all three of them would have been assigned to other and surely more pleasant worlds by now.)

In any event, the whole affair seemed safely and permanently closed, and then I turned up. When I asked Lingo for Lastus' address, Lingo immediately reported to Sledge. Phail was the executive who received the information, and he promptly panicked, afraid I would get the truth from Lastus. It was Phail who sent Malik and Rose to kill me, and incidentally to shut Lastus' mouth for good and all.

This time, when the others learned what Phail had done, there was increased displeasure, beginning when General Ingor pointed out that I might have been able to shed light on my brother's personal code. But it seemed too late to do anything about it, and except for the fact that Phail seemed to have assured himself a dim future with Kemistek everything remained unchanged.

It was three years later when they were on the tour of the mine and first ran into me. (Three years! I reach back for the time, and my memory seems to fall into a hole. Three years, gone forever.) None of them thought of the implications until much later, when it struck Elman that possibly Gar Malone's brother *hadn't* been killed, that possibly the man who had looked like Gar Malone had been Gar's brother after all. Phail refused to consider the idea when it was presented to him, and Triss was doubtful, but General Ingor thought it best to follow it up. By then, of course, I had already made my escape. Still, they had seen me once, and they had a description of me—including the missing hand—and when the story went around Sledge Tower at Prudence about the crazy bearded horseman who had waved a handless arm in fury and chased a helicopter while riding a hairhorse, Phail quickly guessed who the horseman might have been.

Once again, Phail was first. It was he who put feelers out for me everywhere it seemed to him that I might go, including the UC Embassy, and he who sent Malik and Rose to get me and bring me to him.

His initial idea was merely to turn me over to the General, but then he saw a way of regaining lost favor by spiriting me away, putting me to work on the notebook, and eventually going to the

General with the code completely broken, the message read, the site of the great lost strike pin-pointed precisely. In having me taken away from Prudence to the Sledge research ship in the Sea of Morning, he was hiding me primarily from his own people.

But not exclusively his own people. Just as Kemistek had spies at Wolmak, so Wolmak had spies at Kemistek, and these spies at last became aware of some corners and edges of what had been going on. Additionally, the UC request for information on a man named Rolf Malone had piqued Wolmak's interest. Colonel Whistler and his people did not yet fully understand what was going on, but they knew that something was afoot and that Phail was involved in it. Wolmak was currently trying everything in its power to learn Phail's whereabouts.

So. The simple facts that I had been seeking were now mine. Gar had been betrayed by Lastus into the hands of Phail, who killed him out of irritation. This murder was aided and condoned by Triss and Elman and General Ingor. The trails back from Gar's murder led one way to the woman on another world who had been abrasive with Phail's emotions, and led another way to the rivalry of two mining and chemical corporations for new caches of raw materials.

No one had gone out to murder Gar Malone for being Gar Malone.

It was with the same impersonality that I snuffed the life from Triss.

XXXII

I wanted to be angry; it would make it much easier to do what I had to do. I thought about the uselessness and stupidity of Gar's death, about the bungling and panic that had cost me years from my life and led to the loss of my hand, about the lost opportunity that Gar had been offering me. I thought about it all and I couldn't be angry. I could only feel a heavy regret, a weighted nostalgia and remorse.

Everything was much more difficult this way. Without the

blessed blindness of fury, I had to do everything coldly, impersonally, watching myself every step of the way.

Violence done of duty weighs more heavily than violence done out of passion.

I moved through the ship light and quick and silent and unseen, armed with nothing but my hand. From Triss I had learned the location of Phail's quarters and there I hurried; this first part had to be gotten over with as quickly as possible.

I saw no one. According to the artificial time by which everyone on Anarchaos lived it was now late at night, so that only a few crew members were up and about. These I avoided easily, and soon came to Phail's quarters.

The door wasn't even locked. I entered a darkened room, stood silent in the darkness for a while, and finally determined that I was alone; there was no sound of breathing here. I felt my way around the room, touched furniture which indicated it was a parlor or sitting room, and came at last to another doorway, in which the door stood ajar. I paused here, listening, and heard the sound of regular breathing I'd been hoping for.

I moved through the dark to that sound, and reached my hand out, and promptly found his throat. I closed my hand around it.

How the pulse beat against my palm! He woke up at once, thrashing and waving his arms around, but I stood and waited and after a time his struggles weakened. I released him when he was lying limp but the pulse was still beating; I didn't want him to die without being sure who was doing it to him, and why.

I left him, and found a light, and switched it on. His face was so altered by lack of breath that for one bad instant I thought I'd come to the wrong room. But it was him, Phail, with his arrogant face and dry sandy hair. He slept nude, and in his thrashings had kicked the covers off; his body was surprisingly pale and thin.

I brought water from the bath and sloshed it on him, then slapped his face until he returned to consciousness. When his eyes opened, and I saw that he recognized me, I put my hand on his throat again.

246

He didn't move. He lay there unblinking, and stared up at me.

I said, "You murdered Gar Malone. I came to Anarchaos to find you and punish you."

Then I closed my hand.

XXXIII

The rest did not require individual attention. What did I have to say to General Ingor or Elman or Davus or Malik and Rose?

From the kitchens I obtained the knife with which I disposed of the crewmen on duty, beginning with the mate on watch at the wheel and ending with the two engineers on duty in the engine room. All told, seven men.

I smashed the radio equipment. There were six lifeboats and I punched holes in all of them. I damaged the engines with pliers and a hammer, then punctured the great fuel tank and led a trail of flammable objects down the flight of stairs into the pool of it at the bottom.

The ship was no longer moving through absolute blackness. Far ahead of us, and a bit to the left, there was a red glow on the horizon. As I moved about the ship, sometimes having to travel along the deck, I glanced at the horizon and from it got a feeling of urgency, as though it indicated an actual dawn coming up. It seemed to me as though I must be finished with what I had to do before that dawn.

At last everything was ready. The ship still moved forward from its own momentum, but with increased sluggishness. I dressed myself warmly in clothing taken from the dead crewmen, set the fire which would eventually lead itself to the spilled fuel and from there to the fuel tank itself, and went on down to the opening in the hull through which I'd first been brought into the ship.

There were three small motorboats down here, tied to the metal platform, and I scuttled two of them. I found the way to open the hole in the hull, started the engine of the remaining motorboat, and steered my way carefully out to the open sea.

I had taken the mate's watch with me, and it read three-twenty A.M. when I started out in the small boat. I maintained course in the same direction the ship had taken, guiding myself by the light on the horizon far ahead and just slightly to the left, and as I went I looked back from time to time at the faintly seen ship, its yellow lights outlining it in the blackness behind me. For the longest while it seemed to sit motionless and eternal back there, an angular black silhouette in a halo of dim light surrounded by the blackness, but at precisely three-thirty by the mate's watch I saw the first jet of flame. Bright red, shooting upward, it illuminated the ship and the bit of ocean just around it in miniature imitation of the noon light of Hell.

So long as I could still see it, the ship never exploded and it never sank. It merely burned and burned and burned, flaming away like a torch back there in the night. I moved away from it at a good speed, sitting in the stern of the small boat, huddled against the cold wind of my passage, and behind me the red beacon silently roared.

I was finished. After four years, I had done what I had come to Anarchaos to do: learn the truth about my brother's slaying and choose an appropriate vengeance. It seemed that I had lost every battle, and then won the war.

How should I have felt? I felt cold, and empty. I no longer wanted antizone, any more than I still wanted revenge. There was nothing I wanted. Not even the oblivion of the black water rushing by below my elbow had any appeal for me.

I was heading toward Cannemuss, but only because life requires motion. So long as one breathes, it is necessary to move. In a map on the bridge of the ship I had seen where this place Cannemuss was: at the far south-easterly tip of the Sea of Morning, at the mouth of the Black River. Triss had told me it was a frontier town, a trapper's village, a way station for supplies going out to the rim and raw materials coming back.

The last time I looked behind me, when the flaming ship had now receded completely out of sight, the mate's watch read nearly four o'clock. From then on I looked only forward.

Five hours later I reached the coast, barren and snowbound, and two hours after that, by traveling southward along the shoreline, I came at last to Cannemuss. And on the pier at Cannemuss was standing Jenna Guild.

XXXIV

At first, we didn't recognize one another. I, of course, had changed considerably since last we'd met. She had not, but was so bundled against the cold that her face could barely be seen. It was something about her stance that attracted my attention, rather than my noticing anything particularly familiar about her face.

Initially, the town itself commanded all of my scrutiny, it being unlike anything I'd ever seen before. Existing in perpetual twilight, permanently frozen, its population largely transient, Cannemuss had none of the towers I'd seen in the other cities on Anarchaos, nor any of the usual ramshackle huts and aimlessly drifting people. There was an air of bustling industry here, as of a thriving pioneer community eagerly moving into an ever-better future. The withering, the long slow decline obvious in the syndicate cities, had not yet shown itself out here.

I saw the ships in the harbor before I actually came within sight of the town itself. Black River, narrow and deep, emptied precipitately into the Sea of Morning at this point, leaving a broad deep protected bay just to the north of the river mouth. Around this bay the buildings of the town were clustered, and in the bay itself were small and medium-sized boats of every possible description, a range of boats as broad as the range of land transportation I'd seen on first leaving the spaceport at Ni. Outside the bay were a dozen or so large ships much like the one I had been a prisoner on, each with its syndicate name in large letters on the bow. Smaller boats scuttled back and forth constantly between these large ships and the port.

I came down along the shoreline from the north, seeing the large ships anchored outside the harbor first of all, and then seeing the traffic back and forth, then the broad entrance to the bay, and at last the town itself.

Cannemuss was a low-built town. Here and there a two-story structure loomed above its fellows, but nothing in the town was as tall as the ships nested outside the bay. Steeply slanting roofs were standard, because of the frequent heavy snowfalls. There was no open ground; streets and all other spaces around the dark buildings were covered with hard-packed snow. Many more men than women moved about on this snow, mostly dressed in furs, many bearded, practically all with the self-sufficient Torgmund look, the look of the frontier.

I steered my little boat into the bay and to the end of the one long pier that jutted out from the quay. I tied the boat to a ring set into a vertical support, climbed the short ladder up to the pier, and met there a bundled man with a thin nose, who held a clipboard and said, "You'll have to pay rent if you stay there, you know."

"I'll straighten it with you when I come back," I said, since I knew I would never be back, and walked down the length of the pier to the end, where I saw Jenna Guild.

I started by her, then was struck by some feeling of familiarity, stopped, went back a step, and looked directly into her face, framed within the fur hood she wore. She had been gazing steadily out to sea and now she made as though unaware of my presence; she naturally thought I was no more than a potential molester.

I said, "Jenna? Jenna Guild?"

Now she looked at me, and in the blankness of her expression I could see she had no idea who I was. I said, "It's Rolf Malone."

A sudden wariness came into her eyes, and guardedly she said, "You have information about him?"

"I *am* him. Jenna, look at me."

She looked, and looked again, and raised an impulsive hand to touch my cheek. "Rolf! My God!"

"You can still see me underneath," I said, and tried my first smile in ages.

"I would never have known you," she said, studying me in wonderment. "I don't think there's a thing about you that hasn't changed."

"You're still the same," I said. "Not a day has passed for you."

"In my cocoon," she said, with that sudden bitterness I remembered.

I said, "Why are you here? Of all places, why here?"

She laughed, with something odd in the laughter, and said, "Waiting for you, of course! But I didn't expect you to come this way." She looked past me toward the ocean, saying, "Where's the Sledge ship?"

"Gone," I said. "You knew I was on it?"

"We thought so." Then she took my arm. "Come along, the Colonel will be very pleased to see you."

"He's here, too?"

"You're an important man, Rolf," she said. "Come along."

Arm in arm we walked into the town.

XXXV

A great fire crackled in the hearth. Electric lighting cast a smooth and even illumination throughout the room. The furniture was soft and ornate and very comfortable, and all in the richer tones of gold and brown, with polished woods predominating. I had just finished a magnificent dinner and was now sitting in an armchair before the fire, Colonel Whistler in a similar armchair to my right and Jenna Guild to my left.

This was the building the Wolmak Corporation maintained at Cannemuss, one of the few two-story structures in town, with offices downstairs and this suite of rooms upstairs. Jenna had brought me here and I had found Colonel Whistler in a downstairs office with a group of strong, able-looking men who reminded me at once of Malik and Rose. The Colonel had immediately whisked me away to the second floor, but had insisted that no one do any explaining until I had had an opportunity to rest and bathe and change into good clothing and have a decent meal. Now all of these had been attended to, the meal was done, the three of us sat before the fire, and Colonel Whistler said, "We both have questions, of course. I hope you'll allow me the privilege of having my questions asked and answered first."

I said it was all right, and that it would probably be better if I just told everything that had happened since I'd left Ice Tower in Ulik four years ago, rather than answer specific questions one at a time, and he agreed that would be the best way.

The story I told him was the truth, but not the whole truth. I sloughed over the part where Torgmund died, and omitted all details of what I did on the ship. Still, the story took a long while to tell. The Colonel and Jenna listened in silence, not interrupting once, and when I was done the Colonel said, slowly and heavily, "I don't know. I don't know whether to say you've been very unlucky for all of the things that have happened to you, or very lucky for having survived them all."

I said, "I was never more than a small pawn in somebody else's chess game. Most of the time I didn't matter at all. And Gar, too. His being killed is the closest thing there is to accidental murder."

He said, "I hadn't known about the strike, of course, but I never fully believed the story that man Lastus brought back with him. There was always something wrong with Gar Malone's death, but I couldn't be sure what. When you showed up, my suspicions were doubled."

"The way you acted," I said, "I was suspecting you."

He laughed. "I suppose you were. But what did I know about you?"

"That I was an ex-convict."

"I didn't know your brother either, of course. Not well. Not to be sure that he would behave this way or that way. You know what I began to think?"

I said, "I think so. That Gar was alive, that he'd made a strike and was keeping it to himself and I was in on it somehow."

"Of course. Coming around to see what we at Ice thought

252

about your brother's so-called death. When you left, I told Lingo to have you followed, and of course he swore you'd managed to elude the man following you. I suppose he never sent anyone after you at all."

"Not from Ice," I said. "From that other outfit, Sledge."

"I've sent word to have Lingo taken care of. That ought to please you."

It didn't. I was finished; I didn't want to follow the threads back any farther. There wasn't any beginning; it just went back and back, everything that happened caused by something that happened before it. The ones closest to it were settled with now, and the rest could go on without me. But I didn't say so; I just mumbled something and sipped at my drink.

The Colonel said, "It was Lingo who told us you were robbed and killed. The way he said it, it wasn't part of any plot, just another of the anonymous killings on this filthy place. I didn't know any reason not to believe him."

"When did you find out I was alive?"

"When Jenna brought you into this building."

"But—she said she was waiting for me down at the pier."

Jenna said, "The Colonel didn't believe you could still be alive. I did."

The Colonel said, "We have our own spies, you know, in the other corporations. It's a business necessity in a place like this, with so many untapped resources, so many fortunes left to be made. We got word that something was going on at Sledge, it had something to do with us, something to do with a dead prospector of ours named Malone. Their man Phail was involved in it some way, and he seemed to be also the one behind the taking away from a UC Embassy of a man calling himself Rolf Malone. We've been trying to find Phail ever since."

"He had me on that ship of theirs. He was hiding me from his own people, too, General Ingor and the others."

The Colonel said, "You must realize something, Rolf. This is a bad assignment for any man, to be stationed on Anarchaos. The corporations use their Anarchaotic branches as sort of punishment centers. The men who get shipped here are the ones who've already got a record of bad judgment or worse. The combination of bad people in a bad situation often ends with trouble. Nowhere else would you find someone like Phail so high in the corporate structure."

I said, "Everyone here? All the corporations are like that?"

"I know what you're asking, and the answer is yes, me too. My own mistakes have no relevance here. Occasionally a man manages to make amends with his company while here, to build a new reputation for himself and be reassigned elsewhere for a second chance. I hope to be one of those men."

The silence after that was uncomfortable for all of us. There was nothing for me to say. I glanced at Jenna and saw her gazing into the fire with a faraway expression on her face. I wondered; her, too? Was she here because of sins in her own past or was she merely an adjunct of Colonel Whistler, dispatched willy-nilly wherever the ups and downs of his career might take him?

The Colonel finally broke the silence by saying, "When General Ingor and the others left the Sledge tower at Ni aboard a seaplane, we thought there was probably some connection, that Phail was more than likely on the Sledge ship somewhere in the Sea of Morning. That didn't help us much, because we had no way of knowing where the ship was. But then cryptographers from all the Sledge towers were sent down here to Cannemuss—they're still waiting, not two blocks from here—and we knew that meant the ship would be coming here. I was sure Phail was aboard the ship, I guessed that the crypto men had something to do with coded information connected somehow with Gar Malone, but I truly didn't expect to find you aboard and alive."

Jenna said, "I never doubted Gar's death, even though the story of how it happened didn't ring true. But about you I wasn't so sure. You'd left the tower looking so hard and sharp and sure of yourself, I couldn't believe you'd been killed so quickly or so easily. I always suspected you were alive somewhere and would turn up some day with a fantastic story to tell."

The Colonel said, "About your brother's notebook. You brought it with you?"

"Yes."

"And *can* you decipher the code?"

"I don't know; I never tried."

"But you will try, won't you?"

"No. You can copy that page out of the notebook if you want; maybe your crypto people can solve it. But all I want is to get off Anarchaos. I'm going back to Earth."

The Colonel leaned forward, the better to look at me. "Are you sure you haven't decoded the message? You might think you have some personal right to your brother's discovery, and of course you'd be worth a percentage, but you'd be hardly in the position—"

"I don't care about the discovery. It got Gar killed; I don't want any part of it."

The Colonel studied me, frowning, firelight reflecting in his eyes. "You aren't interested in money," he said.

I looked at him, and something about his expression, something about his eyes, put me in mind of Phail, when Phail was trying to judge me and couldn't because our values were so different. I said, "I'm interested in going back to Earth. I've been changed by everything here; I want to see what kind of life I can make for myself on Earth."

"Of course," said the Colonel softly. "We'll talk about it in the morning." He sat back again, and looked into the fire.

We didn't do any more talking.

XXXVI

Jenna came to the room half an hour after I'd gone to bed, as I had known she would, but she never mentioned the notebook until much later, after we had been together a couple of hours. I don't know if that was the result of planning or impulse, though I would say her excitement was genuine. False excitement would have chosen objects other than my scars and left wrist.

When at last she brought the talk around to the business of the night, she began obliquely, murmuring, "I wish you were rich. I wish you were the richest man I knew."

I moved my shoulder, beneath her head, to a more comfortable position, and said, "Why?"

"Because I am a very expensive girl, and I wish you could afford me. I wish we could just pack up, you and I, and go off together, travel from world to world, see everything, do everything."

"You couldn't be a poor man's wife?"

She laughed throatily. "Can you see me back on Earth, in one of those three room project apartments, riding down once a week to market floor for my shopping, setting my own hair, spending my evenings in front of the entertainment wall? Can you really visualize me there?"

"No," I said. "I can't."

She raised up a little and looked at me, smiling. "Can't you ever be rich?" she asked. "Don't you suppose some day you might be beautifully wealthy?"

"I don't think so," I said. "I don't know any way to make a lot of money."

"What about Gar's notebook?"

"You think I should make a deal with the corporation?"

She smiled and shrugged, saying, "I'm not working for the corporation now, Rolf. For all I know someone else might offer you more than the Colonel. Haven't you thought about it yourself?"

"No."

"The Colonel thinks you have."

I said, "What did you do to Gar?"

"What?" Surprise and confusion made her sit up and look around the room as though she'd lost something. "Do to Gar? I didn't do anything. What kind of question is that?"

"In his notebook—"

In sudden agitation she leaped up from the bed, crying, "I don't want to hear about it!"

"You don't want to hear what he said about you?"

"You know I don't!" She prowled about the room, nude and beautiful, like a caged animal. "Do you think I like myself?"

"I hadn't thought about it."

"Listen," she said, her eyes blazing. "Listen to me, I don't know if you're a fool or what you are, but watch the Colonel. He'll never let you get away with that notebook, he won't let you go until you tell him what the code says."

"I don't know what it says."

"You won't get *him* to believe that. He's convinced you've already decoded it."

"I haven't."

She came back and sat on the edge of the bed again, saying urgently, "I never meant to hurt Gar. I wasn't used to his kind of sincerity; I didn't know when it stopped being a game."

"All right," I said. "I can see how it would happen."

"I'll tell you this because you're his brother, to make up for it. The Colonel sent me here tonight."

"I know."

"You know?" She sat back, frowning at me. "Then why didn't you kick me out?"

"I wanted you. It's been a long while for me. Besides, you wanted to be sent here. Does the Colonel think he can hold me prisoner?"

"He won't let you go until he knows where the strike location is." She leaned forward, intent and sincere, saying, "Don't you see? If he can find it, claim it for himself, he can make his own arrangements with the corporation, make up for what he did that sent him here."

I lay back on the pillow and closed my eyes. It wasn't over yet. What was it I'd been told, long ago, before ever coming here? "It was the colony that killed your brother." And in a way that was right. It was the colony that made these situations possible, that created the power vacuum into which these hungry and immoral Colonel Whistlers and General Ingors moved. The spreading

257

responsibility washed back and back, endlessly. It was the colony that killed my brother.

But even that wasn't the end of it. This colony was an abortion, a monstrous growth; without outside assistance it couldn't survive a year. So that if it was the colony that had made the murder of Gar possible, it was the Union Commission, in its turn, which made the colony possible. Without the UC there would be no imports or exports, no monetary exchange, nothing. The colony would die.

I opened my eyes and looked at Jenna. I said, "I cannot kill them anymore one at a time."

"Kill? You mean the Colonel?"

I saw that she hoped I meant to kill the Colonel, that her telling me the truth had been at least partly in the hope that my response would be the Colonel's death. I said, "You know, of course, where he sleeps."

"Rolf—"

"And in his absence," I said, "you have his authority, have you not?"

Doubtfully, she nodded.

I said, "Get dressed."

"Rolf? What are you going to do?"

I got up from the bed and took from under the pile of my clothing on the chair the yellow notebook. I held it up and said, "You were right, I *do* know what the code means. It's a code Gar and I made up together when we were children."

A sudden smile lit her face like sunlight. "Rolf!"

"I was going to go on my own," I said, "but I see that's no good. I'll give you a half share, if you'll help me."

Already I could see the calculation behind her eyes, though she masked it very well. I knew she would stay with me until we were safely clear of Anarchaos, that she would make no attempt to double-cross me while we were still in this lawless hellhole. What she said was, "Of course I'll help you. For the money, naturally for the money; I told you I'm a very expensive girl. But not for the money alone. For Gar, too. And for you."

"All right. Do you have the authority to order a plane for us?"

"If the Colonel isn't around to countermand it."

"He won't be. And there are some other things I want, too. Have them put on the plane."

"Of course."

She said of course, but then she questioned me, wanting to know why I needed such things. I told her I would explain later, and said, "The plane is for you and the Colonel. Everyone else is to continue to wait here for the Sledge ship."

"All right. Shall I carry the notebook?"

"I think not," I said.

We kissed in the corridor outside the room, with a great show of passion. Then she hurried away to make the arrangements, and I went off to strangle Colonel Whistler in his bed.

XXXVII

Everything went smoothly. Bundled up in heavy furs, I could have been Colonel Whistler or anyone. Jenna and I took a corporation auto out to the airfield, where at her orders the plane was already warming up. It was a small plane, with only ourselves and the pilot aboard. I dispatched the pilot after we took off, but kept Jenna for her usefulness. She knew how to fly the plane, and she could clear the way if any questions arose at any of our stops.

The entire circuit took three standard days, and questions did arise. After the first day there was an increasing urgency in the requests for information about Colonel Whistler, who seemed to have disappeared. (I had buried him in the snow not far from the Ice building at Cannemuss.) Jenna had the authority of the Colonel in her own person when he was unavailable, and she did excellent work keeping the corporation employees from growing too suspicious too soon.

We did the circuit almost entirely without rest, going first to Chax and then to Ulik, on to Prudence, to Moro-Geth, and at last to Ni. I told Jenna, when we arrived at Ni, to wait at the

259

company airfield till I returned, as she had done at each of our other stops, and this time she said, "Shouldn't I go on to the spaceport and start arranging for our tickets?"

"You can call them from here, can't you?"

"Yes, there's a ground line, but why not go straight there?"

"Because it would be better to fly in. Phone and order two round-trip passages, for Colonel Whistler and his secretary of Ice, to be billed to the Wolmak Corporation."

She smiled. "That's lovely, Rolf. We'll let them pay our fare."

"We've got to, I don't have any money. I'll be back as soon as I can."

We kissed, and I picked up the last of the five suitcases, and carried it into the city.

When I arrived at Ni spaceport they told me there wouldn't be another ship leaving for two standard days, but there were dormitory facilities if I cared to wait on UC territory. I said I did, and got out the rest of my luggage and money, which had been checked here ever since I'd first arrived. I then went to the UC commander and said to him:

"I'm afraid I have a rather—delicate problem. While I was here, there was a woman . . ."

He smiled, showing that he was a man of sophistication, and said, "It does happen."

"The only problem is, she might come out here looking for me, and to tell you the truth she frightens me."

"You want us to keep her out, is that it? Well, unauthorized local citizens are kept out anyway, so there's really no problem."

"Well, but she isn't exactly a local citizen. She's an off-worlder, works for one of the syndicates."

"Ahh," he said, nodding his head. "I see. So she could come in."

"If she could be told there was no one here by my name, no one"—I held up my left wrist— "suiting my description, I would be very grateful."

"I'm sure it can be arranged," he said, and was very hearty and jolly and man to man with me.

So I had no trouble from Jenna. I waited the two days, a ship arrived, and I boarded it, the only passenger leaving the planet. I'd been somewhat afraid Jenna would decide to book passage by herself after all, but she had chosen not to. What she was doing instead I couldn't guess, except that she had surely given up waiting for me by now. If she hadn't been found out by Wolmak employees already, she was more than likely busy trying to rearrange the facts of the last few days so as not to get in trouble with the corporation. I thought it likely she would succeed, she having the kind of drive necessary for success. As to the suitcases, I hardly thought it likely she would be mentioning them to anyone, since their effects might ultimately reflect back upon her. Besides, she didn't know—and I doubted she could guess—what I had done with them.

The suitcases were my answer to the problem of Gar's death, my final answer. I had tried avoiding the problem, with death or antizone. I had tried giving it a limited response, avenging Gar upon the persons of Phail and the other involved parties from Sledge. But I now saw that it would end only when I had accepted my responsibility to the fullest and completed the vengeance I'd come out here to start.

It was the colony that had killed my brother. That was true, finally. After the specifics of inter-corporation intrigue and lost strikes, there was still the fact that Anarchaos had produced the climate in which Gar's life could end as it had done. Phail and Gar, working for the same corporations on other planets, would never have met one another across a loaded gun.

If the colony was responsible for Gar's death, it followed that I must somehow kill the colony. I had tried to believe for a while that it was best to leave the place to its own slow self-destruction, as in the empty shacks around the perimeters of the major cities, but the rough health of Cannemuss had proved it would be a long while before that slow suicide completed itself. I had tried to believe with Rohstock, who wrote in *Voyages To Seven Planets* that "All are guilty on Anarchaos, and the guilty are invariably punished—by life on Anarchaos," but it is true that man is infinitely adaptable, and if a man knows no life other than the life of Hell, eventually Hell becomes normality and ceases to be Hell. I had tried to evade the issue by telling myself the task was too big for one man, but even as I'd thought it I'd known that the magnitude of a duty is never an excuse for shirking the attempt to perform it.

When I had seen in Colonel Whistler's eyes the look I remembered from Phail, I had known at last there was no choice. Anarchaos was a cancer, and to merely snip off a few of the sick cells was to do nothing. The entire cancer had to be rooted out and destroyed.

Thus the suitcases.

It was my job to kill the colony, and what was it now that kept the colony alive? The Union Commission, bound this way and that by rules and regulations so that it could supply Anarchaos the necessities of its life without supplying the discipline and order it so urgently needed. Some underling members of the UC might be disgusted by the arrangement, might want to do something more forceful, but those at the top were too ensnarled in red tape and the balance of power, aided and abetted by those off-world corporations who were fattening themselves on this rich carrion world.

Well, I had just seen to it that the red tape would disappear. Tourists might be slaughtered, missionaries and merchants might be obliterated, engineers and prospectors and all honest workmen might be slashed and hacked, and the UC, wrapped in its own regulations, would stand to one side and do nothing. But now something was going to happen, and the UC would *have* to move.

According to the timers and my watch, it would happen in two standard days, eighteen hours and twenty-one minutes after my spacecraft lifted off Anarchaos. At that moment in time, the five suitcases would explode, each with enough force to demolish a city block, enough to topple one of those towers.

Four of the suitcases were hidden in the four UC Embassies in

Chax, Ulik, Prudence and Moro-Geth. The fifth was hidden in the spaceport at Ni.

In less than three days, the entire personnel of the UC mission to Anarchaos would be wiped out. Records gone as well, and the heart of the monetary system. And all the equipment in the spaceport.

I wasn't sure in which direction the UC would cut the red tape, whether they would merely pull out entirely and leave Anarchaos to rot in its own juices, or rather move in emphatically, take over full-time governing of the planet, and replace its absurd anarchy with some protectorate government of its own. In either case, *this* colony at Anarchaos was dead. We were even.

Alone in the blank passenger compartment of the spaceship, I sat a while in thought, and slowly boredom crept over me, the boredom of travel by shuttle, until at last I took Gar's notebook from my pocket. Neither then nor later did I look at any of the sections in code. Instead, I opened it to the remembered spot and began to read:

ROLF

I am going to have a second chance . . .